THE LONG RUN

'No one picks through the intelligence maze with more authority or humanity than Allbeury.'

The Sunday Times

'Mr Allbeury is a writer of espionage novels that soar far above the genre.'

New Yorker

'Ted Allbeury is perhaps the best, most authentic and skilled spy novelist in a very crowded business.'

Toronto Sun

'Certain things are constants, and Ted Allbeury is one. In book after book, the prolific British writer of espionage tales has maintained a superior level.'

New York Times

'His novels are very well written, warm and humane ... absolutely worth becoming acquainted with.'

L. O.-bladet, Copenhagen

'Allbeury's people are real in the sense that Greene's or Maugham's are.'

H. R. F. Keating, The Times

'One of the best story-tellers around today ... There is something totally absorbing about the way in which he spins a web of mystery and imagination that never fails to fascinate.'

Sydney Morning Telegraph

'The doyen of contemporary spy writers.'

Daily Telegraph

Also by Ted Allbeury and available in Coronet paperbacks:

Beyond the Silence
As Time Goes By
The Line-Crosser
Show Me a Hero
Other Kinds of Treason

About the Author

Ted Allbeury was a lieutenant-colonel in the Intelligence Corps during World War II, and a successful executive in the fields of marketing, advertising and radio. He has been writing since the early 1970s: he is best known for his espionage novels but has also written one highly successful and highly praised general novel, *The Choice*, and a short story collection, *Other Kinds of Treason*. This is his thirty-seventh novel.

The Long Run

Ted Allbeury

CORONET BOOKS
Hodder and Stoughton

First published in Great Britain in 1996
by Hodder and Stoughton
A division of Hodder Headline PLC
First published in paperback in 1996
by Hodder and Stoughton
A Coronet Paperback

10 9 8 7 6 5 4 3 2

A CIP catalogue record for this title is available from
the British Library.

ISBN 0 340 68215 9

Printed and bound in Great Britain

Hodder and Stoughton
A division of Hodder Headline PLC
338 Euston Road
London NW1 3BH

To lovely Annabel Wright, with love from all of us

But this *long run* is a misleading guide to current affairs.
In the *long run* we are all dead.
by John Maynard Keynes, *A Tract on Monetary Reform*, Chapter 3

CHAPTER 1

The coffin was a roughly-made structure of chipboard and in places the rough splinters had been left untrimmed. The lid was resting against the coffin which was suspended on a couple of carpenter's trestles. The taller of the two men took several photographs of the body in the coffin. There was no lining or support for the body and there had been no attempt to mitigate the swollen lips and the lividity around the throat. With a few more general shots of the garage, the man wound back the film in the Leica M6, released the base-plate, eased out the film cassette and handed it to the other man.

'It's Fujicolor 200. Needs E6 processing.'

The other man nodded and slid the cassette into his jacket pocket.

They travelled in the back of the van with the coffin and when it stopped by the open grave near a clump of silver birches they got out and watched as the workmen lowered the coffin with two ropes into the open grave. When the spoil from the digging had been shovelled into the grave they waited until it had been smoothed into shape. A man who had stood separately, watching the burial, handed a form to the taller man and showed him where he should sign the burial certificate. The name of the deceased was given as Kemal Cadesi and his occupation as 'Turkischer Gastarbeiter.'

The two men walked together to the gravel path that led to the road in one direction and in the other to a small church. The tall man took the path to the road leaving the other man standing as if waiting for someone. As he looked up at the lowering clouds he shivered, but it was quite mild for October in Berlin.

He had been sent from London to witness the burial because he had once worked with Charlie Foster who had gone down on the local records as a Turkish guest-worker, the Germans' rather coy designation *of their foreign refugees. The name he had been given had been taken out of a guide-book and was the name of a street in Istanbul.*

As it began to rain he turned up his coat collar and headed for the road. The SIS car should be there by now. He hoped that the photographs that his opposite number in the BND, the German equivalent of SIS, had taken would be acceptable. He'd have a night on the town with Malins and take the early morning flight the next day to London. He wondered what Charlie Foster had done to deserve ending up in an anonymous grave in a clapped-out cemetery in Berlin. He hadn't seen him in the last two or three years.

CHAPTER 2

As Mason sorted out his change for the taxi fare the cab-driver pointed at the building behind them. 'Looks like one of them Odeons they built in the thirties'. As Mason handed over the fare and a tip he smiled. 'Don't let 'em hear you say that or you'll end in the nick.' The driver laughed and drove off. The building they were talking about was the new headquarters of MI6, or SIS as its inmates preferred. They still referred to it themselves as 'The Firm'.

At reception Mason asked where he could get hold of Millar. The clerk reached for his log-book and opened it at the notes for the day.

'Millar, Millar . . . ah yes . . . you'll find him at the French Embassy, a cocktail party, standing in for the Director-General.' He looked up at Mason. 'OK?'

Mason nodded and walked back to the street. It was beginning to rain and taxis were scarce. Several ignored his waves but finally one stopped and he asked for the French Embassy.

Inside the embassy the first person he saw was Millar's wife, a Frenchwoman, amiable and vivacious. She cleared him through the flunkeys and through the double doors that led to the main rooms. The place was crowded and for a few moments Mason stood by a dais that was occupied by a five-piece group led by a good pianist playing a lush 'stride' version of 'My very good friend, the milkman'. As he cast around he finally spotted Millar and edged his way over to him. When he arrived Millar looked at him sharply.

'What the hell are you doing here?'

'I thought I'd better put you in the picture as soon as possible.'

Millar looked around. 'Let's go into the annexe. Follow me and don't talk until I say so.'

Millar obviously knew his way around the embassy and they finally ended up in a conservatory lit only by candles.

3

'OK,' Millar said, 'What's going on? Where's Loomis?'

Mason took a deep breath. 'He'd changed his mind. Said he wasn't going to co-operate. While we were arguing another guy came in and started threatening me with a knife and Loomis drew a gun. Smith and Wesson .38. I saw the cylinder start to turn so I shot him.'

'Where is he now?'

'He's still there. So is the other guy.'

'He'll go straight to the media and they'll raise hell on the whole bloody thing.'

'He won't. He's dead, Millar. So's the other guy.'

'You mean you killed him – them?'

'Yeah.'

'But surely there was something else you could have done?'

Mason's face flushed with anger. 'Yeah there was. I could have let Loomis kill me. I decided against it.'

'And the other fellow?'

'He cut me with the knife before I put him down.'

'And you left both bodies?'

'Yes.'

'D'you contact the police?'

'No. Of course not. There's no connection to us.'

'This means that the whole operation is down the pan.'

'Fraid so. Somebody talked and somebody got to Loomis and persuaded him to change his mind.'

'Have you had any other contacts since you left the cottage?'

'Only my doctor.'

'Why your doctor?'

'To patch up the cut I got.'

Millar half turned away, lips pursed and frowning. 'The D-G won't be best pleased about this.' He paused, eyebrows raised. 'Are you sure it couldn't have been settled some other way?'

Mason put his clenched fists into his jacket pockets and for a few moments he was silent as he stared at Millar's face. Then he said, 'I'm taking a couple of weeks' leave. Amsterdam and then Berlin. I'll leave my contacts at HQ before I leave.'

Millar nodded and looked over Mason's shoulder. 'So be it. I'd better get back in and do the rounds.'

* * *

As Mason walked in the rain towards Hyde Park Corner he cursed Millar with every obscenity he could lay his tongue on, primitive words used adjectivally, adverbially and straight. Repetitious and ineffective they did nothing to ease his inner anger. So the D-G wouldn't be best pleased. Too fucking bad. But his anger was against Millar who hadn't even cared enough to ask about his cut. A ten-inch-long cut that ran across the hip-bone that he had turned to his attacker to stop the knife plunging into his belly. He would put in a chit for a complete new suit. An Armani special. Medical bill, sick-leave and every other bloody-minded item he could contrive. He remembered something from his training course a long way back. It was Macleod who said it. 'You aren't a professional, Jimmy lad, until you learn that they're all shits. Everyone of 'em who sits behind those bloody desks.' And Macleod was right.

He decided he would draw some money from the Barclay's cash point at Gatwick. He wouldn't even go back to the flat, he'd stay with Candy in Amsterdam and then move on to Berlin for a couple of days.

By the time he was on the plane he had cooled down and his thoughts were back at the cottage on the Romney Marshes and one dead body at the top of the stairs and the other half-way down. He had put the gun in a locker at the airport and had no regrets about killing them. It was Millar who had set it up and he'd made a bodge of it. He'd put his silver dollar on the wrong man. People like Millar, sitting behind a desk, saw it all as a chess-game, a programme of logical moves. But it wasn't a chess-game it was more like a mixture of Australian rules foot-ball and kick-boxing. And the only rule was – don't trust anyone.

He leaned back in his seat, closed his eyes and slept until the pilot was saying his piece about the ground temperature at Schiphol.

CHAPTER 3

Sir Peter Crombie was a man for traditional breakfasts and *The Times* and his mail had to wait until he got to the toast and Robertson's Golden Shred. A throwback to nursery days. He used a miniature dirk to slit open the envelopes and left the large A4 envelope to last. But he took out the contents of that one first. A couple of pages stapled together.

He read it slowly and said, 'Shit', as he finished the last page. He apologised for the expletive without looking up. His wife, Lady Diana, merely raised her eyebrows. She had been raised in a family of rugby-playing brothers and took such stuff in her stride. Finally he reached for the envelope. There was no stamp and no postmark. It must have been delivered personally.

He grunted with the effort as he reached for the small trolley that held the two phones. A black one and a red one. The red one had no dialling facility and that was the one he used.

'Put me through to Harding will you.'

There were a few moments of clicking and then, 'Harding, sir.'

'Are you at the office?'

'Yes, sir.'

'Come round to my place as soon as you can.'

'Right, sir.'

Sir Peter Crombie had been Director-General of SIS for almost six years. He came with no previous experience of intelligence work but he was patently loyal and patriotic and was appointed, as an experienced Staff officer, to tame and reorganise the wilder elements of MI6. He came to admire the loose cannons who risked their lives and ruined their private lives to keep an ungrateful nation safe and secure. He never pried too deeply so long as the next layer down kept him reasonably informed. The definition of what was reasonable was to be their responsibility. His frequently repeated guideline was simple and to the point. 'Let me know *before* the shit hits the fan.'

Sir Peter came from a military family and the army life came naturally with his genes. Some of his senior staff saw him as a bit over the top with his unabashed patriotism. It had been said that when the National Anthem was played at international soccer matches he watched the TV screen to see which members of the England team actually sang the words. A strong contrast, he felt, to the England rugby players who all sang the words. They might be a bit behind or ahead of the band but they sang lustily. And, of course, loyally. Loyalty was the prime virtue in Sir Peter's beatitudes.

He took Harding into his small study and waved to an easy chair. 'Make yourself comfortable,' he said. And holding out the contents of the A4 envelope, he said, 'Read that.'

Harding turned the pages slowly and then read them again. When he looked at his boss he said, 'Where did you get this?'

'It was stuffed in my letter-box. The envelope's over there. No stamp. No postmark.' He paused. 'Any ideas?'

'It looks like extracts from some Stasi documents.' He shrugged. 'Is that all?' He paused and when Sir Peter didn't respond he went on. 'But there's no demand for money or a threat of exposing the stuff to the media.'

'Are you surprised at what it says?'

Harding shrugged. 'Nothing that politicians get up to surprises me any more.'

'So what are you going to do about it?'

'Me, sir. Why me?' said Harding, his indignation making his voice a little shrill.

'A Stasi document. German. You're head of the German desk. Who else?' When Harding remained silent, Sir Peter smiled and shrugged. 'OK. Right now it's my baby. I'll have to show it to the Foreign Secretary and I'm sure he'll discuss it with the PM.' He paused. 'But before that I want you to check what we've got on our files about this wretched man Boyce-Williams. How long do you need?'

'A couple of hours.'

'OK. See me in my office as soon as you can.'

Harding pushed a single page of notes across Sir Peter's desk, who ignored it and said, 'Tell me.'

'Nothing, sir. Police reports of kerb-crawling in Kings Cross area and Paddington. Young girls picked up. Frequent visits to clubs in Soho. That's about it. He gets about a lot as Party Chairman, so it's impossible to cover him all the time. There have been unofficial complaints by young females at Central Office of sexual pressures but nobody was willing to lay a charge. There have been a couple of hints of this in *Private Eye*. All the rendezvous in the thing you've got are so general that they're not likely to be considered suspicious. And we've got very little on Stasi contacts in this country. We concentrate on the KGB bodies.'

The D-G nodded. 'No need for me to warn you to say nothing to anyone about this matter. I've arranged to see the Foreign Secretary tomorrow. He'll want to consult the PM. Could take two or three days.'

'There's another thing I think you need to point out to them.'

'What's that?'

'We may not be the only people who were sent this stuff. If they try to ignore it or sweep it under the carpet it would be very damaging if the story ran in the media.'

'A good point. I'll bear it in mind. There's just one thing I'd like you to bend that devious mind of yours to in the meantime.'

'What's that?'

'What's the motive for all this? What does the instigator expect to get out of it?'

'I'll think about it, sir.'

When Harding had left, Crombie opened the top left-hand drawer of his desk and took out the document, placing it on his blotter and reading it again.

Subject: **904 Stasi P file. Extracts.**
Richard Henry Boyce-Williams. Born 2 Jan 40.
Status: Chairman Conservative Party (see notes on function of Chairman of C.P.) Subject only son of Sir Arthur Langan Boyce-

Williams. Educ. Winchester School, Magdalen College, Oxford Univ. Read Politics and Economics. (2.2). Trainee in family-owned chain of grocery shops. Unconfirmed harassment of female staff. Employed as personal assistant to local MP (Howard Sparks, parliamentary spokesman for Police Federation). Elected safe Conservative seat for Broadwater, Warwickshire in 1972. Latest appointment considered as reward for long and loyal service to Party. Appointment much criticised by back-bench MPs who described him as PM's crony with no knowledge of constituencies.

J.R. Assessment

Outwardly a jolly, amusing personality but is in fact a very nervous man behind the flamboyant bonhomie. Aware that his colleagues see him as a lightweight even more determined to succeed. His predilection for very young girls is probably motivated more by a need to impress both the girls and his men friends than by his sex drive which seems more likely to be deviant. Contact should show respect and appreciation. Lives beyond income.

6 May 82. London. Builders' Arms, Victoria. Contact Rupert.

Discussed PM Thatcher's reaction to events in Falkland Islands. Her anger at sinking of HMS *Sheffield.* French Exocet missile from French-supplied plane. PM Thatcher's private comments on Mitterand.

16 June 82. London. Charing Cross Hotel. Rupert.

Discussed in detail British losses in Falklands. 255 dead. Despite Argentine surrender PM still not forgiven French government co-operation with Argentinians.

1 Dec. 82. London. King's Arms, Chelsea. Werner.

Discussed details of cabinet meeting covering demonstrations of women (est. 20,000) at Greenham Common airbase. US ambassador has made unofficial complaint to Foreign Secretary.

12 June 83. Marlow, Bucks. Compleat Angler. Rupert.

Discussed election results and possible reshuffle of cabinet.

7 Oct. 83. London. Strand Palace. Karl.

Discussed cabinet discussions on Labour Party's choice of N. Kinnock as party leader. Government delighted.

12 May 84. London. Broadcasting House cafeteria. Karl.

Discussed possible further assistance to striking miners. Cabinet considering using troops to quell violence.

15 Oct.84. London. Waterloo Station. Karl.
Discussed IRA bomb at Brighton Hotel and narrow escape of PM.
5 killed. 50 wounded. Discussed action to be taken by MI5.

9 March 85. London. Liberty's restaurant. Conrad.
Discussed cabinet meeting on repercussions from ending of miners'
strike, especially possible action against Arthur Scargill.

26 June 86. London. Royal Court theatre bar. Karl.
Discussed Northern Ireland and action against terrorists.

14 June 87. London. Garrick Club. Johan.
Discussed repercussions of Conservative general election third succes-
sive victory also probable new cabinet.

27 Oct.89. London. Liberty's. Johan.
Discussed quarrel between PM and Nigel Lawson now that Chancellor
has resigned. Discussed European monetary system.

2 April 90. London. Tate Gallery rest. Johan.
Discussed cabinet reaction to poll tax riots. Several of our people
arrested, he will check situation and advise.

23 Nov.90. London. Ritz Hotel. Johan.
Discussed PM's resignation and effect on foreign policy. Gave back-
ground on Hurd and Major.
Note: Cash payments over period $200,000 (see sep.list). Facility visits
Budapest and personal services provided. (Female ex KGB)

On the way back to his office Harding couldn't get Charlie Foster out
of his mind. The *late* Charlie Foster. Foster's threat had been to use
the Stasi records of their Western informants if SIS didn't co-operate
about Tarrant who was being held at that time by the KGB. Crombie
hadn't mentioned Charlie Foster but the possible connection was
there. Who took over Charlie's information? Maybe he'd give Mason
a ring tomorrow. As Sir Peter frequently said, 'Time spent in reconnaissance is seldom wasted'.

CHAPTER 4

Benjamin Porter had had a couple of years as Chancellor of the Exchequer before he became Foreign Secretary and was considered to be a success. A safe pair of hands, not given to seeking public approval or affection, he just got on with the job. Crombie liked him and they were on Ben and Peter terms. But as Crombie watched Porter read the pages of the document the older man's face gave no clue as to his reaction. When he had finished Ben Porter folded the papers and looked across his desk at Crombie.

'I'll have to show it to the PM. You'd better hang on. I'll get my girl to fix it.'

As Porter reached for one of the phones Crombie said, 'Wouldn't it be best for us to discuss it so that we have at least a suggestion to put to him?'

'No.' Porter shook his head decisively. 'Only he can decide what he wants to do. Boyce-Williams is an old friend of his.' He paused. 'Just one thing before we see him. Looking through these contacts it could be contended that what he passed on was no more than a journalist could have passed on. Just well-informed gossip. What would you say to that?'

'Well. First of all any journalist who took comparatively large sums of money for his inside information has stepped well over the line of mere gossip. Even I don't know what Maggie's thoughts were about Mitterand.' He smiled. 'I can guess. But I don't *know*. Secondly we don't know if this material has been sent elsewhere. The newspapers won't treat it as just a chat between old friends. And lastly, even if it were a fabrication, and it was published, in the present scenario Boyce-Williams would be finished.'

'He may be a bit of an ass, Peter, but he's well-liked you know.'

'So was Philby.'

'Oh for heaven's sake. That's history. Times have changed.'

'The bottom line's still the bottom line, Minister.'

'What is the bottom line?'

'That Boyce-Williams is guilty of treason.'

'Could we satisfy a court on that evidence.'

'No.'

'Why not?'

'Because we can't substantiate its source. We don't even know it. A good defence counsel would have it thrown out before it got to court.' He paused. 'But none of that matters. True or false Boyce-Williams will go down the pan if the press get hold of this. All we can do is try to make sure that the PM doesn't go down with him.'

Porter sighed and reached for the phone. Five minutes later the message came back. The PM was in the House for Prime Minister's Questions. He'd see them in his room at 4 p.m.

Porter looked at Sir Peter. 'We'd better go separately, Peter.'

The PM was at his desk talking on the phone as one of his assistants showed them into his office at the House. When he hung up the phone he waved them to two armchairs by his desk.

'That was Mary. Sophie's just delivered a grand daughter.' He grimaced. 'I know I *am* a grandfather but I hate being called that.' Then with a brisk change of pace and subject, he said, 'Your problem, Foreign Secretary?'

Porter handed him the document.

'You want me to read this now?'

'Please, Prime Minister.'

As the others had done in their turn, the PM read the material twice. Slowly and carefully. Eventually he looked up and tossed the papers onto his desk. He looked at the Foreign Secretary.

'How did we get this?'

Sir Peter said, 'Stuffed into my letter-box at home. No stamp, no postmark. We don't know who sent it, nor why.'

'What do you want to do?'

'Confront Boyce-Williams and offer him a deal. He goes quietly and we cover up. But there's the danger that if this crap . . .' he pointed at the papers on the desk, '. . . has gone to the media they'll blow him out of the water.'

'And me too.'

'If he's out of the picture before it comes out that's good enough. Prompt action has been taken.'

'It'll break his heart. He loves all those bazaars and the constituency garden parties.'

'He was a fool, Prime Minister. A dangerous fool.'

'When should it be done?'

'Soonest. Hours not days.'

'OK. Leave it to me. If he won't resign I'll have to come back to you both.'

The rather portly man was smiling and holding up a glass of champagne as he met the press to announce that he was giving up his Chairmanship of the party. The constant travelling had taken its toll, he said, and his doctors had insisted that he took a long break. He had told the PM about his intentions several months ago. The PM had been most gracious about it. And it would give him more time to spend with his family.

'What family?' the man from the *Mail* said to the *Guardian* man. 'The bugger's not even married.'

The *Guardian* man smiled and said softly, 'There's always his dear old mom. They used to call him Mummy's boy when he was at school. Spoils him rigid. Always has done. It's a wonder he didn't end up queer.'

The club was in a basement in Frith Street and a Maltese named Potto was the boss. It was called The Take-Away Club because you couldn't do it on the premises but there were a couple of rooms on the other side of the street that were available for 'entertaining' one of Potto's young ladies.

When the rotund figure of Henry Boyce-Williams made its way down the stairs from the street, Potto took him to his favourite table, waved to one of the girls to bring them each a whisky and turned to his guest. 'Well my Lord, they tell me you're giving up politics for a bit.' He always referred to Boyce-Williams as 'my Lord'. It wasn't flattery. He just assumed that important men like Boyce-Williams were all Lords. He wasn't interested in the politics of his adopted country.

'I'm just sick of the bloody travel, Potto. Opening bazaars and kissing babies.' He paused, 'Speaking of babies, who's the blonde by the bar?'

'Which one?'

'The one in the blue top.'

'And the big tits. That's Jennie. She's new. You fancy her?'

'How old is she?'

Potto laughed. 'Old enough to do it. Just.'

'I think I'll give her a try. But I'll take her to *my* pad. That OK?'

'For you, milord, anything's OK. I'll go over and tell her.' He paused as he stood up. 'You want a taxi?'

Boyce-Williams smiled. 'You think of everything, Potto. The perfect host. Yes, Please.'

He lay back on the bed in his tatty bathrobe watching the girl, Jennie, as she stood there naked, brushing her long hair slowly and carefully. He guessed she was about eighteen but she had been very co-operative. Very active. That was one of the reasons he liked them young.

He reached for the small bottle on the bedside table, and with a tumbler of water in one hand, he took the tablets and sipped the water, until the bottle was empty. He seemed to be asleep as she put on her top and her skirt, and still asleep as she picked up her money, slid it into her handbag and let herself out.

There was a long and amiable obituary of Boyce-Williams in *The Times*. The one in the *Daily Telegraph* was short and uncommitted. The tabloids did their normal job without much to go on and only called it a day when the editors concerned realised that instead of ruining his reputation they were making Boyce-Williams the envy of all their male readers.

It looked like it was all wrapped up. Both the PM and the Foreign Secretary reckoned that it had been dealt with properly. Only the wretched Boyce-Williams had found himself without a chair when the music had stopped.

But Crombie and Harding knew by instinct that there could well be more to come. And they were not going to be satisfied until they found out why the document had been sent and who had sent it.

It was at their second meeting that Crombie finally raised the question of Charlie Foster. He hadn't been involved in the Foster affair and he didn't want to know too many details. He didn't want to be involved but it *was* a loose end.

'I can't get out of my mind that this thing, the document, is typical of what Charlie Foster threatened to do. Do you think he really did have the details of Stasi informants outside East Germany?'

'I'm sure he did?'

'What makes you so sure?'

'Charlie Foster wasn't a bluffer.'

'So what happened to his material?'

'We've no idea.'

'Didn't we follow it up?'

'No. It was a shambles. We just wanted to get out before the Germans made an issue of it.'

'You're quite sure that he's dead?'

'Quite, quite sure.' Harding looked unhappy and rather shifty.

'A witness?'

Harding shrugged. 'You could call him that. It's best you don't pursue it, even with me.'

'It's not all that long ago, couldn't we see if we can trace whatever he had. Did he have time to destroy it?'

'No. No time at all.'

'Is it worth getting someone to do a check? His old contacts maybe.'

'I've got someone in mind. Shall I go ahead?'

Crombie shrugged. 'I'll leave it up to you.'

As Harding walked back to his office he was annoyed that Crombie was being so devious. Pretending not to know. He'd been tempted to say, 'Yes, I'm sure he's dead. I gave the order for Maguire to kill him if he wouldn't play ball. Remember?' But that's how the game was played. He'd go ahead and brief Mason. Even on that Crombie had made clear that he wasn't ordering it. It was up to him. He shrugged. So be it. That's what he was there for. To carry the can.

What worried away at the edge of his mind was that he didn't see Charlie Foster choosing a man like Boyce-Williams as a target.

A politician, a nonentity in intelligence terms. The only consolation he had was that if there *was* anything to find then Mason would find it. He was not only tough but dogged. He'd grind away until he'd got an answer. And it gave him an excuse to transfer Mason away from that fool Millar. He'd handle Mason himself.

CHAPTER 5

Mason took the tube from Heathrow to Victoria, a train to East Croydon, and a taxi to his flat.

James Mason was thirty-two years old. Not handsome, but attractive, mainly because of his blue eyes and boyish smile. But as they so often are, both features were deceptive. The blue eyes gave him an air of innocence that was entirely spurious and the boyish smile was inherited from his father, a rather likeable con-man. James Mason lived alone in the flat on the outskirts of Croydon. He was not one of those lonely bachelors who live on TV meals and don't know how to work a washing-machine. His flat was kept with a precision and meticulousness that came from four years in the army including three years in SAS. He was totally self-sufficient and slightly mean with money and affection. The kind of man that *Marie-Claire* warned its readers about. Men who are born with street-cred and an instinct for survival. His mother was originally German, and German had been the language of his home-life despite the fact that his father, who had been in the army of occupation in Germany, knew only enough German to make a deal or proposition a girl. It was James Mason's German that had caused him to be recruited by SIS nearly ten years ago. Single-minded and ambitious, he had become a highly-rated field agent in a couple of years of hunting down suspected war criminals.

Some people claim that a man's choice of car is very revealing. Mason drove a ten-year-old Healey 3000 metallic blue convertible, with a well-worn hood that made it necessary to drape a towel across his lap if the rain was more than a drizzle. At high revs it sounded like a Buggati because in all Healey 3000s the exhaust assembly had only a fraction over an inch clearance from the road, which frequently caused holes to develop in the long tube. This meant that Healey

3000 owners were sometimes stopped by elderly policemen and cautioned about excessive noise. Younger policemen were more understanding.

As Mason waited for the water to boil for his tea he looked through his mail. A reminder from Croydon library about two overdue books, a special offer from Barclays for an annuity, a wine offer from the *Sunday Times* and three letters from girl-friends, one from Hamburg, one from Australia and one from Los Angeles. None of them was passionate, but all were friendly and eager to hear from him, or even to receive a visit. Which suited him well, for Mason didn't believe in getting involved. He was a natural loner. It suited his job and it suited his temperament. Like the words of the poem – 'He travels the fastest who travels alone'. As the switch went on the Rowenta kettle the phone rang.

'Mason . . .' he said curtly, '. . . who is it?'

'It's Harding, James, is it convenient to talk for a moment?'

'Yeah.'

'I'd like to see you at ten tomorrow at the office, can you do that?'

'Yes of course. Anything special?'

'Just briefing for an assignment. You might enjoy it.'

'Not that bloody security shambles in the Falklands, I hope.'

Harding laughed softly. 'No. Your friend Millar's landed that.' He paused. 'Hang on in suspense until we meet.'

'OK. I'll do that.'

He hung up and went back to preparing his meal. He quite liked Harding, his boss. Harding had been a field agent for years and tolerated inflated expenses chits because he knew what it was like being stuck in some strange place with no contacts and no background. You had to get out and about a bit or you'd go crazy. For some the consolation was *Haute cuisine,* for others booze, and for some it was girls. For James Mason it was a bit of all three. It went down as 'contacts with informants' and nobody expected you to name names or to present supporting receipts. It was taken for granted that one way or another you'd be living off your expenses. And if you were SIS you didn't get hassled by the Inland Revenue or Customs and Excise. They didn't want some creep in a tax office able to build up a picture of who worked for SIS, so even your pay was tax-free. Not that pay scales were particularly generous. Just a bit more than your equivalent rank would get in Special Branch.

Harding had decided that the only lead he would give Mason was Malins. His other concern was to keep Mason away from the BND.

He leaned back in his chair. 'You ever come across a chap named Foster? Charlie Foster?'

Mason shook his head. 'No.' He frowned. 'I've heard the name somewhere or other. Can't recall when it was.'

'Let me give you a brief picture of what happened. Foster ran a successful network into East Berlin but eventually three of his network were picked up by the Stasis. Foster wanted to do a deal to get them released. They weren't British nationals and SIS in Berlin and London wouldn't agree.' He sighed. 'Foster defected. Went over to the other side and worked for the Stasis and for the KGB in return for them releasing his three couriers. He became a key man.

'We sent one of our chaps, Tarrant, into East Berlin to do a recce on where Foster was but to make no contact. Tarrant himself was picked up. For some reason Foster took a liking to him and contacted London to say that unless Tarrant was allowed back with guarantees of his status he, Foster, would release names and details of westerners who had co-operated with the Stasis.

'Legally and every other way Foster had committed treason and London went all "holier than thou" and wouldn't play.' He sighed and shrugged. 'Somebody was sent over to put the frighteners on him.' He paused and it seemed quite a long pause. 'Foster ended up dead.' He shrugged. 'End of story. Except that we want those records.'

'Was he bluffing?'

'I'm sure he wasn't. He was certainly in a position to record anything he wanted to. And he wasn't a bluffer.'

'Are there any leads left in Berlin?'

'Only one, I'm afraid. A chap named Malins. A bit of a crook. Used to be SIS and retired early. Made a pile. Owns several properties in Berlin and Amsterdam, and has several sources of income apart from the property. Runs a porn shop, a travel agency and two night-clubs.' Harding paused and smiled. 'A bit of a rascal, always on the lookout for making a buck, but vaguely likeable.' He shrugged. 'Anyway make up your own mind.'

'Can I use the facilities at our Berlin detachment?'

'No. At least at this stage I want you to be totally independent. But you know your way around in Berlin.'

'What about funding?'

'I've spoken to Facilities here. You'll have your own funds, enough to cover anything you're likely to want and only answerable to me. No questions asked but use your loaf and don't go over the top.' He paused. 'Carter, who's in charge in Berlin, will know you're around but he won't know why and you don't, repeat don't, tell him.'

'When do you want me to start?'

'You've started. As of now. My girl's got an official authorisation which she'll give you along with details of funding and priority facilities here in London. She'll also give you an address and brief background on that Malins chap.' He stood up. 'Call me any time. The girl will give you my contact number. Day or night.' He nodded. 'Best of luck.'

They shook hands and Harding walked him into the secretary's office, leaving him there to pick up the paper-work.

He had lunch at the café near Victoria Station and then took a train back to Croydon and walked to his flat.

Sitting on the bed he read the brief notes on the man Malins. There was a rather grainy photograph of him standing by a Mercedes talking to a man who had his back to the camera. There were addresses and photographs of three properties he owned that were let as flats and the same for his porn shop, the travel agency in the Kurfürstendamm and the two night-clubs which were both near the Zoo Station.

It seemed that Malins had served in SIS for about ten years, the last five in Berlin. He had retired early and still drew a pension but was classified as 'no contact' from the moment he left. It was assumed that he had accumulated his original capital from black-market dealings and, possibly, bribes. Details were given of five bank accounts, two with Deutsche Bank in Berlin, one in the Channel Islands, and two with Barclays in London. There was exactly £300,000 in each of the Barclays accounts but no information beyond account numbers on the others. It was hinted that Malins would have got the boot if he hadn't resigned. There was no information on whatever his connection was with Charlie Foster.

Mason stood up and moved over to the small writing desk under the bedroom window. From one of the small drawers he pulled out a thin piece of card with his standard check-list typed in a column.

* * *

1. Instructions for milkman.

2. Instructions for mail.

3. Contact Mrs Anderson about no cleaning.

4. Arrange car garaging and service.

5. Fix answerphone for access from outside phone.

6. Story for parents.

7. Get electricity meter read before leaving.

8. Set security alarm.

9. Carry passport, SIS ID card, useful phone numbers, cheque book, Barclaycard (office card).

10. Pay outstanding bills.

11. Batteries for radio, recorder and Contax T2.

12. Small arms (calibrate) and ammo. (Check for X-Ray) Ruger 22/45?

It took him most of the next day to deal with his list and he spent the last hour of the afternoon with the armoury sergeant at the shooting range in the cellars of an old house in Clapham. He handed over the Ruger to the sergeant who clamped it on the top of a heavy tripod whose feet were set in concrete. He turned to look at Mason.

'Where you takin' this, sir?'

'Berlin.'

The sergeant shook his head. 'You won't get this through like this, sir. Too much metal. The grip's OK. That's Zytel. It's the stainless steel barrel that's the problem.'

'Anything you can do about it?'

'Give me six hours and I can make the barrel removable and I can convert it so that it looks like a hand-held microphone.'

'Sounds a good idea. It's all yours.'

'I'll need an extra hour for calibration.'

'How about 2 p.m. tomorrow?'

'That's OK.' The sergeant paused. 'Don't risk taking ammo, there's plenty around in Berlin. I can give you a couple of contacts.' He smiled. 'It's cheaper than here anyway.'

It was late afternoon when Mason drove over to his parents' house at Purley, a half-hour drive from his flat. He had taken a dozen chocolate eclairs, his mother's favourite tea-time delicacy.

His parents lived in a comfortable detached house in a street that was pleasantly old-fashioned with lace curtains, stained glass in the front doors, and tiles in the porch that not only gave shelter to callers but housed the electricity meter and the mains-water stop-cock.

As they sat in the front room having tea together he said, 'What's the old man up to these days?'

She smiled and shrugged. 'You know him, boy. He's back to reading the death notices.'

Sam Mason studied the obituary sections of the national and local newspapers with the same care and experience that stock-brokers read the *Financial Times*. Recently bereaved widows were his speciality. It made him a quite handsome living relieving them of most of their inheritance.

He prided himself on the fact that he never cleared them out completely and that they had six months or so of his cheerful company before he folded his tent like the Arabs and silently stole away. He claimed that it was a tribute to his kindness and caring in a time of grief that after thirty years only two women had made any attempt to prosecute him.

As Mrs Mason poured them both another cup of tea she said, 'I'm glad in a way because he has these wild ideas from time to time of starting up companies and conning banks and wealthy people into putting money in as an investment.' She laughed, an indulgent laugh. 'Sees himself as a tycoon but he's out of his league with those people. It's them who would do *him* down in the end.'

'I've often wondered why you put up with him. Why you never chucked him out.'

'Oh no. I'd never do that. I like him. He's always been good to me.'

'Why did you marry him in the first place?'

She smiled. 'For the same reason the widows like him. He says nice things. I'd miss him terribly.' She leaned forward pointing at the silver-plated cake-tray. 'Have another eclair. They're lovely.'

'Not for me, ma. They're for you. I don't really like 'em all that much.'

She laughed. 'Your gran always used to say – "never trust a man who doesn't like eclairs and meringues".' She paused. 'Can I ask what you're doing these days?'

'I'm going abroad for a bit. You can ring that London number I gave you if you need to get hold of me in a hurry.'

'I think about you all the time.' Her voice quavered. 'Hoping you're OK.'

He smiled. 'I'm OK, ma. You know me. I can look after myself.'

'I wish you'd got a nice girl. Somebody to care for you.' She sighed. 'Every chap needs a woman around him. Somebody to talk to.'

He laughed and stood up. 'They're not all like you, ma. Don't worry. I'll get by.'

'How's Mrs Anderson these days? She looking after the place properly for you?'

'She's OK. Does a great job. Always asks about you.' He bent to kiss her. 'I've got to go, ma. Got some clearing up to do. I'll keep in touch. Give Sam my regards.'

She nodded. 'I'll tell him. Don't think he doesn't worry about you too. He cares you know, in his own funny way.'

'I'm sure he does. Don't get up. I'll let myself out.'

CHAPTER 6

As the plane banked to turn into the wind the pilot said, 'Ladies and gentlemen, you can see the famous Brandenburg Gate through the starboard windows and Unter den Linden. A bit further over you can see where Checkpoint Charlie used to be. The temperature on the ground is two degrees Celsius but there's no rain. Thank you for flying Lufthansa and enjoy your time in Berlin.'

He waited at the carousel for his second bag to come around then carried them both to the customs bench. At the check-out at Gatwick the machine had picked up the gun barrel but the guard accepted it as a microphone with only a cursory glance. Here in Berlin the check was even more perfunctory. With the Red Army busy flogging everything from cap badges to Kalashnikovs, there was no great interest in guns. Drugs and brand-new hundred-dollar notes in bundles of fifty were the current targets.

He took a taxi to the Savoy and settled for a double with bath. There was a film festival on and accommodation was heavily booked.

In his room he unpacked one of his bags and put his clothes away but left the smaller bag locked and inside the wardrobe. He ordered sandwiches and coffee from room service and unfolded the paper from his inside jacket pocket to check the information on Malins. The first meeting wouldn't be easy, he'd have to bluff a bit and see what happened, but he couldn't go too far. Malins was still a British national and held a valid British passport. Maybe it would be better to meet him at the garage he owned by the Zoo or at the travel agency on the Ku'damm rather than at his house.

As he ate his sandwiches he read through the Property To Let classifieds in the copy of *Der Tagesspiegel* that he had picked up at Tegel. He marked three possible flats within walking distance of the

Ku'damm. Then he tried the number for Malins' travel agency. They said he was at the garage and he dialled that number.

A girl's voice said '*Autoverkauf Gerhard.*'

'I'd like to speak to Herr Malins please.'

'Just a moment.'

After a few moments' silence the girl came back. 'Are you the gentleman enquiring about the second-hand Mercedes convertible?'

'No. It's a personal call.'

'Can I say who's speaking?'

'My name's Mason. James Mason.'

'Hold on a moment.'

Then a man's rough voice said in bad German, 'Malins. What can I do for you?'

'I'd just like to have a chat with you, Mr Malins. Let's speak English.'

There was a moment's silence and then. 'What's it about? I'm very busy.'

'It's a personal matter.'

'Cut out the bullshit – what personal matter?'

'I wanted to talk to you about Foster.'

'Foster. Who's Foster?'

'Charlie Foster.'

There was a long silence then Malins said, 'Are you from Century House?'

'Kind of.'

'Then sod off, mate. That's a warning.'

'Now who's bullshitting? What's the harm in talking?'

There was another long silence. Then Malins said, 'Where are you?'

'At the Savoy in Fasanenstrasse.'

'Room number?'

'I can't remember. Just ask for me at the desk.'

'I'll see you in an hour but if you're playing games you're trying it on the wrong guy.'

Then just the clatter as Malins hung up.

The desk rang him that his visitor had arrived and Mason asked them to send him up.

Malins was in his late fifties, a broad-shouldered, compact man about 5' 8" and about 160 pounds. Tanned face and brown eyes with the beginnings of a five o'clock shadow which was fair enough as it was well past 5 p.m.

Mason stood aside as Malins bundled into his room as if he owned the place, looking around suspiciously.

'Is this dump wired, my friend?'

Mason laughed. 'Give me a chance. I only got in on this morning's flight. Anyway. This is just a private chat. Like I said. Just between you and me.' He pointed to one of the armchairs. 'Have a seat. How about a drink?'

'I'll have a Bells if you've got one.'

Mason walked over to the mini-bar, poured the whisky and put the glass with a jug of water and a soda syphon on the low table in front of Malins. He poured out a tomato juice for himself and sat down facing his visitor.

'Good of you to spare me a few minutes of your time, Mr Malins.'

'Freddie. Just call me Freddie.' He waved a dismissive hand.

Mason smiled. 'Gives you as Roger Frederick in your "P" file. My name's James. James Mason.' He paused. 'I'd like to find out a bit about Charlie Foster and I wondered if you could help me.'

Malins studied the whisky as he swirled the glass slowly. Then he looked back at Mason.

'I thought you said no bullshitting.'

'I did. And I meant it.'

'Tell me something. What did they tell you about Charlie?'

'They said that he'd gone over the other side to do a deal with the Stasis or the KGB to release three of his agents. Worked for the other side for about two years. Made some threats and then disappeared and he's not been heard of since.' Mason wasn't prepared to be too open at that stage.

Malins leaned back in his chair. 'How long you been in SIS?'

'Quite a few years.'

'So why don't they trust you?'

'I don't understand.'

'Charlie Foster's dead. And your bastards at Century House know that, because they arranged it.'

'Tell me more.'

'I don't know any more and I can't prove a thing. I don't know how they did it or how they disposed of him but you can take it from me – he's dead. But I've got a good idea who did it. I think I know who he was and I once had a brush with him myself, and he was here like you are now, to get Charlie Foster. He was Special Services and I don't doubt he finished off Charlie Foster.'

'Would you recognise him again?'

'Too fucking true I would.' He paused. 'You ain't here about Charlie, my boy, whatever they told you. You're after those records he had.' He looked at Mason's face. 'True or false?'

Mason smiled and shrugged. 'Maybe.'

Malins smiled, a knowing smile. 'When they send you out with only half the story you know you're there to carry the can if anything goes wrong. You want to keep that in mind.' He paused and picked up his glass again, waving it towards Mason. 'They could do it to you too, so keep your powder dry, my friend.'

'How were you connected with Foster when he was around?'

Malins shrugged. 'Let's say we did a bit of business together.'

'Did you know him when you were in SIS?'

'No. I'd left before he came on the scene.'

'How did you come to know him?'

'He contacted me. By that time he was in East Berlin.'

'I was told he'd sold out to the Stasis or the KGB. Had he?'

'He worked for both but his real relationship was with the KGB.'

'What did he do for them?'

'I've no idea.'

When Mason looked disbelieving, Malins said, 'I mean it. I knew he was well in with them but that's all I knew.' He paused. 'The guy who could tell you more is Tarrant. D'you know him?'

'No.'

'There were two Tarrants, father Tommy and son Johnny. It's the son you want. His old man has an antiques business somewhere in the Cotswolds. The son was over here way back doing what you're doing – looking for Charlie Foster. Then he just disappeared and I heard afterwards that he'd taken early retirement. He and his old man were very close, his old man had been in SIS too. Good record. But Johnny didn't have his old man's charm. Tough and pretty ruthless. You should try him out.'

'Could you give me a lead to an ex-Stasi guy who operated in East Berlin?'

Malins laughed. 'Since the Wall came down there's dozens of 'em hanging around. I've got one at the garage working for me – serving gas.'

'Could I talk to him?'

Malins shrugged. 'No problem, but he won't know anything. There's hundreds of 'em swanning around trying to get jobs and hide the fact that they're ex-Stasis.'

'You mentioned Foster's records. Was that just a bluff or did he have something?'

Malins poured himself another whisky and leaned back in his chair. 'Yeah, he had records all right. I don't know what they were but he had access to all their records including their informants. I don't mean just informants in East Germany but people in West Germany and other countries.' He paused and looked at Mason. 'That's why your people knocked him off.'

'So why didn't SIS pick up his records?'

'I'd guess for two reasons. Firstly they were in too much of a hurry to fix him one way or another. He was a loose cannon was our Charlie. And secondly Charlie seemed mild, but underneath he was tough. He wouldn't have talked no matter what they did to him. Nobody knew where his records were.'

'But *you* think he did have records?'

'I don't think. I know he did.'

'How?'

'I'll tell you one of these days if you're still hanging around.' He leaned forward and put his empty glass on the coffee table. 'You doing anything this evening?'

'Not particularly.'

Malins reached inside his jacket and took out a wallet, opening it carefully, one side bulging with hundred D-Mark notes and from the other he took a card and handed it to Mason.

'That's my best club. Come and have a bite to eat with us about eight.'

Malins stood up, folding the wallet and tucking it back into his jacket pocket.

Mason glanced at the card which said, 'The Pussy-Cat Club' and the address was in Charlottenburg.

As he looked back at Malins he was already heading for the door. At the door Malins looked back over his shoulder. 'Just show the card and ask for me. I'll tell 'em to look out for you.' And he let himself out without waiting for an answer.

The entrance to The Pussy-Cat Club was between a massage parlour and a TV and radio shop. The door was open but a heavy curtain inside the entrance was guarded by a large man whose tattoos suggested that he had spent time in the merchant navy. Anchors, knots and the points of the compass covered both bare arms. But when Mason showed him the card and asked for Freddie Malins the man was polite and amiable as he led Mason through another door that was protected by a coded security lock.

Inside, the main room was surprisingly large and clean and the tables were white formica each with a vase of flowers in the centre and chairs with comfortable-looking cushions. At the far end was a long bar and the barman in a bow-tie was busy preparing drinks for the only customers, four Japanese, sitting in one of the dimly-lit alcoves with two girls. The girls were young and pretty and only their very low-cut sweaters were concessions to their business.

The doorman guided Mason to the bar, lifted a flap and passed though more curtains that gave onto a staircase that led up to a corridor with half a dozen doors. The man knocked on the door at the end of the passage and when a voice shouted 'Herein' from inside he opened the door and waved Mason inside.

Malins came forward, hand outstretched and showed him to a leather armchair.

'Good to see you, friend. What'll you have?'

'A Coke if you've got one.'

'Diet or straight?'

'Straight please.'

Malins opened the door of a refrigerator and took out a can, putting it on a tray with a glass and a paper napkin. As he moved it to the low table in front of Mason he said, 'How'd you like my place?'

'I thought you lived in Grunewald.'

'I do. But I'm often here until about 6 a.m. so I've made it comfortable.'

'It's quite a place.'

'Surprised, eh. Thought it would be tatty, didn't you?'

Mason laughed. 'Something on those lines, yes.'

The furniture was a mixture of Swedish and leather, the panelled walls alone must have cost a fortune. There was a small bar and at the far end a table that could accommodate eight people. In one corner was a Bechstein boudoir grand.

'Who plays the piano?'

'Nobody, but I couldn't resist it. It's so beautiful. I sometimes pay a guy to play if I'm entertaining. D'you like music?'

'Yes.'

'What d'you like?'

'I like classical stuff but I only play ballads. You know, Gershwin, Kern and that sort of thing.'

'You actually play?'

'Yes.'

'Play me something.' The enthusiasm was so patently genuine that Mason couldn't refuse.

As he opened the keyboard lid and made himself comfortable on the double-stool, he smiled at Malins who was leaning on the piano.

'What would you like?'

'"Goodnight Sweetheart". D'you know it?'

Mason smiled and started playing and the requests were continuous. 'Manhattan', 'Love walked in', 'You were never lovelier' and finally a couple of Bing Crosby numbers – 'Please' and 'Thanks'. As he closed the lid, Malins was looking at him and there were tears in his eyes. 'You know I'd give a million to be able to play like that.' Then as if to emphasise the truth he added, 'Pounds, Dollars, D-Marks. You name it.'

'Why don't you take lessons?'

Malins shrugged. 'Too many other things to do.' He sighed. 'Let's eat.'

A homely, middle-aged lady brought in a dish of cold cuts and a bowl of salad and there was coffee in a *cafetière* on a tray with a jug of cream and a bowl of sugar.

'Just help yourself, James.'

'Thanks. Has the Wall coming down helped your businesses?'

Mason helped himself to a couple of rounds of cold beef and a sliced tomato.

'Yeah.' Malins smiled. 'They cleared out the porn shop in two days.

There was nothing like that on the other side.' He waved his fork. 'Mind you a chap came over once a week for videos for that old crook Honeker.'

'You mean porn videos?'

Malins smiled. 'We don't sell anything else. The clubs were always busy but in the first couple of months the Ossies didn't have the money. The garage does well. They still can't believe they can just get all the gas they want.'

'This man you reckon knocked off Foster. Do you know his name?'

'Yeah. But I ain't telling you, my friend. That's for sure.'

'Why not?'

'Don't be silly. I don't want to end up floating in the canal. I've got my own minders but they ain't in the same league as that fellow.'

'Is he SIS?'

'He was but they made him freelance. He was a bit rich even for them. By the way I told my Stasi guy to come to the club after he closes the garage tonight. Seems he met Charlie Foster a couple of times.' He looked at his watch. 'Be about another half hour.' Pointing at a bowl he said, 'Try those strawberries, they fly 'em in from Italy.'

'What was Foster like?'

'Funny you should ask that.' He paused and looked at Mason. 'He was very like you. About the same age and build and the same temperament. Much sharper than he looked. Listening but not giving anything away. A tough cookie under the mild appearance.'

Mason smiled but said nothing, and then the phone rang. Malins reached behind him and nodded as he listened, finally saying, 'OK. He'll be down in five minutes.'

He turned back to Mason. 'The Stasi guy's down in the club room. Have your coffee and I'll take you down and introduce you.'

The German was younger than he expected, an open, pleasant face, and when the introductions were over Malins left them alone.

'Freddie tells me that you knew Foster. Did you work with him?'

'No. I was just a guard where the Englishman was kept prisoner. Foster used to come and talk with him.'

'Who was the Englishman?'

'His name was Tarrant.'

'Why was he a prisoner?'

'He had been asking around about Foster. He'd been sent to find him.'

'To do what?'

The man shrugged. 'I don't know but he said he was only required to locate him and not make contact.'

'What was their relationship?'

'At first Foster seemed very aggressive towards Tarrant but after a few meetings it all changed and Foster was very friendly with him.'

'Why the change?'

The man shrugged. 'I've no idea.'

'What kind of work did Foster do for the KGB?'

'I don't know. He worked from a private house. I had to pick him up from there a couple of times when he was visiting Tarrant. I seem to remember somebody said he was into monitoring. Radios and that sort of thing. Maybe it was interception. There were other people at the house. A senior KGB man, a girl and a couple of servants.' He shrugged. 'I don't remember much. I wasn't all that interested at the time. I was just a guard. But I often had to hang around waiting for him and I'd hear them talking.'

'Well, thanks for your help. Would you like another drink?'

'I wouldn't mind a vodka.'

Mason looked around for a waitress and saw that the club was full now. And the waitresses now were topless. He signalled to a girl who jiggled over to the table.

'A vodka and a lager, please.'

'Are you a member, sir?'

The Stasi man said, 'He's Freddie's guest, sweetheart. Get cracking.'

The girl smiled. 'No problem.'

When she had left the German said, 'Are they still worried about Foster?'

'Who?'

'Your people in London whatever they call them. MI6 isn't it?'

Mason ignored the question and then the drinks arrived. He gave the girl a ten D-Mark tip and lifted his glass to the German. 'Your good health, comrade.'

The German shrugged, tossed down his vodka and stood up, holding out his hand and as Mason took it the German said, 'Contact me at the garage if you need anything more from me.'

Mason nodded. 'Thanks, I will.'

As Mason was finishing his lager Freddie Malins joined him at the table.

'Was he any use to you?'

Mason shrugged. 'He gave me some background, that's all. I'll have to think about it.'

'How long you staying in Berlin?'

'Until I've got some hard news about whatever Charlie Foster was using to pressure my lot in London.'

Malins said dryly, 'Could be a long stay, Jimmy.'

'What makes you think that?'

'You won't be the only one who's looking for Charlie Foster's stuff. German intelligence will be looking for it too. If they haven't already got it. Then there's the French and the CIA.' He paused and looked at Mason. 'I doubt if you're even the only one from SIS who's sniffing around.' He waved his hand. 'Don't take it the wrong way, my friend, but you could be just another Tarrant.' He shook his head slowly. 'On your own you won't make it. That's for sure.'

'SIS probably didn't rate Charlie Foster all that highly or he wouldn't have gone over to the other side.'

Malins laughed. 'Fair enough. Good thinking. But remember, it wasn't SIS but the KGB who saw him as an asset. It isn't just your lot who want Charlie Foster's dope. There are others, the KGB and the ex-Stasis who could find a good use for it.'

'You sound as if you know what Charlie Foster's information was.'

Malins laughed. 'I'm bloody sure I know.'

'So what was it?'

'Like I said. If we get to know one another better I'll tell you.' He shrugged dismissively and changed the subject. 'Do you want a bit of female company for the night? You won't find anything better outside.'

Mason thought for a moment and then said, 'Thanks for the offer. But I'd better get on my way. Are you going to be around tomorrow?'

'I'm around every day. Give me the card I gave you.'

Mason searched his pockets, found the card and handed it to Malins who wrote a number on the back of the card. 'This number can put you through to me wherever I happen to be. But be careful what you say. The police and the BND all use scanners to monitor calls on mobiles.'

He pushed back the card to Mason and stood up. For a moment he was silent and then he said softly, 'We could put something together you and me. Think about it.'

Back in his hotel room Mason sat at the small writing desk making notes on a sheet of hotel notepaper. It was a slow process as he let his mind go over his conversations with Malins and the ex-Stasi man.

It took over an hour before he had finished. There wasn't much. Nothing concrete. But this sort of job always took time to get moving. He read the list of points again. It was a short list.

1. Ex-S man knows house where F lived.

2. Malins knows more about F's information than he has told me.

3. Ex-S man referred to F's girl-friend. Who was she? Where is she now?

4. Contact Tarrant. (Check his 'P' file).

5. Check M's 'P' file thoroughly.

6. Identity of man who M claims killed F.

CHAPTER 7

The call came in just before lunch from the editor of *The Times*. He would only speak to the Director-General. After two or three minutes of fencing so that Sir Peter could be warned, the editor was put through.

'Sir Peter Crombie?'

'Speaking. How can I help you?'

'Gartside. *The Times*. We're going to print a piece on Boyce-Williams, I thought it might be useful to speak to you first.'

'Boyce-Williams? For Christ's sake. He's dead.'

'I know, we did an obit on him.'

'So what's the story?'

'The story is that he was a paid informer for East German intelligence, the Stasis. Briefed them on the inside thinking of the government of the day. Covers quite a long period.'

'Sounds libellous to me.'

The editor laughed. 'Who's going to sue us?'

'When are you printing the story?'

'Probably tonight.'

'Maybe you'd better come and see me and show me whatever evidence you claim to have.' He paused. 'Somebody *may* sue you, despite what you're told.'

'When?'

'Come over right now. I'll lay on a couple of sandwiches.'

As Gartside switched off the recorder he looked at the two reporters. 'He's scared all right. Or he'd have told me to get stuffed.' He paused. 'Keep it till tomorrow but make it part of a general sleaze story. Dish up all the recent stuff and make this a "last straw" story. How corrupt can you get and still govern the country?' He shrugged and smiled. 'You don't need me to tell you how to do it. Exclusive to us.'

* * *

Despite having had a fifteen minute talk to Harding, Sir Peter knew he wasn't winning. It was the same document that he had received that *The Times* had shoved across his desk. He went through the motions of reading it carefully and then pushed it back.

'What else have you got?'

Gartside grinned. 'What more do you want? You've got dates, places, subject discussed and how much pay-off.'

Sir Peter leaned back in his chair, shaking his head. 'Any political lobbyist could have given 'em that stuff.'

'From inside the cabinet? No way. Not just experienced guesses. Not just speculation. But the actual details.'

'May I ask where you got it?'

'From an American journalist. He'd offered it to the *Washington Post* who told him that hanky-panky by British ministers was of no interest to their readers. They'd had a belly-full.' He laughed. 'Got enough of their own stuff.'

Sir Peter shrugged. 'Maybe your readers are sick of it too.'

'If I give you a copy would you like to have it checked out?'

'You think I'm going to waste the time of my people on checking if Boyce-Williams was seen having a cup of tea in Liberty's tea-room years ago?' He smiled a wintry smile. 'You must be joking.' He paused. 'Have *you* checked it out?'

'No. We'll just leave it for the public to make up their own minds.' He sighed. 'Would you like us to say that a senior spokesman from SIS denies it all?'

'No, dear boy. But you'll probably say it anyway.'

The Foreign Secretary admired Arthur Ramsey. He was a good Prime Minister but he seemed to have lost touch with what the public were thinking about the Party. His friends likened him to Harold MacMillan and the adjective the media always used was 'patrician'. There *were* similarities. They were both Scots, they were both wealthy with large Scottish estates measured in thousands of acres. They both spoke with what most people felt was an affected accent and they never panicked no matter what happened. An amused smile had always been enough acknowledgement of bad news. The commentators always said that the Foreign Secretary was the only member of the cabinet who was heeded by the PM. He seldom ventured advice and there was no indication that it *was* ever heeded. The constituency parties loved Arthur Ramsey. For them he was a figure of self-confidence and optimism, and a man above petty political game-playing. The sniping from the Opposition was dismissed as proof enough of petty minds at work. Not a real politician of any substance among them, let alone a solitary statesman. Best ignored and humoured in their foolishness when the TV cameras were covering PM's Question Time.

Ben Porter had arranged the meeting with the PM, himself and Sir Peter and although he knew it was necessary he didn't look forward to it.

They sat in the small garden at the back of 10 Downing Street, the PM's official residence; and the meeting had not provided a solution. The PM had enough other things to worry about and didn't want to spend time discussing what he considered to be muck-raking by the media. The Foreign Secretary wanted a lead.

'Both Sir Peter and I feel that the constant sniping by the Opposition and the media is beginning to have an adverse affect on the Party's standing in the country.'

'Oh come now, Ben. Nobody's going to give credence to that stuff. They are obvious nincompoops. A jab at us now and again might work. But day after day . . .' he shook his head '. . . there's a kind of Gresham's Law about political twaddle – the weak currency drives out the strong.' He smiled. 'But if you're all that worried have a word with the Whips. I've not heard any complaints from the back-benches.'

'Of course not. They wouldn't raise the subject with you.'

'Why not, for heaven's sake?'

'Because you're you, Arthur. Too revered, too admired to be upset by bad news.'

'You really feel that it's that bad?'

'Yes. We both do.' He nodded towards Sir Peter.

The PM was silent for a few moments and then he said, 'What do you want to do about it?'

'Hit back at them.'

Arthur Ramsey shrugged and smiled amiably. 'I'll leave it to you chaps then.' He looked at his watch. 'I'll have to go. Mary's taking me to see the new granddaughter.'

He put his arm round Ben Porter's shoulders as he walked them both to the back gate.

As they stood at the foot of the steps to the main doors of the Foreign Office, Ben Porter said to Crombie, impatiently, 'Why can't the Whips keep these bastards under control?' He paused. 'And for that matter, why is there never a whiff of warning on these things from your people at SIS or from the Security Services?'

'Ben. Calm down. How can any organisation keep tabs on several hundred MPs, their staff, and their private lives now and in the past. Twenty-four hours a day?'

'But why always our people? The other lot are just as delinquent so why are they never seen coming out of massage parlours or taking bribes for asking questions in the House?'

There was a long pause and then Sir Peter said quietly, 'We could guide a few arrows their way if you felt it might help.'

Porter stood brushing dust from his jacket. 'So what do you want me to say – go ahead?'

'Yes. If you wish.'

'I can't say yes. You know that. I'll just have to leave it to you.'

And so far as Sir Peter Crombie was concerned that was enough.

The story broke in *The Times* and the *Guardian* three days after the meeting with Crombie and, inevitably, it came up at Thursday's PM's Questions at 3.15 p.m. It was the second question to the PM and they'd gone through the formula of him being asked his movements for the day.

'I refer the Honourable Member to the answer I gave to the previous question.' He sat down and knew what was coming on the supplementary from the Opposition back-benches, delivered in a grating Glaswegian accent that made its contents barely understandable and with a venom that sent drops of saliva flying onto the heads of members on the lower benches. Hansard recorded it without the elaborate arm waving and frenzied delivery.

'Madam Speaker. In view of the report in today's copy of the Tories' own paper, *The Times,* giving details of the monies received by the late Chairman of the Conservative Party for his traitorous connections with the East German security services. Does the Prime Minister not accept that this calls for his resignation? Are there no depths of sleazy behaviour and corruption that stick in the gullets of the members opposite? For the sake of the country it is time for a general election.'

Arthur Ramsey stood up slowly, his notes ignored on the bench beside him.

'I find it not in the tradition of this House to besmirch the reputation of a former member, now dead; using an unproven, uncorroborated report in a newspaper. The Honourable Member must be singularly gullible and singularly uncouth to have raised the matter. (Pause) Let us hope that he himself is never the target of a smear campaign.'

There was much waving of order papers from the government benches and the questions moved on to the NHS and rising crime figures.

Crombie had watched from the Strangers' Gallery and thought that the PM had done well in the circumstances. The press had obviously lapped it up. It would keep the story going and there wasn't much real news at the moment. He thought that the Opposition had taken on board the veiled hint of a threat and were slightly subdued. He would get his people checking out MacTavish right away.

CHAPTER 8

Peter Crombie had booked into the Compleat Angler at Marlow just after mid-day and now stood on the edge of the weir hooking up the long green strands of weed from the steps. He cast out his line and sat down. He was not an expert angler but he found fishing a great solace after the Machiavellian manoeuvres of his normal work.

Until he had taken up his new appointment he had no interest in politics unless it affected the Army. He despised the politicians who produced nothing but affected the lives of so many ordinary people, justifying their misdeeds and mistakes on the grounds that they had been elected by the people they governed so badly. Winston Churchill was his only exception and even he had had to move from party to party in desperation. And now it was politically correct to criticise the man who had led them to victory. The catchpenny scribbles of critical biographers who claimed to be historians, most of whom hadn't been born when the war was being fought.

For some time Crombie had been worried about the way the country was going. It seemed to him that the media had become a self-appointed government. Everything that the real government did was categorised as catastrophical and against the people. They seemed to have a panel of people they could call on to prove that the health service was useless if not deliberately harmful, that identity cards that might help the police were a breach of civil rights. Ministers and leaders of industry were traduced in the gutter press. And if someone suggested that the media should be controlled in some way they were labelled as Fascists. No government was always right but even the most inept government was likely to be right from time to time. But not in the eyes of the opposition and the media.

Public figures, even the Royal Family and quite ordinary people were done over by the media with virtually no chance of rebuttal or even correction. The media's response to criticism was 'OK, sue us', knowing full well that virtually nobody had the money to mount a libel case. You could win your case and still go bankrupt from lawyers' costs. No newspaper would give you space to criticise another newspaper. The old motto 'Dog don't eat dog' still applied.

Uncorroborated slanders could be voiced in the House under the protection of parliamentary privilege and could then be quoted by the media with impunity.

Criminals were lauded and became rich from books and films of their murderous lives, and any fanatical lunacy of 'political correctness' could be given space and time. The government seemed powerless to stop it. Grateful for a couple of days respite from experts who claimed in the media that somehow record production figures meant a rise in mortgage rates. Was this the 'Land fit for heroes' that men had fought for in two world wars? The country under Winston had fought for fourteen months alone, with no allies after the French surrender. And now the President of the USA said that if there *was* a 'special relationship' it was with the Germans. And the French swaggered around the corridors of power in Brussels openly deriding the British. The opposition, despite their venomous attacks on the government, were totally ineffective. They had no power and they knew it. Behaving like bullies in a school playground was their only consolation. The opposition's new man looked like a real leader but the rest of them were the old hacks, the spokesmen for their paymasters, the unions. But nobody seemed ready to do anything about it. He knew from his army experience that when there was a problem that seemed insoluble it was always one man who provided the solution. Like David Stirling and the Long Range Desert Group that became the SAS, and Winston Churchill with Special Operation Executive. Not forgetting Bletchley Park and Enigma, civilians not soldiers.

Maybe he should be the instigator and do something before it was too late. But it would take more than one man to tackle this problem. He would have to give it some thought. It was at that moment that a pike took his line. He didn't like pike and he had no compunction in clubbing it with the handle of his keep-net.

He had dinner alone at the hotel and drove back refreshed and content. Even the M4 was virtually empty. It was after midnight when he got to Chelsea.

There was a note stuck with Blu-Tack to the hall mirror.

'There's another of those envelopes. I've put
it on your desk in the study. Must have come
between 9 – 10.30 p.m.
Don't fret.
Love,

Di xxxx'

He sighed as he walked upstairs to his study. Maybe it was just an ordinary letter. But if it wasn't, who would it be aimed at this time?

He tore the envelope open and pulled out the contents. It was three pages this time. He pulled up a chair, moved the table-lamp nearer and read the pages.

Subject: Nelson Overy   10.24.40

Place of birth: Richmond, NY

Status: After university (Boston) took Law Degree (Yale) and joined lawyers Stauffenberg and Collins at their Washington Head Office. Specialised on fraud and general litigation. Became partner. Saw service in Vietnam. Infantry. Promoted to Captain and awarded C. Medal of Honour. Served as attorney for CIA. Appointed dep. director CIA by incoming President. Resigned after two years on grounds of ill-health. A year later was appointed as 'Roving ambassador' by President.

J.R. Assessment.
Subject is ostensibly an out-going personality but in fact is tortured by self-doubt which leads him to need sustaining as being valuable. Driven by multi-faceted ambitions. Generous with money but feckless. Subconsciously constantly seeking approval of peers and superiors. Subject to short periods of severe depression.

Feb 7 1982 Meeting in Washington 105 George St. with Anton Blum. Gave details of Reagan budget deficit and assessment of effect on defence procurement.   1.5K

May 4 1982 Discussed likely government reaction to proposed mass protest in June in New York. Outside United Nations. Favourable response. Meeting with Reiss at Marvin Centre Cafeteria in Washington. 3K

Aug 1 1982 Meeting in LA. Pett's Pizza. Attending Olaf Lund. Gave details of intended landing of US troops in Beirut and PLO evacuation. 25K

March 17 1983 Meeting in New York at China Grill with Steiner. Discussed Reagan's plans on development of anti-missile system to destroy missiles before reaching targets. Called 'nuclear shield'. Assesses as highly dangerous and suggested proposals violate 1972 ABM treaty with Soviet Union. 15K

Oct 25 1983 Meeting at Broadway Diner in N.Y. with Kaufmann. Discussed White House reaction to bombing of marine compound in Beirut with 200 deaths. Indicated likely actions to be taken. 10K

Sept 14 1983 Meeting at YWCA Cafeteria, Washington with Blum. Discussed White House reaction to shooting down of Korean airliner. Indicated intensive propaganda campaign against Soviet Union. Suggests no military action likely. 20K

Oct 23 1983 Meeting at Cafe Plaza, Washington with Blum. Gave warning of impending invasion of Grenada by US marines. Congress expected to react unfavourably. Reagan will use remit by organisation of Eastern Caribbean States as giving authority. 20K

June 4 1984 Meeting in Washington, Astor Restaurant with Blum. Gives details of Reagan's visit to Peking (see detailed notes). Reagan agreed to sell Peking nuclear reactors. 15K

Feb 15 1986 Meeting in Washington, Astor Rest. with Stone. Gives details of explosion of Shuttle Challenger. 20K

April 7 1986 Meeting in Washington at The Gallery with Blum. Gave details of American bombing of Libya. Some aerial photographs. 30K

Nov 9 1986 Meeting in Washington. Kays Sandwich Shop. Blum. Exposure imminent of US arms deals with Iran. Trouble with Congress expected. 10K

Jan 6 1988 Meeting in New York, Market Diner with Blum. Discusses Reagan's visit to Moscow. White House hopes for friendly atmosphere. 15K

June 3 1988 Meeting in Washington at The Nanking with Blum.

White House plans pressure through UN on Iran to end Iran–Iraq war.   5K

Note: Further meetings on record up to Nov 27 1989. Figures represent cash payments in US dollars. Direct payments to Swiss and Cayman bank accounts amount to 750,000 US dollars.

Like the first time, there was neither covering note nor a demand for money, and no explanation of what the sender expected him to do with it. Why send it to him? Why not to the Director of the CIA? He wasn't surprised at what he read. He had met Nelson Overy a couple of times. He was always described as the White House's trouble-shooter but in fact he was a 'fixer'. He did deals. Trading influence for favours. The favours were supposed to be for the benefit of the administration and sometimes they were but sometimes they were for Nelson himself or one of his associates. He had heard that in the early days old Nelson had made five hundred bucks a time just for fixing for some petty businessman to be photographed standing alongside the President. He wondered what the CIA would do about it. They'd play for higher stakes than just a discreet resignation. And some of them wouldn't grieve too much if the President himself went down the Swanee with Nelson Overy. Washington played the political game by the big boys' rules. Maybe it would be better to pass this directly and personally to the President.

He stood up slowly, put the envelope and its contents into the drawer of his desk and turned the key, holding the key in his hand as he stood there wondering about whether he would show it to his own people. He decided that he'd best leave it until tomorrow to make a decision.

He looked in on Lady Di but she was fast asleep, the bedside light still on and a paperback copy of Linda Barnes's *A Trouble of Fools* on the floor beside the bed.

As he undressed in his own room it passed through his mind that maybe his thinking should also include something to stop the ridiculous bureaucracy of Brussels and the European Union. When the public had been given a referendum on it all those years ago it had been for a Common Market, not another government consisting of little groupings of self-selected French and Germans laying down laws for others without any intention of obeying them themselves. He read a couple of pages of Hawking's *A Brief History of Time* and was asleep five minutes later.

* * *

One of the few concessions Sir Peter had made to new habits for old was using an electric razor. It wasn't only that he didn't need to wait around to get in the bathroom. He could sit on the edge of his bed and shave as he listened to Today on BBC 4. It never failed to anger him hearing some little whippersnapper harassing some Minister who was trying to get a word in edgeways.

He glanced in the mirror to check that he had left no patches on his jawline, and then he sat back on his bed and checked the contents of his jacket. Wallet, credit-card case, money-clip, house keys and office keys, ball-point, cheque-book, and a small handful of loose coins for parking meters. He looked at his watch. Five minutes before he went down to breakfast. He knew now what he was going to do. And it would suit Diana too. Always wanted the sun. He had another two years to go before retirement and he'd go early. Just do another year, And in that year he'd carry out his plan. He already knew the man to help him do it. It would probably take at least twenty operators to cover the main operation and they would have to be carefully chosen. But first he would have to go through the ritual dance with the Foreign Secretary. He wasn't seeking approval. Just a nod and a wink would be enough. After that a couple of weeks' leave for getting things on the rails.

He caught the Foreign Secretary at Heathrow. He was on his way to New York and the United Nations. He persuaded him to leave the VIP lounge and move into one of the empty immigration offices.

As he cautiously outlined what he had in mind the Minister's face was impassive, and when he was through Benjamin Porter said, 'Have you told me everything?'

'No. Not everything.'

'Was this prompted by our few words after seeing the PM the other day?'

'The campaign by the media and the Opposition has concerned me for quite a time. It seemed to be getting out of hand.' He paused and looked at Porter. 'You seemed to be concerned about it too.'

'I was concerned. Still am, in fact. And I share your suspicions about it being deliberate and planned. But what you've described to me would be equally a conspiracy. Some folk might say – fair enough. Fight fire with fire. But cast your mind to what kind of situation would arise if it came out that the Foreign Secretary had ordered, or gone along with, an operation by the Secret Intelligence Service to counter-attack the media and some of the Opposition. There would be . . .'

Crombie interrupted him. 'I wouldn't be using SIS facilities or staff and I'm not asking for your approval. Let us say that what I described was merely hypothetical . . .' he shrugged '. . . just imaginative speculation.'

Porter was silent for a few moments and then said quietly, 'Don't expect me to cover up for you if it goes wrong. I totally sympathise with your outrage at what's going on but see me as no more than an onlooker. And . . .' he paused '. . . and we never had this conversation. You just came as a courtesy to see me off.' He paused again, then said, 'Take care, old friend. Have a good leave and give Diana my love.'

Porter turned and Crombie watched him walk slowly back towards the VIP lounge.

Crombie used his cell-phone to tell his driver to bring the car round to the main exit. He checked in at the office and then was driven home.

In his study he sat reading the sheet about Nelson Overy again. The meeting with Porter had gone much as he'd expected. A little better if anything. It was all part of the political chess-game, where blind-eyes and deaf-ears were turned when there was a whiff of danger in the air. Danger to reputations. Danger to status and territory. Porter liked being referred to as 'a safe pair of hands', but for Crombie it was just moral cowardice. Honour, personal or political, was no longer a feature of public life. Power was all that mattered. But they were, away from politics, just ordinary men. Not talented but priding themselves on representing the views of their constituents. But never realising that the ordinary members of the public were not interested in the niceties of exporting weapons and technology, nor in the composition of quangos, and when the chips were on the table not much concerned about which party battened onto their earnings. All that mattered was how much they took.

CHAPTER 9

Crombie was put straight through to Swenson, his opposite number at the CIA.

'Hi Peter. How's things?'

'So-so, as usual.' He paused. 'What's the set-up with Nelson Overy at the moment?'

There was a longer pause. 'Are you using the X-phone?'

'Yes.'

'Well press the other button and I'll do the same.'

There was a gap but no clicks and Swenson came back. 'OK. He's giving us a lot of problems at the moment. Advocating drastic cuts in the organisation on the grounds that there's no Cold War etcetera, etcetera. The usual garbage. Rumour says that the White House are going to form a committee under his chairmanship to cut us down to size.' He paused. 'I guess you've got the same attitude in the UK.'

Crombie said quietly, 'I could solve the Overy problems for you permanently if we could meet.'

'Nothing will shift him from the President, Peter,' Swenson said with obvious regret. 'They're old boys from way back.'

'Nevertheless. Like I said, I could give you what I'm sure will get rid of him for good if we could meet in the next forty-eight hours. But I can't come to you. You'd have to come here,'

There was a long pause and then Swenson said, 'Give me a hint, Peter. Just an indication.'

'A Stasi report on your friend. Times, places, money paid. Over a period of ten years.'

'I'll get tonight's Concorde.' The reaction was instant. 'Meet me in and book me in at the Connaught.'

'OK. Will do.'

* * *

Olaf Swenson and Peter Crombie had known one another for years and as they settled down in Swenson's rooms at the Connaught Crombie didn't waste time. He handed over the envelope and said, 'Read that stuff.'

As Swenson sat there reading Crombie wondered what his reaction would be. Swenson's face gave no hint of his feelings. Finally he put the pages back in the envelope and passed it back to Crombie.

The American said quietly, 'Where did you get it, Peter?'

'It was shoved in my letter-box at home. No stamp, no postmark. It was the second lot I got.'

'What was the first?'

'Chairman of the Tory Party, Boyce-Williams. Went through the motions of resigning for health and family reasons and then took an overdose.'

Swenson nodded. 'I remember a report from our embassy.' He paused. 'What are you going to do with this stuff about Overy?'

'I want to do a deal with you. I need some help in another direction.'

'Tell me.'

It took nearly half an hour to outline his plan to challenge the media and the political muck-rakers. When Crombie had finished Swenson looked at him, half-smiling.

'Are you really going to do this?'

'Of course. I ought to have done it at least a year ago. This isn't how a country should be run.'

'I could give you the names of a couple of dozen influential people in the States who've had similar thoughts but without the guts to face them out. How many guys would you need from me?'

'Two. They'd have to be totally loyal and maybe access to half a dozen specialists who could be called on when needed.'

'How many people have seen this Nelson Overy stuff?'

'Just me. I haven't reported that I received it. I would pass it to you with no conditions as my part of the deal. You can shred it or use it any way you want. As far as our deal is concerned it doesn't exist. But if you use it you don't ever reveal that it came from me.'

For a few moments Swenson was silent, then he said, 'OK, my friend. It's a deal.'

'Will you use it?'

'You bet I will. That bastard's done a lot of damage. If this stuff got to the press in the States it would almost certainly bring down the

President. He may be a fool but he doesn't deserve that.' He paused. 'Let's talk about the guys you need.' He smiled. 'I'm going to enjoy seeing your operation working. Anything I can do, I'll do. Just tell me.'

They talked and planned until the early hours of the morning and Swenson flew back to Washington via Toronto. Well satisfied with his meeting and in the unusual position of not only ensuring the downfall of the CIA's main detractor but also deciding who to bring down with him. He admired the Brit's intensely patriotic attitude. The outrageous thinking was more American than British yet he wouldn't have dared to put up a similar plan to fight the bad effects of the media in the US. But the Brit was right. It was time for someone to draw the line and if Crombie was ready to do it he would help in any way he could.

Meantime he'd have to think carefully about how to deal with Nelson Overy. He could go direct to the President and show him alone the evidence. But he knew all too well what would happen. It would be swept under the carpet and Swenson was determined to prove that not even the President's cronies could indulge in treason and get away with it. Just thinking about doing it gave him incredible pleasure. Two days to think about it, and the implications, and then he'd press the button.

CHAPTER 10

Mason looked at four furnished apartments and chose one in Marburger Strasse over a restaurant, and signed a four-month lease, payment in advance. It was sparsely furnished but clean and newly decorated with a well-fitted kitchen with a dish-washer and clothes washer. In the sitting room there was a TV and VCR and a Sony compact hi-fi stack.

He moved his kit from the hotel the same evening and telephoned a booking on the early morning flight to London the next day.

When he signed in at mid-day the next day there was rumour that SIS's move to Vauxhall Bridge Road had been postponed again. And he found that Harding had just started a week's leave and was only contactable in an emergency.

At Archives he wrote out the request for Tarrant's 'P' file and the clerk fed his ID number into the computer before calling up the number of Tarrant's file.

He looked at Mason. 'There are two people named Tarrant with "P" files. What initials have you got?'

'I can't remember. One is the father, the other the son. It's the son's file I need.'

The clerk looked back at the computer screen and said, 'I'll bring it to you in the reading section. It's supervised reading by the way. No notes, no copying. OK?'

Mason shrugged. 'OK. If that's how it is.'

It was five minutes before the clerk handed him the buff file and a numbered ticket for a reading position.

The file of John Rowan Tarrant was just two A4 pages of double-spaced typing. He read both pages quickly and then turned back to the first page. It gave the basic details of date of birth, current address and date of recruitment into the Intelligence Corps. There was the usual fruit-salad of training courses that Tarrant had taken and a reference to the fact that his father was ex-SIS and Intelligence Corps. A file reference for his father was given. There was very little about Tarrant's service postings but he had been with the SIS detachment in Berlin for fourteen months. But the time he was there didn't cover Foster's service there or his defection. Tarrant appeared to have been brought back to London and then transferred to Port Security at Liverpool. The final entry was an indication that Tarrant had suffered some disability in the course of his duties which necessitated him retiring aged thirty-four with a full pension and a tax-free special payment of £20,000. There was no indication of what the disability was or where it was sustained. What puzzled Mason was why Tarrant's seemingly innocuous file was in a restricted category. He recognised from long experience that this particular 'P' file was not intended to be really informative. Somebody was putting down a marker. A piece of insurance in case some action or lack of it was queried in the future. He memorised the latest address that had been given, handed the file back to the archive clerk and wrote Tarrant's address on the back of an envelope. It was a house in a village just outside the village of Broadway in Worcestershire in the Cotswolds.

He hesitated between going to Croydon to get his own car or hiring a car in London. He decided that it was a long enough journey to make the pleasure of using the Healey worth the inconvenience.

At Broadway he stopped for a snack at the Lygon Arms and got directions to Tarrant's address.

The cottage was on a small estate that had once been a stables and parked at the main house were three Jaguars, two XJ6s and a convertible XJS. As Mason parked his car a man came out of the cottage and walked towards him.

'Nice crate you got there,' he said, pointing at the Healey.

Mason smiled and patted the car's bonnet. 'Thanks. I love her.' He paused. 'I'm looking for Mr Tarrant if he's around.'

'I guess that'll be my old man. He's the vintage cars and antiques man.'

'It was Johnny Tarrant I wanted to speak to. Is that you?'

'Sure is. What can I do for you? I'd better explain that we only deal with Jaguars and my father does all the buying.' He smiled. 'I'm just the mechanic.'

'Could I take you for a drink somewhere?'

'I can give you a beer in my place.' He pointed at the cottage.

'That's very kind of you.'

In the kitchen Tarrant opened the refrigerator and turned to Mason. 'Worthington or Boddington's?'

'Worthington please.'

Tarrant put the two cans on the kitchen table with two glasses.

'Take a seat and help yourself.'

Tarrant drank from the can and Mason did the same. When Tarrant put down his can he wiped his mouth with the back of his hand and said, 'What can I do for you?'

'I wanted to ask you about Charlie Foster.' And as he spoke he opened his leather ID card case and showed it to Tarrant.

He saw the surprise on Tarrant's face turn to anger before Tarrant turned his head away, looking towards the open window and a net curtain that was moving slowly in the breeze. Then Tarrant looked back at him. Angry and suspicious.

'Which of them sent you?'

'Nobody sent me. They told me to try and trace what had happened to Charlie Foster's records and your name came up when I was in Berlin.'

'Who from?'

'A German named Laufer.'

'I've never heard of him.'

'Used to be in the Stasi. Said he was one of your guards when you were picked up and held by the KGB.'

Tarrant shrugged. 'I never knew their names.'

'He said Charlie Foster visited you a number of times when you were in custody.' He paused. 'What were you doing in East Berlin when they picked you up?'

Tarrant half-smiled. 'Same as you. Looking for Charlie Foster.'

'What do you think happened to him?'

'They killed him.'

'Who's they?'

'London. SIS. He used to visit a chap named Malins. They waited for him, shoved him in a car and took him away.'

'Why did they do that?'

'He had information which they said could cause a lot of trouble. Stuff about Stasi and KGB informants in the West.'

'What happened that made you take early retirement?'

'I got shot in my shoulder in the Foster business and kicked around mentally, and they thought I knew too much. They wanted to make sure I didn't talk.'

'If they killed Charlie Foster they could have killed you too.'

Tarrant shook his head. 'No way. My old man was in SIS. They'd never have got away with it.' He paused. 'I had to sign a document that I'd never talk about what went on. They could do me just for talking to you.'

'They couldn't. You obviously signed under duress. A court would throw it out in five minutes.' Mason paused. 'Could I talk a little more about Foster?'

'If you want.'

'I noticed a pub in the village. Could I ask you and your father to have a meal with me there?'

'Dad's in America escorting two XK120 Jaguars but I'll have a meal with you.'

It was only when he had to help Tarrant on with his jacket that he realised that he could barely use his left arm, and Tarrant said, 'Thanks. They made a bit of a mess of my shoulder.'

During dinner at the pub they talked of nothing but cars. They found they were both fans of 1965 Mustangs but they had to be red. The landlord agreed to find James Mason a room for the night and they drove back to the cottage with a six-pack of Boddington's and a bottle of Chateau Latour.

When they were settled, Mason asked, 'Tell me about Charlie Foster.'

'When he first came to see me after I was arrested he was very antagonistic. Against SIS and me too. But after a couple of meetings he was more relaxed. Even friendly. Made them give me better conditions and talked about me and my father and him and his family back in England.

'He told me about his girl-friend. Her name was Gala and she was half-Russian. Her father was one of the Soviet Union's top film directors. He was seldom around. Had houses in Paris and LA and apartments in Moscow and Portofino.'

'Can you remember her father's name?'

Tarrant frowned as he thought. 'His first name was definitely Sergei and I think his family name was something like Leon.'

'Leonov?'

'Yes.' Tarrant looked surprised. 'Have you heard of him?'

'Yes. He's famous. Most people assume that he's an American. He looks like one and talks like one. His films are rather like Fellini's films. Extravagant, over the top, but beautiful. Gets criticised for showing corruption and decadence without condemning it.'

'Another guy he mentioned was Hartmann. He didn't live with them but he was part of the group. I think he was a German, a link between the KGB and the Stasis.'

'Did you know the man named Malins?'

'No. I'd heard the name. I think way back he was SIS and I heard talk that he was thrown out.'

'Because of a connection with East Berlin?'

'No. I think it was black-market. Not just the usual stuff that every-body does, but on a big scale.'

'How did you get your shoulder?'

'Foster had helped me to escape. I was hiding in a girl-friend's apart-ment in West Berlin and the German security people had been watching it. They mistook me for Foster and when they burst in the guy had a gun. I shot him but he plugged my arm first. The BND guy was dead and SIS got me to hospital and shipped me home the same night on an RAF plane. Both SIS and the Germans wanted to keep it all quiet.'

'Did Foster give you any idea of what the KGB or the Stasis used him for?'

'He was definitely working for both but his clout came from the KGB. He had been in Signals before he was transferred into the I Corps, he'd been monitoring Soviet and East German military radio. He was bilingual German–English. I'd guess he was doing that sort of thing for the KGB. A sort of technical consultant.' Tarrant reached over and filled Mason's glass with the last of the wine. As he put down the bottle he looked across at Mason, lifting his own glass. 'Cheers.' When he put down his glass he said, 'I got the impression that apart from Gala the person who had most influence over him was a chap at the university named Rosen. He was a professor of something or other.

Psychology I think. People told me he was often on TV talking about current affairs.'

'Did Charlie Foster talk to you about him?'

'He said he was a man who had ideas that could change how we live.'

'In what way?'

Tarrant shrugged. 'I didn't follow any of it. It didn't interest me. I was more interested in Charlie's promise to have me released.'

'Why do you think he took so much trouble to get you released?'

'I'd told him about my wife who was seriously ill and I think that made him sympathetic.' Tarrant smiled and shrugged. 'And of course he hated the people in SIS.'

'Going back to Rosen, what part did he play in Charlie Foster's work with the KGB?'

'My impression is that Rosen also worked for the KGB and that was how they met.' He paused. 'Don't get me wrong when I say Charlie was impressed by this guy. He definitely didn't like him. He was impressed by him but he said he thought he was a dangerous man.'

'In what way?'

Tarrant shrugged. 'I've no idea. Just said he was a fanatic and Hitler was a fanatic and all fanatics are dangerous.' Tarrant sighed heavily and Mason felt that he was tiring the man unduly.

He stood up. 'I'd better get back to the pub.' He held out his hand. 'Thanks for your help. I'll let you know how it all turns out.'

As Tarrant shook hands he frowned and grimaced and said, 'Don't. I'd rather not know.'

The next morning Mason phoned Ricky who looked after the Healey and fixed for him to pick up the car from the short-stay parking at Gatwick. Mason was back in Berlin late that afternoon.

CHAPTER 11

When Swenson asked for half an hour of the President's time it took nearly a week before a meeting could be arranged. The President was relaxed but defensive.

'Morning to you. What's the problem?'

'It's several problems, Mr President.' He paused and pushed the pages across the President's desk. 'I think you'd better read that before we talk.'

He watched Carson as he read the pages twice and then tossed them to one side.

'Where did you get this rubbish?'

'It's not rubbish, Mr President. I've had some of it checked and the information came to me indirectly from the source – Stasi records.'

'And . . . ?'

'I want to make sure that when Nelson Overy is arrested that we can keep you well clear of any dirt that will come out.'

'Meaning what?'

'Meaning that you personally instruct me to arrest Overy and get him up in front of a grand jury inside a week. When I talk to the media I'll make quite clear that you are angry at an old colleague abusing your friendship.'

'And if I veto this proposed action?'

Swenson took a deep breath and said, 'I've called a press conference for 4 p.m. today, sir. Copies of that Stasi report will be made available to the press. Arrangements are already in train to do that.'

The President leaned forward looking grimly at Swenson. 'You ain't gonna last long, my friend, if you go on with this crap. I'll see to that.'

'We'll have to see, sir. Right now I am concerned to see that the

President of the United States of America comes to no harm from this affair.'

'I'll think about it. I'll let you know.'

'It's already on-going, sir. I didn't come here for approval of Overy's arrest. I don't need it. Treason is treason and I guess he'll get a fair trial. I just wanted you to be forewarned.'

'Will you give him bail?'

'No, sir. That wouldn't be wise'

'He'll have the best lawyers in town.'

'He won't. I've already briefed the best lawyer in town.'

'Who? Burke?'

'Yes, sir.'

Carson turned angrily in his chair to look out of the window. There were blooms already on the magnolias and the spring sunshine made the white stone walls even whiter. For a few minutes Carson was silent and then he turned back slowly to look at Swenson.

'You've been trying for this for years haven't you?'

Swenson didn't reply.

'OK. Go ahead. You have my approval. But I warn you, you're going to regret it. It's not only your people who can play dirty. Now get out of my office. In future I'll deal with your deputy.'

Swenson stood up. 'Thank you, Mr President.'

He walked to the door leaving the pages on the President's desk. He despised the man. He didn't even have the political *nous* to pretend to go along with Overy's arrest.

The CIA's Public Relations section had done an excellent job. But with a sitting duck they couldn't really go wrong.

The TV crews were there to show an angry-looking Overy being escorted from a conference of businessmen in the Watergate building. Plain clothes officers bundling him past out-thrust microphones.

The press conference at the CIA's HQ at Langley was calmer and downbeat. Always a sad moment, Swenson said, when a previously respected man close to the White House was found wanting. The law must take its course etcetera. Questions were limited and the answers bland.

By mid-evening a covering statement had been issued by the FBI indicating that Overy had been under suspicion with them for nearly a year.

The White House statement was bland. On the lines of 'these things happen in the best of families'.

The President himself made a glancing reference to what had happened when he addressed a dinner for businessmen that evening. It was on the lines of not rushing to conclusions. It was for the courts to decide. And convict, if appropriate, he added, almost as an afterthought.

Crombie watched it all on CNN on satellite. There was only a brief reference to it on News at Ten.

By the next morning there had been a complaint from the German Ambassador to the State Department, alleging that it was not made clear that Overy's dealings were with the old East German government and the charges against Overy had been categorised as espionage with a German state organisation. Bonn demanded a correction and an apology.

The President received hate mail and phone-calls damning him for having friends who were traitors, and others cursing him for not defending an innocent man whose sole purpose was to relieve the tension between the two countries.

The TV breakfast shows featured TV crews outside Overy's mansion and the newspapers ridiculed a President whose closest associate had been spying under his nose. By the evening editors referred to Overy as spying for the Soviet Union.

Overy's lawyer told the press that it was 'much ado about nothing' and his client was the victim of internal feuding between government organisations.

The grand jury assembled on the Saturday morning and found good cause for the case to go to trial.

The Sunday papers in London gave double-page spreads that rounded up Overy's career and went on to Aldrich Ames via Philby and the inability of expensive intelligence organisations on both sides of the Atlantic to catch their traitors until it was too late to do any good.

The German media gave the affair only the briefest coverage. They were up to their ears in spies and they were bored with spies no matter whose they were.

The President levelled things off with the CIA by insisting that the investigations to be carried out regarding Overy's contacts should be done by the FBI not the CIA. It was after all, he said, a domestic matter, and therefore the FBI's legal responsibility.

CHAPTER 12

Sam Wheeler was in his late sixties. Tanned and fit, and working harder now that he had retired than when he was running his own press agency. He had worked for a number of press agencies in his time, PA, Reuters and two US agencies concerned solely with politics. He had a son who was a travel writer and a daughter who was an artist. He was a grandfather several times over. His wife, Mary, had died five years ago and Sam lived on his own with daily help from a young woman who lived on a nearby estate.

His speciality had always been politics and what, for want of a better description, he called 'current affairs'. And current affairs so far as Sam Wheeler was concerned were the stories behind the stories of the corridors of power. Not just in London and Washington but in most of Europe. There had been many times when SIS had looked to Sam Wheeler for the real facts behind yet another story of alleged corruption in some foreign government. And his knowledge of what was going on in the background of the movers and shakers was better than that of prime ministers and presidents themselves. He had never used his knowledge to provide scandal stories but to assess and forecast what was going to happen in world events. When he retired and set up on his own he was courted by scores of editors, politicians and journalists. He was well-off but far from wealthy. As he frequently said when asked about money he believed that above a certain fairly modest limit, the only use for money was to be able to say 'get stuffed' when he felt like it.

He had served his national service after the war in the Black Watch and although they had served at different times, that was Peter Crombie's old regiment. They had met frequently in the last few years and had great respect for one another.

Sam Wheeler had not been surprised when he got the call from

Crombie asking if he could spare him a couple of hours and pick him up from Orpington Station.

Sam lived in a small, neat bungalow in a quiet area of the London commuter suburb and that was where he had taken Crombie after picking him up from the train.

Sam Wheeler was not an avid gardener but he was fond of, and a collector of, geraniums; pelargoniums to the pedants. They did a tour of the specimens in the conservatory as Sam praised the old-fashioned, vivid red Paul Crampels as being far superior to the newcomers with their emphasis on variegated leaves rather than the flowers. And eventually they made themselves comfortable in cane armchairs around a low glass coffee table with mugs and a thermos of tea. When the tea had been poured, sugared and milked, Sam held up his mug.

'Cheers, old friend. Tell me what I can do for you.'

Crombie took a deep breath. 'I want to ask you a silly question, Sam.'

'Off or on the record?'

'Off. Totally off. Even the question, let alone the answer.'

'So, ask away.'

'I'm worried, Sam. I think the country's going to the dogs. And it's the media that's doing it. Mischievously, wantonly and recklessly. They're taking away our character and our pride in ourselves. They have become like spiteful children. They've brought down several ministers and now I think they wonder if they couldn't bring down a prime minister. And after that maybe they could bring down a government.' He paused. 'Am I right? Or am I getting paranoid in my old age?'

Sam Wheeler leaned back in his chair until it creaked, closing his eyes as he let the sunlight fall on his face. It seemed a long time before he opened his eyes and looked at Crombie.

'First of all. You ain't paranoid, Peter, and never will be. You're not the kind. You're right about what's happening. And it's both serious and dangerous.' He paused. 'But I doubt if it's a concerted thing, and it's the government who have let it become serious. It's become a feeding frenzy, like sharks with the smell of blood. The government should have put a stop to it two, maybe three years ago.' He sighed. 'And I know now what you're going to ask me to do.'

'What?'

'Put up a plan of campaign to stop it.'

'And?'

'And you're gonna tell me that despite what's going on the government haven't the guts to do what's necessary. They are too used to backing off.'

Crombie fiddled inside his jacket and brought out a typed sheet which he handed to Wheeler, who put on his glasses and read the page slowly. When he had finished he smiled and handed it back.

'You couldn't deliver, Peter. They wouldn't let you.'

'If I said that I've already had the nod that I can go ahead – including using SIS special contingencies' funds – would that convince you?'

'Whose nod?'

'The Foreign Secretary.'

Sam Wheeler's disbelief was obvious. 'Are you telling me that he agreed to do everything in this outline plan of yours?'

'Of course not. He knows in general what I'm aiming at and it's up to me. If it backfires – it's me, not him.' He paused. 'And I suspect the PM has had a hint by now.'

'Why are you doing this, Peter? Why stick your neck out when you're near to retirement with a good record. Politicians aren't worth it. None of them.'

'I'm not doing it for politicians, Sam. I'm doing it – or trying to do it – for ordinary people. The ones who lose their jobs because of some stupid regulation. The ones who are buggered about by men who couldn't build a hen-coop to save their lives. The ones the media sneer at because they prefer Cliff Richard to some obscure gang of yobs who call themselves a group but can't play a chord on a guitar. The ones who don't use four-letter words in front of their families.' He paused. 'I love 'em and they deserve better than they're getting.'

'You won't end up doing what you're aiming to do but I guess you could probably frighten the bastards so they're always wondering if it will all happen again if they try it on again.'

'Will you help?'

'What support would I get if I do?'

'Bodies, cash – whatever you need.'

'I'd need very experienced bodies. Journalistic backgrounds and experienced surveillance people.'

'They're available from when you say yes. *If* you say yes.'

'What made your people change their attitude?'

'They haven't said they have changed. But the attack on Boyce-Williams and the arrest of Nelson Overy in the States have had their effect.'

'What's Overy got to do with it?'

'I supplied the proof to Swenson at the CIA.'

'Tell me more.'

Crombie told him the Nelson Overy saga and the basics of the operation in Berlin. When he had finished Sam Wheeler said, 'Do I have a free hand? No interference? Not even from you?'

'So long as you keep me in the picture. The less I know, the better.'

Sam Wheeler was silent for long moments and then he said, briskly, 'OK. Rent me a house somewhere near London. Detached. And open a bank account in my name – about ten, fifteen grand to start with. Not Barclays. That's where my personal account is.' He paused. 'When can I meet Swenson to go over his offerings?'

Crombie shrugged. 'Soon as you want?'

'OK. Give me his number and a number that'll get you any time.'

Crombie wrote two phone numbers on a seed catalogue and handed it over. 'The money will be in Lloyds this afternoon. Their branch in Victoria Street.'

As Sam Wheeler was driving Crombie back to the railway station, Crombie said, 'No matter how it turns out I won't forget today. I'll see it's not forgotten.'

Sam Wheeler laughed. 'I'm going to have some fun, Peter. And all in a good cause too. Don't let 'em get cold feet as soon as it starts working. They've got out of the habit of hitting back.'

'They'll co-operate all right, Sam.' He smiled. 'Even if they don't know they're doing it.'

CHAPTER 13

When Sam Wheeler answered the brief ring and opened the front door he didn't recognise the man standing there. But he noticed the Rover parked outside the house.

The man said quietly, 'Sir Peter told me to contact you.' He hesitated and held out an envelope. 'He's written you a note about me.'

Still standing at the door, Wheeler took the envelope and slit it open rather untidily, opening the single sheet and reading it carefully.

> Dear Sam,
> The bearer, Hugo Renton, is in my confidence
> on the matter we discussed. He could be
> useful.
>
> Yours aye,
>
> Peter.

Wheeler looked at the man's face. He guessed he was in his mid-thirties, fresh-faced and casually dressed.

'Have you got any ID, mister?'

'Of course.' He smiled as he fumbled in his jacket pocket to bring out a thin leather wallet, which he handed over unopened. There was a Barclaycard, a Marks and Spencer's card, a folded driving licence valid for another three years, and a Territorial Army identity card made out to Captain Renton. The last pocket contained a card identifying Hugo Renton as a staff member of the Conservative Central Office.

Wheeler folded up the wallet, handing it back as he said, 'You'd better come in.'

He led his visitor into the kitchen and waved him to a chair at the kitchen table. He wasn't happy that Crombie had made somebody else privy to the operation.

'How did Sir Peter think you could help?'

'Well, sir. As he explained it to me he thought you might find me useful as a sort of bird-dog to indicate prospective co-operators.'

'What's that mean in plain English?'

Hugo Renton smiled amiably. 'I think he means that you may need help in deciding which Member of Parliament would be happy to drop some particular bombshell on a member of the Opposition or even, perhaps, on the media. Biting back rather forcefully at an impolite interviewer – on camera perhaps.' He paused. 'I know them all because of my job and I know their little ways.' He smiled. 'They'd take something as authentic if it came from me. And I wouldn't have to reveal where it came from.'

Sam Wheeler relaxed. It was good thinking. Hugo Renton could be very useful. He looked across the table at his visitor.

'Are you aiming to be an MP eventually?'

Renton looked shocked. 'Good God, no, sir. A politician's the last thing I'd want to be. I think they'll die out eventually.'

Wheeler laughed. 'An interesting thought. Why should they die out?'

'They're useless, sir. They don't contribute to society, just hinder things. If we still have MPs in twenty years' time it will be seen as a form of punishment.'

'Punishment for what?'

'For making "The Market Forces" take over men's lives.'

'You sound like you should be with Her Majesty's Loyal Opposition.'

'I thought of it, sir, but it would be pointless. For them being an MP is all they want. A bit of status, a bit of pretend power. It's the Tories who make things work but they make them work for the establishment, not for the people.' Renton smiled. 'You'll say I'm a raving Red, sir.' He went on. 'It's all there, sir. The Opposition complaining that Tory ministers go off to good jobs in industry and commerce. What they're really complaining about is that nobody in industry or commerce wants *them,* people who can't do anything but talk. It's plain as a pikestaff.'

'Has Sir Peter told you what we're aiming to do?'

'Only roughly, sir, just a general outline. No details.'

'Do you think it will work?'

'It could calm them all down a bit. Like throwing a bucket of water over a couple of dogs fighting.' He smiled. 'Worth a try anyway,' he said encouragingly.

As Wheeler looked at Hugo Renton he was aware that he never much liked young men who said in their ignorance what you had been thinking for years. But instinct told him that Crombie was right. Hugo Renton could be very useful. He knew first-hand which of his brood had a smattering of courage but wasn't stupid. For the first time he noticed that the young man had red hair and the pale skin and freckles that went with it. It gave him a kind of youthful, innocent air that could be useful.

'Where can I get in touch with you, Hugo?'

Renton took out a card. 'There's the Office number and my home number.' He smiled. 'At your service.'

'How did you come to know Sir Peter?'

'He's my uncle, my mother's brother. He paid for my education when my father died.'

'What was your father?'

'He was an SAS officer. He was killed in Northern Ireland.'

'I'm sorry.' He paused. 'And what are *you* going to do?'

Hugo Renton smiled. 'You nearly said – "when I grow up" – I'm not sure what I'll do. I'd like to be a historian or maybe an archaeologist.' He shrugged. 'Something to do with the past.'

Sam Wheeler smiled. 'Sounds like the intellectual's version of growing roses or geraniums.'

They chatted for ten minutes or so about the activities and mechanisms of Conservative Central Office and then Hugo Renton left.

Later that day Sam Wheeler checked three properties and settled for a detached house with big grounds in Clapham. It was ideal for what he wanted. Handy for London, parking space for half a dozen cars and as most similar houses in the area were already divided into flats there would be nothing strange about four or five men going and coming at all hours of the day and night.

Crombie had arranged for a fax machine, a computer and modem and several phones to be installed and the first two Americans were due in two days' time. They were both experienced journalists with several years experience in the past in the FBI, and Swenson had guaranteed their discretion. They had been used in similar roles in Washington and

New York and had been frequent visitors to London in the past few years. They were both in their fifties.

Back at his own place Sam Wheeler sat at the kitchen table and went over his target list. It gave the name, home address, home phone number, office number, brief details of career and photograph of seven editors on leading national newspapers; and the same details of ten TV and radio journalists, all of them well-known political interviewers.

A separate list was of opposition MPs who constantly made smear allegations about government ministers and officials.

Helen McKay was Sam Wheeler's first recruit. She had been born in Edinburgh and had a tendency to distrust Glaswegians despite that city's strenuous efforts to out-do Edinburgh as a cultural centre. Two years in Glasgow city's police force had convinced her that its male-dominated society was not for her. But the two years' experience had shown that she had a natural talent for investigation. Her mother said it was just natural nosiness. When Helen McKay set up as a private investigator she was an instant success. Used by local businesses and the courts, she made a good living for a young woman in her late twenties. Sam Wheeler had been one of her first clients. It was a brief to compile a list of names and addresses of councillors on all of Glasgow's local councils. Her latest assignment from him was a lot more interesting. A look in depth at the financial background of James MacTavish, MP.

Sam Wheeler met the two Americans off the plane at Heathrow. They could have been brothers but Chuck came from Boston and Marty from Houston. They had identified themselves by both carrying a paperback copy of Tom Wolfe's *The New Journalism*. And they had insisted on only their first names being used.

He had taken them for a meal at an Italian place on Lavender Hill and they had gone back to the house with a couple of six-packs of Budweiser.

Afterwards Sam Wheeler had spent an hour talking about their part in the operation. The questions they asked showed that they had well understood what was needed. When their chatting moved on to why it was necessary it was obvious that they felt that their own country was similarly under threat from the media and hundreds of pressure groups.

Sam Wheeler asked. 'When did it start in the States?'

It was Chuck who responded. 'I don't have any doubt when it started. It started November 22, 1963, when they murdered Jack Kennedy.' He leaned forward, his face intent. 'You know they've shown those scenes of the shooting in Dallas thousands of times. I've seen it myself a hundred times. And every time, Godammit, I've prayed that it was just a film and it wasn't gonna happen. There's gonna be a happy ending.' He sighed deeply and settled back in his chair. 'The country couldn't believe it – they still can't believe it.' He paused. 'And after that came the sleaze. A frenzied press and TV looking for dirt – and politicians, made to order – ready to supply it.'

Wheeler said, 'What about the American Dream?'

Marty smiled. 'That was Hollywood's dream. The films formed our ideas of what America was all about. Chicago was factories and gangsters, New York City was slums where tough kids played, colleges were all covered in ivy and pretty cheerleaders. That's how foreign countries saw us too. When *Saturday Evening Post* stopped using Norman Rockwell that really marked the end of the dream for ordinary people.'

Sam Wheeler said, 'So why doesn't somebody do something about it?'

Chuck looked at Marty who just shrugged. Chuck said, 'Who would do it? You've now got three separate groups. The politicians who want it just like it is. The media who've never had such influence. And lastly, ninety per cent of the people who can't do a thing except vote every four years as to which gang of crooks has the next turn in Congress.' He turned to look at Sam Wheeler. 'Helping you with your game might give us some ideas.'

Marty said, 'Which do you want first – newspaper guys or TV?'

'Any way you want.' Wheeler paused. 'Any problems?'

Marty laughed. 'No way. We're used to the bastards and their little ways.'

'Where will you start?'

Chuck said, 'Cleaning ladies, telephone operators, junior office girls and, of course, their neighbours at home.'

Marty said, 'You'd better lay on a couple of cars for us then we don't have to use our passports.' He smiled. 'They're both Canadian.'

Sam Wheeler stood up, stretching his arms. 'OK. I'll do that.' He nodded towards the kitchen. 'The refrigerator's full of food and you've got my number. I'll leave you to it and see you tomorrow.'

In Washington the President's move of shifting the prosecution of the case against Nelson Overy from the CIA to the FBI seemed to have worked and the lead attorney for the prosecution had finally agreed to a meeting with Overy's lawyer, Waring. The meeting was arranged to take place in an office at the courthouse.

Schenk was a tough Brooklyn type who didn't normally handle FBI cases and had been chosen to prosecute for that reason. He sat, hunched up on his chair, watching Waring arrange a pile of law books on the low table between them. He noticed all the marker flags stuck in the case-law volumes. It was Waring who had asked for the meeting and Schenk was intent on making Waring start the talking.

Eventually the books were arranged and Waring looked across at Schenk.

'I thought we should talk, Charlie.'

Schenk shrugged. 'OK. Talk.'

'I guess you've had enough time to realise that you're walking on very thin ice in this Overy business.'

'You must be kidding. But tell me more.'

'All that crap you're putting up about alleged meetings with East German security people won't stand up for a minute once we get into court. In fact I'm seriously considering applying for a pre-trial review on the grounds of a complete lack of evidence on any of the counts in the indictment.'

'Did you come here from your office?'

'No. I came from a client meeting in the Hilton.'

Schenk reached in his brief-case and pulled out a plastic folder, handing it to Waring.

'There's a copy of that waiting for you at your office. We've got two of the contacts. Both willing to testify and already signed sworn statements. We've also applied to Overy's Swiss bank for freezing his funds and releasing information on the grounds that we can prove that the money was obtained by criminal activities. It's all in the folder.' Schenk went on, 'We're going to *subpoena* all his records claiming that what you've produced so far is demonstrably incomplete.'

Waring sighed and was silent for several moments as if he were thinking about what he would say.

Finally, he said, 'Don't drive me to it, Charlie. I don't want to involve the Man.' Schenk could hear the capital letter.

'Why not?'

'You know damn well why not. He'd be impeached and whichever way it went he'd be finished. There's an election in eighteen months' time and your party would be slaughtered.'

'And Nelson Overy walks? You're crazy. And I ain't any party. Never have been.'

'That's what I want to discuss with you.' Waring nodded. Then, as one conspirator to another, he said, 'I know you've got to put on a show. Me too.' He smiled. 'Friend Overy's a difficult man to deal with. He still hasn't got the message.'

'Carry on.'

'How about I assemble a whole raft of evidence that involves the CIA and its methods, question the source of this material and so on. And you quote *New York Times v United States* – the Penkovsky Papers case. The precedent says that you can ask the court to restrain us from publishing our stuff on security grounds. You then go ahead on one count only. We offer a plea-bargain deal. Guilty on the one count. He gets a year and a hefty fine and it's all over.' He shrugged, arms spread wide. 'He'll be disgraced anyway.'

'Hogwash. You'd appeal against the sentence. And you'd come back to me again and want another deal. He'll confess to everything but in strict confidence. He'll reveal names and testify if necessary. He'll walk and you'll have all his old buddies, especially one, swearing he was framed. He'll sell the rights to a book for a couple of million plus film rights.' Schenk shook his head vigorously. 'No way.'

'So you've no objection to me involving the man in the White House?'

'No comment. It's up to you what you do and it'll be on *your* head if you do involve him.'

'Is there any deal you'd consider?'

'Sure there is. He pleads guilty on all the charges and we'll ask only a token jail sentence on the grounds of his co-operation having helped us identify a number of other East German intelligence agents.' Schenk smiled. 'Provided he does co-operate.'

Waring stood up, loading his law books into a leather bag. As he closed the bag he looked at Schenk. 'Who's laying down the ground rules?'

'My office.'

'I don't believe it. Somebody's calling the shots way over your head. Don't blame me when you find yourself with your arse out in the snow.'

Schenk shrugged. 'I won't, my friend. I won't.'

Back in his own office Schenk slung his jacket over the back of his chair, loosened his tie and sat down, reaching for his pad to make notes of his meeting with Waring.

Right from the start it had been a real dog's breakfast. The President had passed the investigation and prosecution of Overy to the FBI. A perfectly legitimate move. The FBI were responsible for the security of the State. But it was intended to be an open insult to the CIA. It also meant that Burke, the attorney chosen by Swenson when it was still in the CIA's hands, would not now be responsible for the prosecution. There was already enough rivalry and tension between the two intelligence organisations without the President's blatant slap in the face of the CIA. He had already heard rumours that the President was just biding his time to find an excuse to remove Swenson.

However, despite the old rivalries, the Director of the FBI had gone out of his way to make clear to both the media and the public that the prosecution of Nelson Overy was a joint FBI/CIA operation. They didn't like President Carson and they were not going to play his game. That's why Schenk had been appointed. He had never acted for either the CIA or the FBI. He was a senior counsel in the District Attorney's office, a specialist on criminal law. Deliberately chosen as a neutral.

But the case he had been given was as flimsy in legal terms as to be non-existent. He couldn't identify the source of the Stasi extracts, he had only two statements and Overy's defence counsel could claim that the meetings were just chats about the world in general. Somebody's lying but who do you believe, a well-known politician or the agent of a discredited foreign intelligence organisation?

He had heard on the grapevine that Overy was raging about being in jail and threatening all concerned with his arrest. But Schenk knew that he could ensure that Overy was in jail for at least a couple more months and a lot could happen in two months.

The phone rang as he was leaving his office. For a moment he contemplated ignoring it but he walked back to his desk and picked up the phone.

'Schenk.'

'Hartley, *Washington Post*, counsellor. You got any comments on this new development?'

'What new development?'

'Looks like the White House pulled the levers for Overy to be let out on bail. Quarter of a million dollars. Seems it was paid in cash by an anonymous guarantor.'

'When's he coming out?'

'He's out already. Due to give a press conference tomorrow some time.' There was a pause. 'Do I gather that you didn't go with this?'

'This is the first I've heard of it.'

'Can I quote you on that?'

'Up to you. You will whatever I say. What reactions have there been?'

'Utter surprise, disbelief – and anger. Most people see the White House finger-prints all over it.'

'Have you contacted the White House?'

'Yes. A firm "no comment". The spokeswoman sounded pretty grim.'

'What line are you taking?'

'Outrage.'

'Thanks for letting me know.'

'What action will you be taking?'

'Raising some hell, kicking some butt.' He paused. 'Who was the judge who heard the application?'

'Guess.'

'Kominski?'

'That's the boy.'

As Schenk hung up he knew that only a miracle would keep the case alive. Kominski was under consideration for the vacant place on the Supreme court and openly the President's nominee. Instinct told him to take no immediate action. There would be turmoil enough from Overy being granted bail and he wanted to see where the chips were going to fall before he decided what to do.

* * *

TV crews and the usual pack of media people waited outside Overy's house all night and it was 2 a.m. when several black limos pulled up outside and a group of people emerged hurriedly from the house, the bulky figure of the politician barely visible, heading for one of the cars, with his coat collar turned up and a scarf around the lower half of his face. TV lights came up and the flashes from still cameras punctuated the shouted questions. The cavalcade of cars was followed by the vans and vehicles of the media. Two or three who still lingered on the sidewalk saw the lights in the house go out ten minutes later.

At 3.30 a.m. a car pulled up in the now empty street and two people, a man and a woman, got into the rear seat of the car. It went over the Arlington Memorial Bridge and then took the Arlington ring road and turned off at 244. On a farm not far from Burke Lake the lights from the large ranch-style house made the night sky seem darker and the tall trees that were a wind-break cast long shadows across the lawn.

Al Simmons, the owner of the farm, was in his early sixties. Overweight but tough with a beer drinker's belly and red hair that was cut in an old-fashioned crew-cut. He was standing at the main window with a portable phone in one hand and a can of beer in the other. There was a tattoo on one hairy arm of an American eagle clutching a rifle in its talons.

When the phone beeped he put it to his ear.

'Yeah – OK. When they get here bring the two passengers to me right away. Don't talk to them. Take the luggage across to the hangar and load it. OK. Roger and out.'

He laid down the phone on top of a TV set and waited until he saw the car headlights as it made its way up the long drive to the house.

Al Simmons took them into the gun-room to give them a drink and hand over the documentation and a bundle of what would soon be their local currency. He didn't like President Carson and he liked Nelson Overy even less. Washington politicians were anathema to Al Simmons, but he had used Overy many times, with appropriate rewards, to preserve the status of the National Rifle Association. But even more important was using him to stop the militia from being outlawed. All he was doing now was paying off his debts with Overy.

The money was no problem and the guarantor he had chosen would just pay what the court decided. The legal boys would make sure that there was no prison sentence handed down.

Nelson Overy had walked along the row of tall glassed-in cases that housed dozens of rifles and hand-guns, including automatic weapons that were in use by the military in every country in the world. He was no longer the experienced fixer but a man who was leaving the world he knew for a life in a country where he was barely known, didn't speak the language, and only had the influence that money could bring. Colombia was not his kind of country and he had only stayed there once overnight when there had been a strike at Bogotá's El Dorado International Airport. He was aware of Simmons' barely disguised hostility but the man was delivering and that was all that mattered.

After a couple of drinks Overy and his wife were led out of the house and along a cement path that led to the massive barn that had been converted into a hangar for a couple of planes. A crop-duster and an ancient but well-cared-for Cessna 210. There would have to be at least two stops for fuel on the way but credit had already been established. The co-pilot checked their seat-belts for take-off and a tractor hauled the aircraft onto the air-strip.

Al Simmons was still drinking beer as he watched the plane roll forward. He saw Overy waving at one of the windows but he didn't respond. When the plane was airborne he made a couple of phone calls and then went to bed. It was already quite light outside.

CHAPTER 14

―――――

It was Freddie Malins who contacted Mason to tell him that Gala's father, Sergei Leonov, was in town for a week and was staying at Kempinski's. It took Mason three telephone calls to persuade a secretary to give him ten minutes with the *maestro*. She had insisted that he stated his business and when he'd mentioned Charlie Foster there was a short silence and then she gave him a slot with Leonov the next day. 5 p.m. at the hotel.

Sergei Leonov had a suite at Kempinski's and a TV crew were gathering up their equipment when Mason arrived. It was a crew from RTL and the interviewer was still talking to Leonov in a small alcove near the windows.

Leonov was a big man both physically and temperamentally. He dominated the whole room, gesturing all the time he was speaking, arms waving to emphasise some point he was making. It was five minutes before he waved Mason over as the TV crew started carrying out their equipment.

Leonov looked at Mason closely as if he were auditioning for a part. Then he said, quietly for him, 'Why on earth do you want to talk about poor Foster?' He raised his eyebrows. 'You know he's dead, don't you? His own people killed him.'

'I knew he was dead but, as I'm sure you know, he had been working for the Stasis and the KGB and he had compiled information about collaborators in the West. It was never found.' He shrugged. 'I'm trying to find it.'

'And who are you – BND?'

Mason smiled. 'No. I'm a Brit.'

'You speak better German than I do, my boy.'

'My mother was German. It was German we spoke at home.'

'And who suggested you contact me?'

'Several people.'

'Why me?'

'Because of your daughter, Gala.' He paused. 'I just want to build up a picture of Charlie Foster's life.'

'Charlie Foster never had a life. He had a great talent for work but no talent for life. I could never understand what Gala saw in him.' He shrugged. 'But she loved him and they planned to marry.' He paused and waved to his secretary to bring him a drink. Then turning back to Mason he said, 'The only person who could tell you about his work is that wretched man Rosen.' He paused. 'Have you talked to him?'

'No. I've not met him. What was his relationship with Charlie Foster?'

'You know about him? His background?'

'Just that he's a Professor of psychology and appears on TV and radio talk-shows.'

'He was a consultant to both the Stasis and the KGB on psychological assessments of potential collaborators.' He shrugged. 'I used him myself on a film about a serial killer.' He paused, shaking his head as if in disbelief. 'He's a very strange man.'

'In what way?'

'On the surface considerable charm and charisma, but behind it all he's a fanatic. A fanatic with a mission.'

'What kind of mission?'

'No idea. But as a Russian I perceive the touch of a Messiah, there. Even an element of Rasputin. The TV talks and all that, border on demagoguery.' He smiled wryly. 'We Russians don't like demagogues. We've had too many of our own.'

'How did he and Foster get on together?'

Leonov shrugged. 'They were professionals. I don't think Charlie Foster was much interested in Rosen's philosophy. All he was concerned with was that Rosen was pretty accurate at his assessment of informers. And on Rosen's side he just saw Foster as a possible source of information or influence if he needed it.'

'What did you think of Foster?'

Leonov hesitated for a moment. 'He was a good fellow in many ways. Honest, loyal . . .' he shrugged, '. . . all the virtues. But, like I said, I didn't see him and Gala as a pair.'

'Why not?'

Leonov smiled. 'Like most virtuous people Charlie Foster was a bore. At least *I* found him a bore. I think she would have got bored with him in the end.' He waved a hand. 'Don't get me wrong. She loved him. No doubt about that. And I guess he loved her in his own way. But he wasn't a man for emotions and I think she was Russian enough to need more open affection.'

'Do you think it's possible that Charlie Foster gave Rosen the information he'd collected?'

'I think it's far more likely that Rosen had all the information already. He was just as well-in with the Stasis as Charlie was.'

'Thanks for talking so frankly.'

'That's OK. But bear in mind what I've said – Rosen for all his charm is a fanatic – and a dangerous man.' He stood up. 'I must go. Let me show you out.'

As they stood at the door of the suite he took Mason's hand as he said softly, 'People who know about these things say I've got a sixth sense like women have, and all the time we were talking my mind was on Rosen, and I kept thinking of the lines from that poem by Yeats – "*And what rough beast, its hour come round at last, slouches towards Bethlehem to be born*". Rosen and those words somehow sit together at the back of my mind.' He smiled. 'So take care young man, we don't want Charlie Foster's history to repeat itself.'

CHAPTER 15

Sam Wheeler drove his car into the driveway of the rented house and noticed that there were bluebells in the thicket of trees by the garage. There was no answer when he rang the bell so let himself in.

The main living room had been turned into a work-place. Apart from the computer they had fixed up two trestle tables, the kind that paper-hangers use, and they were covered with piles of newspapers and magazines. He heard the sound of a car outside and walked to the window. It was Chuck and Marty easing their bulky bodies out of a 'J' registered Ford Fiesta. He walked over to the door to let them in.

Ten minutes later they were sitting round the kitchen table with an array of Coke, Budweiser, coffee and Marks and Spencer's sandwiches. Beef, tomato and cheese. They were none of them food connoisseurs but had taken a liking to English beer which was represented by a case of Boddington's.

'This gal who did this MacTavish stuff for you's very good. I've given a teaser chat to one of the tabloids.' Marty grinned. 'They'll pay a couple of hundred for it. Maybe more if they buy UK rights and exclusive.'

'Is what she's put together enough?'

'It sure is. She's got the whole *enchilada* here,' he said pointing at the plastic file. 'Breaks every law there is. Planning, Fair Rent, Fire Precautions, harassment of tenants, and tape-recorded threats of physical violence. And his brothers are on all the appropriate council committees. She says it's like the Rachman case, whatever that was.'

'Evidence?'

'Signed statements, photo-copies of police reports, court proceedings, rent-books and two tape-recordings and transcripts. The tapes are no use in court but they clinch this story so far as the media's concerned.'

'Did the tabloid check anything you gave them?'

'Yeah. Confirmed all of it.' He paused. 'Shall I go ahead?'

'OK.' Sam Wheeler paused. 'What's the state of the game in general?'

Chuck looked at a list they'd made out.

'Two tabloid political reporters, one broadsheet editor, two TV news interviewers, the Shadow spokesman on crime and an Opposition back-bencher who specialises on Health disclosures.' He smiled at Sam Wheeler. 'You know, these people don't give a shit, they're up to their little games almost openly. Everything under the sun. Our people wouldn't dare do it except undercover. These guys must feel they're special and untouchable.'

Marty chipped in. 'The other thing you ought to tell your boss is to tell the Prime Minister and other ministers not to rise to the Opposition bait so easy. Somebody starts some rumour and you've got some government guy assessing it inside the hour. Ignore the bastards. Don't respond. Play hard to get. Don't deny rumours. Just sweat it out. It's obvious that your media will attack anyone with no grounds at all. It's like they're drugged with their power.' He shook his head in disbelief. 'Why does the government let 'em get away with it?'

Sam Wheeler shrugged. 'Good guys but weak leadership. And the media have got a lot of power if you don't make them toe the line. Right now they're out of control.'

The tabloid held the story over the week-end so that it could run for at least the full week. As soon as the story appeared there were threats of writs but none was received. MacTavish didn't take his seat in the House for two days and when the Speaker allowed him to make a personal statement on the third day it was received in silence by both sides of the House. Several newspapers recalled the Prime Minister's comments to MacTavish about smear campaigns when he had raised the subject of Boyce-Williams in Parliament after his death. Just one carried a headline – 'The biter bit'. It sat easily at the head of a column. Two if you used a photograph. MacTavish's constituency chairman and committee announced their unanimous decision not to nominate MacTavish as their candidate for the next election.Grampian TV put together an 'investigative' documentary on the subject of tenement landlords and their abuse of poor, working-class people. And a group that was formed to support MacTavish broke up in disarray a few days after its formation. A police spokesman announced that the evidence had been evaluated and passed to the Procurator-Fiscal.

Hugo Renton arrived at the Clapham house an hour after Sam Wheeler phoned him. As always, Sam chose the kitchen for his meetings.

'I've got a problem, Hugo. My chaps have got a good story. Could be used in the Commons but we need someone to say it who isn't a minister.'

'What's the subject?'

'Nurses' pay.'

'That comes up next Wednesday. What have you got?'

'There was an item on BBC TV's newscast yesterday evening. Showed over a hundred nurses with banners outside one of the London hospitals. A couple of friends of mine did a quick check. There were roughly a hundred and thirty demonstrators. Only twelve were nurses, thirty-two people there had nothing to do with any hospital or health service and the rest were cleaners and non-medical employees. The commentary referred to them as "disgusted nurses". The usual heartstrings stuff. A blatant distortion of the facts.' He paused. 'We also got the names of a man and a woman in the crowd who are used by TV crews to get people to mount these displays. They get paid for their so-called assistance.' He laughed. 'They used to specialise in protesting students at LSE, and they helped with the Poll Tax riots.'

'Have you got their names?'

'Yeah. And addresses, and their contacts at TV Centre.'

Hugo Renton was obviously delighted. 'I've got just the chap for this, Mr Wheeler.'

'It probably won't go far in the media but it's a warning to all TV news and documentary people.'

'It'll be a great morale-booster for our people too. Lessons all round.'

It wasn't until early evening on the day after Overy's flight that it was realised that he had disappeared. The media's search for someone to blame ranged from the President, Judge Kominski who had heard the application for bail, the FBI for its lack of supervision and security, and finally settled temporarily on Hector Loundes who had been the guarantor for the bail. He had had to deposit half the bail money with the court and that money had been forfeited immediately by order of the court. This led to an open conflict as to which court should receive the money. Hector Loundes appeared to be a mild, elderly man from Oklahoma City who had made a fortune on the Chicago futures exchange. The press investigated everyone who had ever known him from school-days on, and finally spat him out when nobody would say a bad word about him. The records showed that he'd never voted in his life. In his photos he looked rather like Harry S. Truman.

On the second day a newspaper in San Antonio published a report that a teenage ham radio operator had heard on his scanner, messages from the pilot of a private plane asking for a fuelling stop where the fuel bill would be paid by someone referred to as N.O. Stringers in all South American countries were alerted to try and locate the fugitive and obtain an exclusive story. Money no object.

CHAPTER 16

As the Chief Whip took his seat he was a little uneasy. He had been told that not only was Sky News keeping its cameras on for at least an extra hour, but BBC 2 and ITV were doing the same. Even for the Tuesday and Thursday PM's Question Times that was a lot of coverage. What seemed more surprising was that the press gallery was packed, not only with the usual parliamentary correspondents but run-of-the-mill reporters who usually only attended when some minister was resigning. But the afternoon's business was the National Health Service and it seemed that the Minister was merely going to give out the latest figures on waiting lists, operations and emergency beds available in London. There would be the usual anecdote from some Opposition member about some old dear who was left in a corridor while they found her a bed in a specialist ward, but the media wouldn't be able to run that for more than a couple of days. Then he remembered his horoscope in the *Daily Mail* that day – 'Uranus is entering your sign. This is not a good time for Scorpios'. He closed his eyes, folded his arms and leaned back in his seat as the Minister reported on improved conditions, more money spent and the rest of it.

He heard Madam Speaker say 'Mr Cartwright' and then the strident tones of the Shadow Health Minister. The NHS was falling apart, everybody knew it except the Minister, etc, etc. It was routine stuff but the speaker knew he had to say it. When he came to his closing jibe he was cheered on by his own back-benchers.

'Did the Minister not feel ashamed at seeing the nurses outside St Mary's hospital pleading for an increase in their pay that would bring them up to the poverty line . . .' He saw a government back-bencher stand and was glad to give way. 'I give way to the Honourable Member,' he said as he sat down. Slightly surprised because the intervener was smiling.

'Madam Speaker, I am most grateful to the Honourable Member for giving way. He asks if we have seen the TV news shots of so-called nurses assembled outside St Mary's hospital with banners asking for more pay. I would like to put his mind at rest. Out of a hundred and thirty protesters, only twelve were nurses. Thirty-two people there had nothing whatever to do with either St Mary's hospital or any part of the NHS and the rest were cleaners, porters and auxiliary staff. I also am assured that two of these people outside the NHS were paid by somebody to organise that assembly. They do it regularly. This particular couple specialise in demos for nurses and teachers.'

There were a few moments of silence as the member sat down and then pandemonium from both sides of the House. Government members waving their order papers guffawing at the Opposition front bench and their friends screaming unparliamentary words like 'liars' and 'cheats'.

The Chief Whip decided that he'd better check what his horoscope was like in the *Mirror*. Maybe it was time to change newspapers.

The TV news channels gave it a mention with no pictures. Their viewers had already seen the real thing from the cameras in the House of Commons. But the newspapers had a field-day. Especially those whose owners had no stake in a TV channel. On phone-in programmes a few Opposition supporters spluttered their disbelief but the majority of callers said that they were not surprised at the organised news item. But a Mori poll three days later indicated that although the Opposition party had lost 2 percent of its support, the government had gained nothing. The 'don't knows' were the true gainers. Their percentage almost as big as that of each of the two main parties.

It took Mason fifteen minutes to be passed from department to department and faculty to faculty at the University and finally end up with Rosen's secretary. The faculty was categorised as 'Humanities'.

'Professor Rosen's office.'

'Could I speak to Professor Rosen please?'

'Personal or academic?'

'I guess personal.'

'Just a moment.'

There was quite a long silence and instinct told Mason that they were using the code to check where the call was coming from.

Then. 'Rosen speaking.'

'Professor, my name's Mason. James Mason. I wonder . . . could I see you for a brief chat?'

'How come your German is so good with a name like that?'

'My mother was German. I was brought up speaking German.'

'Very useful. Why do you want to see me?'

'I wanted to ask you about a man named Foster.'

'Is he a student or what?'

'He was a man you knew. A Brit. Charlie Foster.'

There was a brief silence and then, 'Where are you?'

'The city centre.'

'Let's see. It's five past eleven. How about you come over here at twelve? I'll meet you at the reception desk. OK?'

'That's fine. Thank you.'

They'd gone to a pub, *Zur letzten Instanz*, that Mason knew well. In the old days it had been a haunt of Stasi top brass and their informants.

When Mason had ordered their drinks and sandwiches, Rosen said, 'You seem at home here.'

Mason smiled. 'I was at one time.'

Rosen smiled a knowing smile. 'Before the Wall came down?'

'Yeah.'

'So why come to *me* about Charlie Foster?'

'A little bird told me you might help me.'

Rosen smiled. 'Never trust little birds.' He paused. 'What do you want to know about him?'

'Anything. How you came to know him. His world.' He shrugged. 'Anything.'

'Are you working for German intelligence or the British?'

'SIS.'

'I guess you know as much about Charlie Foster and what he was up to as I do. What you really want to know is – where are his records – yes?'

'That too.'

'They were Charlie's insurance. Months before the Wall came down, he and the people around him could see that East Germany was finished. Nobody guessed how it would end but they knew that its days were over. SIS or the BND could have had his records for a reasonable pension for Charlie. No hassle. No killing. Just a trade.' He smiled a rather cold smile. 'But governments don't do it that way, do they?'

'Depends on the government concerned.'

'It doesn't, dear boy. It doesn't. They're all the same. They are in the power and control business. They hate being challenged.' He shrugged. 'I warned him. He was a very bright young man. Very straight. Very upright. And very naive. Doomed to be a loser. A gallant loser. But a loser all the same.'

'How did you come to know him?'

'I was a reference point for his records. Who mattered and what to do about them if the chips were ever on the table. I picked them out for the Stasis originally. I did the same for Charlie Foster. Just used different criteria.'

'Do you know where his records are now?'

Rosen laughed. 'You're a very brash young man, aren't you? Straight to the point. No messing. A strange mental mixture. A German would have taken months of getting to know me before asking that question. A Brit would have needed to contrive some pressure point to make me talk. But you. Well.' He smiled. 'The world is going to need men like you, James Mason. The new movers and shakers. By the way. Who did give you my name as a contact point?'

'Several people.'

Rosen sighed. 'Ah well. Enough for our first meeting. We must meet again. Do keep in touch.' He took out a card. 'There's my home address and telephone number. Keep in touch. I mean it. We've got interests in common.' Rosen stood up. 'I've got an account here. I'll look after the bill. *Ciao.*' And he threaded his way through the tables to the counter, talked for a few moments, then left.

Mason sat there finishing his drink and wondering what his next move should be with Rosen. He could see why people found the man charming. He had that rare virtue of listening as you spoke to him. Maybe that came from his experience as a psychologist but Mason sensed that the man was a natural and overt charmer. He was a recruiter. A man who wanted to convince you that you shared his rather dogmatic views.

CHAPTER 17

The azaleas at Rock Creek Park were beginning to fade but Swenson walked through the woods until he came to the place with the rough wooden table and benches in the clearing for picnics. Pike and Thompson were already there and Swenson settled down on the bench facing them. They were both ex-CIA and both in their forties. It had been arranged for half a dozen agents to retire for various honourable reasons five years back. The object of the exercise was to have a small number of suitable men who could be called on to carry out tasks that would not sit too happily in Harry Truman's original brief for the CIA.

Louis Pike was not a big man but his bare arms were well muscled and his eyes were the eyes of a man given to action rather than discussion. He was wearing a blue denim shirt with the sleeves rolled up, loose blue slacks and trainers. Thompson was a pleasant-looking man in a clean white shirt, black trousers and well-polished black leather shoes. It was Thompson who spoke.

'The guy who put up the bail money was a Hector Loundes, age sixty-four with around two hundred million bucks, maybe more. All made legitimately. Not even a driving offence on his records. Oklahoma born and bred. Well liked in the community and a big contributor to the National Rifle Association. Has made no complaint about having half his bail money confiscated. Refuses to talk to the media. Lot of acquaintances but no buddies. I checked his phone calls for the last year. Over the last month he's made daily calls, sometimes more than one, to a guy named Al Simmons.' He nodded towards Pike. 'Pikey took over Simmons.'

Pike shifted on the bench, uneasy at having an audience. 'Lot of money. Lot of clout and spends a lot of his time, most in fact, organising NRA groups. Gives talks at meetings. Claims that government is the enemy taking away our freedom and abusing the citizens. Got plenty of buddies. All influential, including Congressmen and Senators of both parties. Loathes President Carson and refers to Nelson Overy as "that slimy scumbag". But has used them both to prevent the gun laws being revoked or modified. Looks like Al Simmons was paying off some old debts when he arranged for Overy to do the disappearing act.'

'Can we prove he was implicated?'

'He wasn't just implicated, chief. He was the whole thing. Organised everything. They used his personal place.'

'Do we know where Overy is?'

'We know from air-control records that he flew with two refuelling stops to Bogotá International. Beyond that we don't know.' He nudged Thompson with his shoulder. 'And Tommo here said that wasn't part of our remit from you.'

'Have you got any contacts down there?' Swenson said, looking at Pike.

'A few.'

'Are you free to go?'

'When?'

'Right now.'

'I guess so. I'd like Tommo with me, he speaks good Spanish, mine's only simple stuff.'

Thompson smiled. 'Like, where are the hookers, *señor*?'

Swenson was silent for a moment and then said, 'Are you still in funds for expenses?'

'Yeah. No problem.'

'OK. Check where he is. What sort of set-up. What security. Local attitude. And phone me on the number soon as you can.'

'Can I think in terms of sub-contracting?'

Swenson hesitated and then said, 'Only if there's no other way.'

As Swenson walked back to where he had parked his car he stopped and sat on a bench watching the people playing tennis. He wondered what their reactions would be if they knew what went on in their names in the defence of their country. The public were agin politicians of all stripes and they were cynical about the graft and corruption that was the life-blood of Washington. Hoover had been a monster as Director of the FBI, nevertheless the public had seen him and the FBI as defenders of their security and their way of life. But these days the FBI were as loathed as were the politicians, seen now as just one more enemy, working more often outside the law than in. Despots who had the power to do whatever they wanted.

The CIA, thank God, were not seen quite the same way. That was probably because they saw the CIA's role as external. Dealing with foreigners. Foreigners intent on destroying the American way of life. The inevitable criticism of the Agency was that it was ineffective. Not warning the White House of Soviet missiles in Cuba or that Sadam Hussein was about to invade Kuwait. Not spotting Aldrich Ames until ten CIA men had been killed by the KGB. The public saw the CIA's role as being the modern-day equivalent of soothsayers and mystics. All that used to be enough but times had changed. It seemed as if suddenly American society was falling apart. Sometimes when he was feeling low he would read through the Constitution, amendments and all, and you could see history at work. The original constitution was all about a citizen's rights, especially to freedom. But almost imperceptibly the amendments had begun to be laws rather than morality.

Swenson stood up slowly, glancing at the players. Some grimly determined to win, some laughing because, after all, it was only a game with friends.

As he got to the car he was back in the real world. Doing his job. Flouting both laws and constitution because the end justified the means. OK. Hitler had said that, but he, Olaf Swenson, wasn't Hitler and his ends really were justified.

CHAPTER 18

There were dainty, triangular sandwiches on several platters on the table in 'Hospitality' and one by one the members of the panel were lured into make-up. The two women knowing exactly what they wanted done, the two men rather embarrassed but inwardly rather fancying themselves with a Barbados tan. Spouses, friends, colleagues, girl-friends and mistresses stayed on in 'Hospitality' and the performers moved into the small Green Room.

Phil Harrison, the panel chairman and presenter of 'Speaking out of turn' chatted briefly to each panel member in turn.

When he came to Greg Matheson, MP, he was smiling the smile that got him all the fan-mail.

'Hi, Greg. Nice to have you on the show again. It'll be much as usual. Health service, unemployment, crime – and . . .' the smile was broader '. . . I'm afraid I'll have to touch on the question of sleaze in the government ranks but I'm sure you're used to coping with that these days.'

'Don't you think the public are sick and tired of the media's passion for sleaze?'

'No way. They love it.' He laughed. 'You chaps have been a godsend to us all.' He turned to look at the clock. 'I'll have to go. You'll all come in in about five minutes. A quick check on cameras and voice levels and then the intro.'

The other members of the panel were a pleasant, sensible woman from the Opposition, a man from the London School of Economics and a spokeswoman from one of the myriad of animal protection and ecology groups.

They were fifteen minutes into the show and the ecology lady was defending the recent violent attacks on a milk depot.

'But why attack a milk depot, Angela?' Harrison smilingly chided her.

'You don't understand do you? Milk is produced by cows and cows only give milk when they have calves. And the calves are torn away from their mommies and shipped to France to satisfy farmers' greed.'

'But if they didn't have calves and cows didn't give milk there'd be no milk and therefore no cows. What's wrong with milk for heaven's sake?' Harrison waited in vain, looking, smiling, to camera. 'Maybe we'd better go to the next question.' He paused, then pointed, as arranged. 'Right sir, the gentleman in the check shirt . . . yes, you, sir. Your question?'

The cameras went to a man in the third row back. A man with heavy glasses and an earnest expression.

'With all these Ministers and government people being exposed for their sleaze, isn't it time the government resigned and we had an election?'

Phil Harrison smiled in Matheson's direction.

'I'll leave you to last Greg . . .' He nodded to the Opposition woman MP.

'I have no intention of commenting on this subject,' she said frostily. 'So far as I am concerned peoples' private lives should remain private.'

There was a ripple of applause from the audience but there were cynical minds who immediately wondered what such a plain woman had to hide.

The man from LSE wasn't going to get impaled on this sort of thing and he grinned as he said, 'I can only go back to what our old friend Professor Joad used to say. "It all depends on what you mean by sleaze".'

Harrison turned slowly to look at Matheson. 'So what *do* we mean by sleaze?'

Matheson smiled and shrugged. 'Who knows. How do *you* define it?'

Harrison raised his eyebrows in simulated surprise and shock. 'I think we all know what sleaze is, Greg.' He waved his arms rather vaguely.

'Adultery by supposedly happily married men for a start?'

'Are you married, Phil?'

There was a wave of amusement from the audience who were well aware that the presenter was married to an exceptionally attractive fashion model, the mother of two lovely children.

Harrison smiled to acknowledge the audience's response.

'Yes, Mr Matheson. I'm married.'

'But you have a mistress. A teenage girl, Mary Hawkins, a secretary here at the TV Centre. You pay the rent for her flat in Sussex Gardens and your name is on the lease and you eat together two or three nights a week at Bertorelli's in Edgeware Road. Isn't that sleaze too? What's the difference?'

Harrison appeared stunned and he could hear the producer on his ear mike saying, 'For Christ's sake say something you stupid bastard.'

Harrison was white-faced as he struggled to take hold of the situation.

He said menacingly, but his voice quavered. 'I'll pass on to the next question but you'll be hearing from my lawyer.' Then, inspired, he said, 'Perhaps you meant it all as a joke.'

Matheson smiled and nodded towards the audience who were still silent. 'That isn't what they think, old chap.'

There was a final question on rising crime in the cities and the lights were lowered so that only the cast's silhouettes could be seen under the closing credits.

When the lights went up in the studio, the presenter's seat was empty and the hubbub from the audience as they left was deafening.

When Matheson went back into make-up to have his tan removed, the girls were obviously highly amused at what had happened. Not that details of Phil Harrison's life were news to any of them. He'd tried it on with at least two of them.

There were several TV crews already outside the studios and there were some cheers and shouts of approval as Matheson struggled through to Hugo Renton's car. The show got extensive mentions on all the TV and radio late-news broadcasts and there were newspaper reporters waiting for him at the House of Commons, at his club, the Army and Navy, and outside his house in Chelsea. It made all the front pages next day. After that the media concentrated on Phil Harrison.

Mason's trip to London had been short. Harding had said that he wanted a meeting to review the situation but he hadn't seemed all that interested in Mason's report. He seemed uneasy as if there was something else on this mind. Mason had been in the business long enough to realise that something was going on that he hadn't been told about.

He sensed that for some reason what he was doing seemed to have taken on a new importance, a new urgency.

Back in his flat in Berlin there was a message on his answer-phone inviting him to drinks at Rosen's place the following evening.

When his taxi pulled up at Rosen's address, Mason was surprised at the size of the house. It stood in its own grounds of about half an acre with a brick wall on the street side at least six feet high. And the house itself had obviously escaped the war-time bombing. It must have been the home of a wealthy merchant before the war and he realised how valuable Rosen must have been to the Stasis and the KGB to be given such a house and one so near to the city centre.

One of the tall wrought-iron gates was open and as Mason made his way up the paved pathway to the house he saw small groups of people on the lawns and on the patio. Rosen himself was standing, drink in hand, with a group of young men with shaved heads, T-shirts and Levis. When he saw Mason he raised his glass and strolled towards him.

'Welcome, so glad you could come. What'll you drink?'

Mason asked for a diet-Coke, the token booty of German reunification. He was introduced to half a dozen small groups of mainly young people who looked more like bikers than philosophy or psychology students. Mason noticed that there were at least thirty men and only three females.

The talk was surprisingly mundane, the end of the football season and the problems of promotion and relegation in the Bundesliga. There were very few from Berlin. Dresden, Wiesbaden, Munich and Dusseldorf were mentioned as home territory by a number of them. At least three of them were Americans. Rosen was obviously the one who mattered and Mason found it odd that a man like that should so dominate men who were far removed from his academic background.

Mason was standing by a small pond talking to one of the girls when two of the Americans joined them. The tall one said, 'Hi, it's Jim, isn't it?'

Mason nodded. 'Yes. Jim Mason.'

The man smiled. 'Jake says you're a spook for the British. What the hell do you do now there's *glasnost* and *perestroika*?'

Mason smiled. 'I get by.'

'Are you helping Jake with his crusade?'

'I didn't know he was on a crusade.'

The American laughed. 'You ain't letting on. Wise guy.' He turned to the other American. 'What d'you think, Andy. Can we trust him or is he a plant by the Brits?'

The other American stared at Mason and said, 'You play games and you'll get hurt, my friend. You can bet on it.'

Mason did what he always did when he was tempted to violence and put his hands in his jacket pockets. He turned to the other American and said quietly, 'Maybe you should warn your little friend that he'd be wise to shut his big mouth before somebody does it for him.'

Then he turned away and walked to where Rosen was talking animatedly to a group of oldish men wearing Harley Davidson sweat-shirts. Rosen was in lecturing mode, insisting that burning the houses of Turks or other immigrants or killing them was pointless. The targets had to be the politicians who had passed the laws that let these people enter Germany in the first place. Even the state's employees, the civil servants who paid their unemployment or social services payments were more desirable targets than the immigrants themselves. They must remember that it was other politicians and other officials who had driven the immigrants from their own countries. Even Mason sensed that there was a twisted logic to Rosen's arguments but Mason was well aware that the men being lectured enjoyed killing and rioting for their own sakes. They were just as ready to slaughter their own countrymen. Surely Rosen, he felt, must know that.

When the group wandered off, Rosen said, 'Do you understand my argument, James?'

'I understand it.' He smiled. 'But I don't agree with it. Those people weren't revolutionaries, they were rioters. The kind who love killing. The kind who set fire to the blocks of flats and looted the shops in Dresden last week. They're hooligans, thugs, psychopaths. Remorseless.'

'But people have got to learn that it is politicians and the State that control their lives, make them jobless, penniless and homeless. Ordinary people who just want to be left alone to get on with their lives. You have to have a tax card to get a job. You must be insured against accidents at work, for illness for health. You have to pay VAT and Turnover tax. You even need a permit to start a small business or drive a car. For Christ's sake. Who are these people to control every aspect of people's lives. Judges, politicians, bureaucrats, police, lawyers, bankers . . .' Rosen's voice broke with emotion and for the first time Mason realised how consumed Rosen was by this driving sense of injustice. Sergei Leonov had said that Rosen was like Hitler and Hitler had made sense to millions of Germans. Even now there were people who believed Hitler's ranting and raving. But today they wore biker's kit, not swastikas.

Mason eventually left about 10 p.m. and although there were two taxis parked outside Rosen's house, Mason went with his instincts and decided to walk to the cathedral before taking a taxi.

CHAPTER 19

They met in Baumann's house in Linden, a leafy suburb of Cologne. There was Baumann himself, representing the BND, the German intelligence agency. Nolte from the Chancellor's office, Weber from the Foreign Office and Lemke from the CDU's party office.

Nolte had taken over as Chairman. There was no protest from rivals around the table.

'I think everybody knows the situation but you'd better give us the latest, Herr Baumann.'

Baumann sat with his broad shoulders leaning forward with his elbows on the table.

'In the past two weeks we have received documents purporting to give information on four people who acted as informants or spies for the Stasis and through them to the KGB. Two contain revelations of alleged sexual scandals and two concern fraud. Financial fraud by an official of the Bundesbank and financial fraud by the head of a large company.'

Weber looked at Nolte. 'Has the Chancellor been informed?'

'Yes.'

Lemke said, 'Where do the allegations come from and what are their demands?'

Baumann shrugged. 'No indication of the sources and no demands for anything.' He paused. 'I have to advise you that this information might go to, or maybe already has gone to, the media both here in Germany and possibly overseas.'

There was silence for a few moments and then Nolte said, looking at Baumann, 'What do the BND suggest that we do?'

'I have discussed this with my top people at Pullach.' He paused. 'Pullach sees this as essentially a political decision. We have our views but they would only be advisory.'

Weber said waspishly, 'Interesting to hear that the top brass of German intelligence feel that dealing with spies is a politician's problem.'

Nolte, ignoring Weber, said, 'What do your people advise, Baumann?'

'Our views on this being a political matter isn't a ploy to avoid comment but we recently had the Federal Court decision that Herr Wolff, the former head of the Stasi organisation, who is now in our custody, cannot be successfully prosecuted because he claims that what he did for the East German State was legal under their system . . .'

Nolte interrupted. 'All the Court said was that Wolff was committing no offence under the laws of his country, East Germany, at the time. But West German citizens who were agents for what was then a foreign country are still guilty of treason and can be prosecuted.'

Lemke coughed nervously before speaking. 'Have we evidence enough to prosecute and succeed?'

Baumann said, 'We've certainly enough evidence to prosecute but that doesn't mean we win the case. But when the public heard the evidence the people concerned would be finished.'

'Why has it taken so long for this to be considered? You said it had been going on for two weeks.'

'We had to do some checking to make sure that the allegations had some basis of fact.'

Nolte pursed his lips and then said, 'Are the sexual things just the usual screwing secretaries and the like?'

Baumann sighed. 'I'm afraid not. One is under-aged girls and the other is sado-masochism – with photographs.'

'So tell us,' Nolte said rather testily. 'What you recommend us to do.'

There was a long silence as they waited for Baumann's reply. Then he said slowly, 'I think you should take all four to trial.'

'Why?' It was Nolte again.

'To teach others a lesson. And if we do nothing and this stuff goes to the media and shows that the government knew but did nothing, then the government would be finished. The other parties would leave the coalition to avoid being tainted.'

Nolte nodded. 'Pass the evidence you have to the Federal Prosecutor and ask him to do what is necessary.' He looked around. 'So, gentlemen. I'll keep you informed.'

Nolte stayed behind with Baumann until the others had left and then he moved to an armchair.

'Tell me what kind of person or gang is behind this, Franz? And what's the motive?'

'We've put in motion some efforts to trace the source but there's not much to go on. Forensic confirm that there are no fingerprints and no biological material for DNA examination. So it's professional. The only indicator is that the person or group aren't just acting from some morality stand-point. All four targets are gross embarrassments to the government.'

'What's that tell us?'

'It says look at anti-government groups.'

'Like what?'

'Like neo-Nazis, ex-Stasis. Even immigrant groups, but they probably wouldn't have the resources. My guess is political. A cult, a group. Something like that. Remember, these folk could have offered a deal and could have screwed us for a lot of D-Marks.'

'Will you keep me in touch on a day-to-day basis?'

'Sure. If that's what you want.'

When Nolte drove off, Baumann phoned the details of the meeting to his HQ at Pullach just outside Munich. The sex offenders they had known about for months but frauds were never visible until something went really wrong. Their anti-fraud unit was under-funded and was manned by the wrong kind of people. You needed maverick thinkers to catch fraudsters. Espionage seemed a decent business compared with electronic fraud. Even the sex games seemed more acceptable until you started wondering why a rich and influential man would pay 10 D-Marks a lash to have his back left bleeding from twenty minutes in a concrete basement in Berlin.

Mason was having breakfast coffee and a sandwich in the cafe in the Europa Centre. He was reading a copy of Detlef Blettenberg's *Blauer Rum*. As he turned a page he felt a hand on his shoulder and he turned to see who it was. It was Professor Rosen who looked down at him, smiling as he said, 'May I join you?'

'Of course.' Mason closed the novel and made space on the table for Rosen's newspaper.

'You like thrillers?'

Mason shrugged. 'I like Blettenberg's anyway. Have you read any of them?'

'I read his first, the one that won the Edgar Wallace Prize. Excellent. But I don't have much time for reading fiction.'

The waitress came for Rosen's order and he asked for coffee and a Danish pastry. 'I'm no good at making myself breakfast,' he said, laughing.

Mason looked surprised. 'Are you not married?'

'No. We divorced some years back.' He smiled and shrugged. 'She said she'd had enough of me pontificating about how the world should be run.' He shrugged again. 'I guess there were other things too.' He said quietly, 'What about you?'

'Not married. Never have been. My job doesn't fit in too well with married life.'

'How long were you in the army?'

Mason frowned. 'I didn't say I *was* in the army. What makes you think I was?'

Rosen smiled. 'Because when you're standing up you always stand to attention.' He went on. 'And how's your search for Charlie Foster's legacy going on?'

'Very slowly.' He smiled. 'Maybe you could speed it up.'

'Why do you say that?'

'I'm pretty sure that you know what happened to Foster's records.'

'There *are* no such records. I can tell you that for sure. You're on a wild-goose chase.'

'You mean he was bluffing?'

'Oh no. He collected material all right.' He smiled. 'In fact I contributed quite a lot to his collection.'

'So what happened to it?'

'There were four sets of copies made. But they were encrypted and if the persons who had them even realised what they were they still wouldn't be able to decrypt them.'

'Did you have a copy?'

'Yes. I destroyed my copy.' He smiled. 'The information I had was far more extensive and for a much more important cause than threatening British intelligence in London.'

For a moment Mason was silent and then he said, 'Would you be prepared to make a statement for my people in London?'

'No way. They aren't significant to me.' Rosen smiled. 'Keep in touch all the same. Maybe at some stage we could assist one another.'

'Some stage of what?'

Rosen laughed. 'Of history, my friend.' He stood up, picking up his bill. 'See you,' he said, leaving Mason sitting there as he walked to the check-out to pay his bill.

Crombie noted with quiet satisfaction the string of revelations that had embarrassed not only the Opposition but the media themselves. On phone-in shows the public were openly criticising not only politicians of all parties but the media too. Accusing them of talking-down every achievement the country made and of turning every item of good news into a disaster. Sam Wheeler and his colleagues had done more in a few hectic weeks to change the public's views of current affairs than all the sound-bites contrived by political PR advisers had done in years. Maybe another couple of months would be enough.

But Crombie's feeling of satisfaction was shattered when he got four more pages of extracts from Stasi files. They came in one envelope and like the earlier two there was no stamp, no postmark and no demand for money or indication of what purpose they were expected to serve.

One was a detailed report on the information passed to the Stasis by a well-known, homosexual, left-wing MP. There were two other reports identifying their targets as being Stasi informants and giving details of money-laundering by a government junior minister on behalf of drug dealers in Turkey. The other was the details of a ring of homosexual paedophiles and the activities with them of another left-winger.

But the main problem was a detailed report of a respected US Senator who was leading a campaign for a more lenient public and official attitude to illegal immigrants. There was very detailed information of his connections and protection of juvenile drug and prostitution rings in Miami run by Cubans, most of whom were illegals.

One thing Crombie knew for sure was that he'd better put Harding in the picture now about all the Stasi stuff. It must be coming from a German source and it fitted in all too well with the Charlie Foster business. He wondered what excuse he could offer for not having taken Harding into his confidence right from the start. The reports that Harding had given him about his chap Mason's work in Berlin were pretty inconclusive. They'd better notch up the priority for Mason.

Meantime he'd put the new Stasi stuff on the back burner for a couple of days.

Harding hadn't asked why he hadn't been shown all the Stasi material earlier. He had little to offer from Mason's mission that was positive. He emphasised that that wasn't Mason's fault. If you're looking for the proverbial needle in a haystack progress was going to be slow. But the Stasi papers could help. Crombie didn't show him the American item. Copies of the other pieces were handed over to Harding and he was told that if extra bodies or facilities could help they would be made available.

Crombie was about to go to lunch when the call came through from Bonn. He didn't recognise the name Baumann but the operator said that he was BND and that was enough. He had given the inter-service password for the day and been put straight through.

'Sir Peter?'

'Speaking.'

'Sir Peter, I'd like to have a meeting with you. Official but off the record, and fairly soon if that's possible?'

'May I ask the subject matter?'

'Let me just say an exchange of highly confidential information.'

'OK. When can you get over?'

'Today. So that we could talk early this evening if that's possible?'

'All right. I'll make myself available. Give me your ETA and I'll send a car for you.'

'The embassy are giving me a car and a driver and they'll be accommodating me. I could be at your office about six-thirty.'

'OK. I tell you what. Go direct to the Traveller's Club and I'll be waiting there for you.'

'Thanks. I'll do that.'

Crombie called for the file on Baumann. Franz Horst Baumann was forty-six years old. A graduate in forensic science of Göttingen University. He had joined the Kriminal Polizei straight from university and had been recruited a year later to the BND, the Bundes

Nachrichten Dienst, the Federal Intelligence Service. He had spent four years at the BND's headquarters at Pullach just outside Munich and had been mainly concerned with the surveillance of both legal and illegal immigrants, particularly groups having political objectives that were considered to be to the detriment of the Federal Republic. For the last two years he had been in charge of the surveillance and penetration of neo-Nazi groups both in East and West Germany. With the Wall down and reunification the neo-Nazis were still his main responsibility. He spoke fluent English and had a good working knowledge of French. He was married with two daughters and lived in one of the more rural suburbs of Cologne. His rank in the BND was the equivalent of lieutenant-colonel. There was a passport-size photograph that showed a typical German face. Blond hair and rather American good features. The eyes and mouth both looked as if they could smile.

Crombie recognised Baumann as soon as he walked into the foyer. He had a dispensation from the club committee that allowed him to not sign in his guests and he took the German to a small private room that he had taken where there were sandwiches, fruit, and a variety of drinks laid out, with cups and a *cafetière* on a small separate table.

When they were sitting the German said, 'It was good of you to see me at such short notice but it could, perhaps, help both our organisations.'

Crombie smiled. 'Help yourself to the food and drink.'

As Baumann helped himself to a beef sandwich, he said, 'I've brought some documents for you to see. We received them just over two weeks ago. They are denunciations of four West German citizens. I'm sorry to have to say that they seem to be true and based on fact. Not the usual stuff we get from jealous wives or jilted girl-friends, but serious stuff. It purports to be based on Stasi records but always when we get contacts from ex-Stasis offering information it is either in return for cash or some privilege. There was nothing with this material. No demand for money and no threat of publishing it if we didn't comply with some demand.' Baumann paused. 'My experience and my instinct suggests to me that this is political. If I'm right in my surmise I think that other governments will have received similar material.' He paused as he reached for his brief-case, unlocked it and drew out a file which he handed to Crombie.

Crombie read the first two pages then closed the file and handed it back to Baumann.

'You're right. We have received this kind of material that purports to be from Stasi records. The Americans have received at least one similar denunciation that I know of.'

'Was that the Nelson Overy business?'

'Yes.'

'I thought that looked very odd.' He paused. 'What did you do about your cases?'

'We only had one. The chairman of the government party.'

'The suicide case?'

'Yes.' He paused. 'I got four more this morning. They're all serious problems. Two concerning Opposition MPs.'

'Have you and your people any theories on what this is all about?'

'Only pretty vague ones which we're pursuing.' He paused. 'Have you got any ideas on the subject?'

Baumann hesitated for a moment and then said, 'At the risk of being told to mind my own business, may I raise the subject of Charlie Foster. If I need a justification perhaps I can remind you that one of my men was killed in the final stages of that mess.'

'It's Charlie Foster's records we're looking for so go ahead.'

'I did a study of Charlie Foster after it had happened. It's mandatory for us after an episode like that. But it's highly confidential. After looking into all the circumstances I came to rather admire our friend Charlie Foster. He was a very competent technician but more important he was an old-fashioned, honest man. His vulnerable point was that he was a romantic. He would have hated the description but it was a fact. His actions to save his couriers and to help Tarrant were admirable even if they were also naive.' He paused. 'Having looked at Charlie Foster under my microscope, I'm pretty sure that this business has nothing to do with him or his Stasi–KGB records.'

'Where do you think they've come from?'

'Ah, that's not so easy. I think it's a German source, from one side or the other of the old Wall and it's like I said earlier – political.'

'What kind of politics?'

Baumann shrugged. 'Who knows? Extreme. Could be Left or Right wing.' He paused. 'And I think they mean business. And I think they've got more Stasi–KGB information than Charlie Foster managed to put together. A lot more.'

'What makes you think that?'

'Can you imagine a fellow like Charlie Foster having an interest in bringing down Nelson Overy or the Chairman of the Tory Party? I doubt if he'd ever heard of them.' He shook his head. 'No. We're looking at a much more sophisticated source than Charlie Foster's legacy.'

'Like what?'

'I don't know. But bigger than our two organisations have had in mind up to now.'

'Have you got something in mind about taking action of some kind?'

'That's why I'm here, sir. With the approval of my top people in the BND. But we need to persuade our politicians that it's a serious matter that is aimed at them themselves. We thought that maybe this could be a joint operation – either officially or at least unofficially approved.'

'When do you have to go back?'

'I'll stay as long as we need.'

'Did you know I had somebody looking for Foster's material?'

'Is this the chap with a flat in Marburger Strasse?'

'I don't have details of where he lives. He's independent of the SIS detachment in Berlin. He's been checking out anybody who knew Foster, but without much success so far.'

Baumann was silent for several moments and then said, 'Don't think I want to interfere but I think your man doesn't realise that he's in considerable danger.'

'Why?'

'Some of the contacts he's made aren't what they seem to be.'

'Are you thinking of Freddie Malins?'

Baumann smiled and shook his head. 'No. He's a crook but he's no problem so far as this business is concerned.' He shrugged. 'Anyway,' he said as if dismissing the problem. 'We'll keep an eye on your man, and if we combine operations he could be very useful.' He went on, 'You know, it would be better to do this unofficially. Politicians can't believe that people have had enough of them. They'll hinder us at every stage. Especially the Washington people. And I think that it's going to be their problem in the end.'

'What makes you think that?'

'Just analyse who the targets have been and we can rule out Foster's stuff. An individual would have been looking for blackmail money or personal revenge. There would have been a demand with the documents. Every target has been involved with politics. Take the German targets. The fact that they were Stasi informants would have been enough. So added to that is the sex stuff and the fraud. They are all politicians. You said that your recent targets have not been just government but Opposition politicians as well.' He paused for emphasis. 'The common factor here, in Germany, and in the USA, is that they are all politicians.'

Crombie said, 'So what are your conclusions?'

'I think we're dealing here with the first moves of a conspiracy.' He smiled and shrugged. 'I understand your smile but I genuinely believe that the people behind this will go to any lengths.'

'To do what?'

'To destroy politicians. To bring down governments.'

'And then what?'

Baumann shrugged. 'Then chaos. They aren't interested in what comes after. I came across a leaflet in Dresden and the heading was – "Anarchy is the life-blood of democracy". We're lucky in Germany. We have many, many problems but the media are reasonably responsible. The public may be either critical or merely indifferent to politicians, but they don't hate them. Here in the UK your media are totally irresponsible. They've been allowed to get away with lies and insinuations for far too long. Politicians are scared of them. And in America, God help them, it's worse. There are people in the States, millions of them, who've been made to believe that the government are against the people, deliberately using their power against ordinary citizens. And in Germany we have the seed-bed of the neo-Nazis for revolution. Don't see the neo-Nazis as just crazy German louts. They have links all over the world and they're not only thugs. There are crooked but clever minds controlling these people.' He paused. 'I'm talking too much.'

'It's a frightening scenario you describe.'

'That's why I'm here. To try and stop it before it's gone too far.'

'You think we should draw in the Americans?'

'If we can. If they'll come in.'

'How long do you think it will take?'

'At least a year. Maybe two or three years. It's going to be a long, hard fight and don't let us kid ourselves, these people have all the arms they need. Not for a war maybe. But it's never going to be a war. It's going to be a long-drawn-out guerrilla fight. Vietnam, Bosnia and Chechenya rolled into one.'

'Who knows you're here?'

'Several people, but it's officially scheduled as a courtesy call and a chat about immigration and extradition problems.' He paused. 'The guy you've got in Berlin looking for Foster's stuff. Remind me of his name?'

'Mason. James Mason.'

'Is he any good?'

'Yeah.'

'Tough guy or a thinker?'

'A bit of both.'

'Could I see his reports to you?'

'I guess so.'

'And I'll show you my people's reports on what he's been up to.' He paused. 'Have you got a high-security fax facility?'

'Yes. At the office and at home. Which do you want?'

'Best use the one at home.'

Crombie wrote his number on the back of the bill and passed it to Baumann. As he slid it into his pocket Baumann said, 'Can I contact you tomorrow morning?'

'Yes. I'll be at home.'

Crombie was about to have breakfast when Baumann phoned and he'd invited him to come over and join him. Baumann had passed the faxed sheets to Crombie who had passed the thin file on Malins and the Foster's job to the German.

They both read as they ate and when Crombie was pouring their coffees Baumann said, 'Anything you didn't know already?'

'I didn't know about the hookers he takes back to his flat.' Crombie raised his eyebrows. 'Do you really do all this checking up on them as routine?'

'Sure.' Baumann grinned. 'German thoroughness. *Vorschprung durch Technik.*'

'He seems to spend a lot of time with Malins.'

'Freddie Malins is an easy guy to get on with. I'm told he likes our friend Mason and he could be helpful.'

'Anything useful for you in Mason's notes?'

'A couple of things. The ex-Stasi guy Laufer and the people he met at Professor Rosen's pad.' He paused. 'Can I contact Mason? Officially. With your blessing. Just informally?'

'D'you want me to get him over?'

'No. That's not necessary. I'd prefer to see him in Bonn or Berlin. I've got some photographs I'd like him to look at.'

'I'd better put him in the picture about what we're going to do. Agreed?'

Baumann shook his head. 'I suggest not. Not yet anyway. Let's have our meeting with the Americans first. I think our friend Mason could be a very useful entry to the opposition provided he doesn't know what he's being used for.'

'Have you got some plan already worked out?'

Baumann shook his head. 'I wish I had. No. But I've got a feeling that Mason could be our Trojan horse into the other side. If I could have a brief chat with him it could help. Before we meet the Americans.'

Crombie shrugged. 'OK. I'll pass the word down the line.'

'When can we have a full meeting with the Americans?'

'As soon as they agree. I'd guess it will take at least a week to arrange it. I'll contact Olaf Swenson today and then contact you in Bonn to fix a time and place for the joint meeting.'

'We'll know they're serious if they include their C-TC unit.'

When Crombie frowned, Baumann said, 'It's their Counter-Terrorism Centre. It's very experienced and very competent. They keep it tucked away inside the CIA and very few people, even inside Langley, know of its existence. We have a similar unit which we shall be prepared to make available.' Baumann looked at his watch. 'I'll fly back on the early morning flight. When I've spoken with your chap Mason I'll let you know my thoughts on using him.'

Crombie hailed a taxi for his guest and then another for himself. As he sat back in the taxi his mind was on the meeting with Baumann. The German made him feel old. He was so full of energy, eager to get things done and thinking ahead of what the problems would be and ways to solve them. He wondered how Baumann would get on with Swenson. The German had the self-confidence that came from having cleared his intentions with both his seniors at Pullach and the politicians in Bonn. Swenson would probably have to work covertly, with politicians, the White House and even some people in the CIA, against him. And, as always, the media ready to take to spurious moral heights to denigrate or disparage any significant government agency. And he himself, Sir Peter Crombie, Director-General of the Secret Intelligence Service, or MI6 if that was how you liked it, unable to rely on the Foreign Secretary, his official boss, or the Prime Minister, to support him in an attempt to block off overt attacks by subversives. He would have least standing of the three of them because he had no authority and few resources. Maybe it would be best to accept the task of being co-ordinator or Chairman or some such thing.

As he paid off the driver his mind went to Sam Wheeler. He had been neglecting him and maybe he'd better think again in the light of this latest involvement. He sighed as he put his key in the lock. Maybe he was getting too old for these games.

CHAPTER 20

Mason was still in bed when the phone rang and he glanced at his watch as he picked up the phone. It was 8.05 a.m. When he spoke he just gave his number.

'I hope I haven't woken you up. My name's Baumann. I think you've had a message from London about me. Yes?'

'Yes. What's it all about?'

'I'm in Berlin for the day. Could I pop in and see you?'

'Yeah. OK. When do you want to come?'

'How about in half an hour?'

'Make it an hour. Have you got my address?'

'Yes. Thanks. See you in an hour then.'

Baumann arrived promptly at 9.15 a.m. looking as if he had been up a long time. In fact he had flown up from Bonn on a Luftwaffe fighter plane that morning and had landed at Tempelhof.

Mason took in the well-cut clothes and the black leather brief-case. He reckoned that the German was about five years older than him and looked as if he were police or military. He nodded towards the kitchen.

'There's coffee in the kitchen and we can sit at the table.' As he led the way into the kitchen, Mason said over his shoulder, 'So. What's it all about? London didn't say much.'

Baumann pulled out a chair and sat down and as Mason poured the coffee Baumann reached inside his jacket pocket and pulled out his BND identity card. Unlike most people shown the card, Mason looked at it carefully, especially the line that gave the holder's rank as Lieutenant-Colonel.

As Mason sat stirring his coffee Baumann put his card away.

'Your people in London told me you were scouting for Charlie

Foster's records.' He paused. 'Not an easy task. My people have been looking too and despite our resources we haven't made much progress.'

Mason shrugged. 'So how can I help?'

Baumann smiled and loosened his tie. 'It's warm for April, d'you mind if I take off my jacket?'

'Help yourself.'

When Baumann had slung his jacket over the back of the chair he reached for his brief-case and took out a leather-bound book. With his hand on the closed book he looked across at Mason.

'We weren't quite sure who you were when you arrived in town but somebody recognised your photographs from previous visits to Berlin when you were openly SIS. We made some discreet enquiries with the SIS Berlin detachment but they said you were in London.' He smiled and shrugged. 'So you were put under casual surveillance.' He paused. 'A few things came up from that, and I thought it would be useful if we compared notes. Peter Crombie gave me the go-ahead.'

'Must have been pretty boring tailing me.'

'Not really. A couple of things were interesting.'

'Like what?'

'Tell me about the party at Rosen's place. The people who were there.'

'I never knew their names. They were mostly Germans. Three Americans. Rosen was obviously the one who mattered. Most of them looked more like bikers than students. I left pretty early.'

Baumann pushed across the leather folder. 'See if you can recognise any of them.'

There were twenty pages with six or seven photographs on both sides of the page. The photographs were black and white rather grainy shots of various men. None of the photographs was posed. They were the type of shots produced by photo-journalists or surveillance teams.

Baumann sat patiently as Mason leafed slowly through the pages, sometimes turning back a page to check a face again or make a comparison. When he had finished he said, 'There were three I recognised.'

'Great. Give me the frame numbers.'

Mason checked and gave the numbers which Baumann wrote down.

'Who are those men – criminals?'

'No. The American you recognised is a lecturer at one of the smaller mid-west colleges in the States. The others I'd have to check our records but I'd guess that we've got them down as subversives.'

'And Rosen himself?'

Baumann smiled. 'I'd like to hear your account of him first.'

Mason thought for a few moments before replying.

'I found him a strange man. Very vital and energetic. Eager to convince you that his strange views were not only right but that you should embrace them without argument.' He smiled. 'But I rather liked him.'

'What did you think his views were?'

'Oh, that politicians are the root of all evil. That government's only aim is to control the people. Therefore governments and the State should be challenged on all fronts.'

'Would it be fair to describe him as an anarchist?'

'No doubt.'

'Anarchy with violence?'

'I don't think he would initiate violence but I think he would condone it if it brought down the State.'

'So why did you like him?'

'He's charming. A natural charmer. He listens to what you have to say even if it's totally against him. He's like those cult leaders in America and Japan. His followers would obey him without question.' Mason smiled. 'Now you tell me what he's really like.'

'I go along with most of what you say but I know more about his background than you do. He *is* a charmer. No doubt about it. And like most charmers he's irresponsible. He's busy lighting fuses but he neither knows nor cares where they lead. He was well-in with the Stasis *and* the KGB. He was very useful to them. He could probably have saved Charlie Foster from being killed. He knew something that your people would have traded for Charlie Foster. Charlie knew it too but wasn't prepared to sell the person concerned down the river.'

'Who was the person concerned?'

'Freddie Malins. Both Rosen and Foster knew something about Malins that your people in London would have found very useful.'

'What was it?'

Baumann hesitated. 'If I tell you I want you to promise to keep up your relationship with both Malins and Rosen. You don't let on what you know. OK?'

'I guess so.'

Baumann shook his head. 'Not good enough. I need a promise.'

'OK. I promise.'

'Freddie Malins was a Stasi informer. Both when he was in SIS and after he left or was thrown out.' Baumann paused to let the news sink in. 'If they had known they could have put him in jail for life or they could have turned him and used him as a double-agent into East Germany.' He looked at Mason. 'Can you go along with the two of them now?'

'No problem. They're just part of the game so far as I'm concerned.'

'You've seen the Stasi stuff that's been sent to your boss in London?'

'Yes. I only got it yesterday.'

'If you read it carefully it gives you a clue as to where it comes from. Not proof. Just a clue.'

Mason's voice had an edge to it as he said, 'Colonel, if you and I are going to work together let's not play games.' He paused. 'What's the bloody clue?'

Baumann smiled. 'OK. You remember that when it comes to sharing information with me. Yes?'

Mason nodded.

'The first part of the report is a mini-CV of the target and then, half-way down the page, there's a heading – "JR assessment". JR is Jakob Rosen and my guess is that it was he or somebody connected with him who sent the stuff.'

'How did it get into Crombie's letter-box?'

'That's no problem for the Professor. He's got contacts all over Europe and the States who'll carry out his instructions. There's another thing that points to him. There was no demand with any of this material for money or the release of prisoners but there has to be *some* pay-off for sending it. The pay-off for Rosen is destroying politicians.'

'But why Brits?'

'It isn't just Brits. We've had them too in Bonn. The Americans have had at least one.'

'Why didn't London tell me about the others?'

'I guess because they didn't see the connection with JR. He's just one of several contacts of yours.'

'Did you point out the connection to them?'

'No. You can tell them. But that's why I want you to keep up your relationship with Rosen and Malins. And don't underestimate either of them. Malins is protecting his fortune and Rosen is quite ruthless under all that charm.'

'Do I gather from this talk that London and Bonn are co-operating on this?'

'At the moment it's just you and me but in a couple of weeks it'll be more official. More resources and more bodies. And the Americans will be part of it. Meantime if you need help or information from me just contact me. I'll give you a twenty-four-hour call number. Don't hesitate to use it.'

'Anything else you need to tell me?'

Baumann said, 'Yes', and fished into his brief-case and pulled out a small spiral-bound notebook and searched the pages. When he found what he wanted he looked up at Mason. 'A girl – Margo Kempe – you met her at a club in Bleibtreu Strasse. She makes her big money black-mailing. Just thought you ought to know.'

Mason laughed. 'And I suppose you've got ten by eight glossies of the photographs, or was it a tape-recording?'

'Neither, I assure you.' He grinned. 'Anyway it's illegal to do that sort of thing under our laws.'

They went together for a quick meal in the restaurant a few doors away from Mason's place and spent the time discussing sports cars and convertibles. It seemed that Baumann had a white Mercedes 300 SL and loved his wife enough to let her drive it.

CHAPTER 21

Joe Logan looked at the blue denim shirt on the hanger in the closet. It needed pressing, but what the hell, they didn't care how he looked or what he wore as long as he went on crunching the numbers for them. He dressed without bothering to shave and headed the ancient T-bird south down the Washington – Baltimore highway. roughly half-way between these two cities was a sprawling complex of heavily-guarded buildings that housed the National Security Agency. Some people still called it SIGINT City. With a resident population of 4000 Fort George Meade was larger than 130 other cities and towns in the State of Maryland. Its population increased roughly twenty times during working hours and inside the high-security perimeter it had its own bus service and its own police force. You could get a decent haircut, do your banking, book a holiday, use the library and buy cosmetics. But beneath the normal-looking surface was the grim reality of monitoring and recording every radio and telephonic signal produced anywhere in the world. There was no enemy, you covered the lot. Just getting rid of the discarded print-out was a major problem. Somebody had worked out that you could build a condo a week on what it cost to preserve the security of those tons of unwanted print-out. Even what was kept was a major problem but it was worth far more than what it cost to get. To hear what two Politburo members were saying about Yeltsin as they left the Kremlin in an official Zil, or even what the Mayor of Paris was saying about the President of France as he talked to his young mistress in the pretty apartment in the 16th Arrondissement, were all grist to the mill.

Logan pulled up at the main entrance and switched off the engine and waited. The entire complex was surrounded by a ten-foot cyclone fence with multiple rows of barbed wire. Inside that was another electrified fence and guards with dogs and closed-circuit cameras with telephoto lenses monitoring every foot of the space between.

After the initial check he drove in and parked in the lot that served the Headquarters Building.

He was checked by two blue-uniformed Federal Protective Service guards, both of whom knew him well. But for the purposes of the security check he was a stranger. Not to be trusted. They passed his piece of plastic across a screen and handed it back to him. It took him fifteen minutes to get to his office through the door that was labelled DIRNSA, in a corridor nicknamed Mahogany Row, past the secretaries and through to the office where he worked with one other mathematician in an office with the number 390 on the door. It opened smoothly as he pushed in his smart card.

He nodded to the man in the separate alcove and said, 'Morning.' His colleague nodded back. 'You're late again.'

'So?'

'So nothing. Just you're late.'

'You oughta be handing out parking fines not wasting time here.'

'And you sound like you're not getting any.'

Logan sat down in his own alcove and switched on the computer and booked in his programme. The screen scrolled and then settled at a display that was blue on a white background and said STOCHASTIC 904. Logan put on his headphones and pressed ENTER.

Joe Logan had been awarded his Ph.D. for a study he had done on the use of stochastic mathematics in code-breaking. Stochastic maths concerns the mathematics of randomness and Logan's original study was now long outdated. Logan himself had made it so. There was only a handful of mathematicians at NSA who could understand Logan's latest work on breaking down encryption and his work was partly financed by the CIA. A token payment was made by the NSA's sister organisation GCHQ at Cheltenham in the UK. The problem Logan had been working on for the last three months was posed by the CIA. There were people using the Internet who were using a code that the CIA's own top code-breakers couldn't break.

The problem was now a concern at White House level. The Federal Communications Commission, the FCC, and the State Department had been asked by the CIA to introduce legislation that would make it illegal to use encryption that was not accessible to the CIA and NSA itself. But there were snags. Several snags. At least one of them insuperable – the First Amendment – abridging the freedom of speech. Another was completely out of the control of the US government. Internet operated all over the world. Nobody and no government could stop what was transmitted to anywhere in the world. The final snag had been pointed out by the lawyers. How would the CIA feel about putting up their top cryptographers in court swearing that there was encoded material that they couldn't break when it was transmitted by some kid who had been tracked down by the FBI or the FCC and refused to reveal his unbroken code? Apart from the embarrassment, what law was being broken? Some bright spark had suggested that a new law could be promulgated, claiming that it was necessary in order to prevent the transmission of pornography. They had tried it out on a specially chosen group of Senators and Congressmen who had said they would be made laughing-stocks if they tried to get such legislation through Congress.

The problem had been passed to Logan to see if there was some way to break any code that could be devised. But Joseph Logan Ph.D. had no intention of finding a solution. It was traffic transmitted using a code of his devising that had been monitored by the FCC and the FBI. Another problem for the two organisations was that the code was being used in transmissions from at least ten different locations, all of which, except two, appeared to be mobile. The two were reckoned by the FCC to be base stations of a network.

For the rest of the day Logan played with the idea of basing a code on an algebraic formula. Not an exotic one but one that would be in the mental data-base of anyone doing maths at university level. At 5 p.m. he closed down and headed back to the parking lot for his car. There was a slip of paper wedged under one of the windscreen wipers – it was yellow, about the size of a raffle-ticket. The number in black was 5. He cursed softly as he removed the paper and stuck it in his jacket pocket. It meant going down to Baltimore for the night and staying at the bed and breakfast place on West Mulberry Street. Not that there was anything wrong with bed and breakfast at Mulberry House. At least he'd get a good sleep and a great breakfast. The snag was Martin. Always doubting, always looking for problems, trusting nobody, on the look-out for a chance of violence. But it was Martin who decided where they should meet.

Tonight's subject was the German and the British network. Not lively enough for Martin's taste. And by lively he meant violent.

They had booked in, had a snack at a cafe, and then walked down to the waterfront area and sat on a crate in front of one of the warehouses.

'I wanna get something big in the three places. And all on the same day.'

'That's your bit, Martin. I'll do the communications, the rest is up to you. You're the one who works the bangs.'

'Are you sure those FBI bastards can't read our stuff?'

'Quite sure. Nobody can who doesn't know our reference.'

'Who *does* know it?'

'In the US of A just me and Snowy. In Germany, Rosen and Heller. In the UK, Bailey and Pops.'

'What if one of you gets knocked off?'

'The network would carry on but jointly decide on a replacement.' He paused. 'I've nominated somebody here and Rosen and Bailey have done the same.'

'There's gonna be need for a lot of traffic in the build-up in the next coupla months. We'll have to have a few preliminary trials on other targets.'

Logan shrugged. 'It's up to you, man. The communications traffic's no problem.'

'You don't go with the rough stuff do you?'

'No.'

'Why not?'

'Because I'm darn sure that in the end it's that that'll bring the roof down on us. I like more subtle means.' He paused. 'Like we did with Nelson Overy.'

'But you went along with smoking the two senators.'

'Sure. What I'm against is *innocent* people being killed. For me they're off-target and off-limits.' He shrugged. 'But that's your bit not mine.'

'Rosen's the same as you. I don't trust him all the way.'

Logan smiled. 'You don't trust me either. But you'd be back to couriers and tapped telephones without us.' He paused. 'Anything else?'

'No. When do you have your polygraph test?'

'Had it ten days ago.' He laughed. 'Clear as a bell. No problems.' He paused. 'How about you?'

Martin laughed. 'Business is good. I'm OK.'

'What about that bimbo of yours? She still giving you trouble?'

Martin flushed with anger. 'Leave her out of it. She's nothing to do with our thing.'

Logan sighed and shrugged. 'Up to you, man. But don't talk in your sleep.'

As Logan eased the T-bird into the heavy traffic on Interstate 95 the white Ford Bronco was two cars behind him. It followed him back to his apartment and waited until he left for work. The man in the white Bronco pressed the test button and listened to the transmission from the mini-transmitter clamped to the reverse side of the T-bird's number plate. He made a note that the battery needed changing but it was movement activated and it would last out for a couple of days more.

CHAPTER 22

Swenson had booked them into the Marriott Hotel just across Key Bridge from Georgetown. It was Friday night and they intended to work all through the weekend if it were necessary. There would be just Swenson, Baumann and himself and Swenson had asked that if all went well he could be allowed to bring in the Vice-President, Joe Healey, to give some official recognition of the operation from the White House level. The President was not being informed.

Crombie stood at the big window looking across towards the river but seeing nothing, his mind was on the meeting. They had already asked him to chair the meeting and to be the administrative co-ordinator of whatever joint operation they mounted. He was embarrassed that he had so little to contribute apart from advice and the Charlie Foster background. He was also feeling guilty at not having found time to talk with Sam Wheeler before he left. Especially as he had received a note from the Leader of the Opposition asking for a meeting to discuss what his shadow cabinet ministers felt was an organised and vicious attack on their MPs.

He was less ready to admit to himself that he was incensed because he suspected that Swenson and Baumann were having talks on their plans without reference to him. Swenson was to show them some film after dinner. The Vice-President was going to join them. Many Washington observers reckoned that Joe Healey would be the next President. A Harvard alumnus, senior partner in a respected law firm and self-confident enough to have a relaxed easy-going attitude to senior people in both parties. And under that easy manner was the kind of wisdom that Americans missed in today's public figures.

Crombie had twenty minutes alone with him soon after arriving and had liked him immediately. He was patently a man who could be trusted. In politics, but not a politician.

The Vice-President had joined them after dinner as they sat around a small table drinking Californian Cabernet Sauvignon and talking about the significance of jazz in the image of America in the rest of the world.

It was Joe Healey who brought them back to reality. 'Gentlemen,' he said, 'I appreciate you keeping me informed on this problem and before Olaf Swenson shows us the film clips I want to tell you of a clipping from a newspaper that I keep permanently on my blotter in the White House. It's a clipping from *The Times* of London about a year or so back.' He paused. 'The heading reads – "Hostile mood in US puts officials in fear of lives".' He paused and sighed. 'It quotes our old friend Gordon Liddy of Watergate fame, who advises listeners to his radio programme facing arrest by force to – I quote – shoot law enforcement officers in the head.' He paused. 'It goes on to quote the instance of when a woman was contacted by police over an expired car licence, the police were confronted by armed paramilitary militia members.' He looked at the three men facing him. 'I keep that cutting on my blotter to remind myself of what's going on. It shames me and it's time the government did something about it. I'm sorry that you people, who are taking the first steps, have to do it covertly as if the forces of law and order were the criminals not the defenders of the public who want to live without fear of violence against themselves and their homes.' He paused. 'I'll sit through the film clips. I've seen them scores of times before but it's as well to be reminded of what we've come to.'

Joe Healey stood up and walked with Crombie and Baumann to the chairs in front of the screen. Swenson was manning the projector himself.

The film opened with several minutes of the FBI's bungled attack on the heavily armed Branch Davidian compound in Waco, Texas. It moved to rescuers working in the ruins of the Oklahoma City bombing, and then on to downtown Dallas and the self-styled Conspiracy Museum run by the eighty-one-year-old R.B. Cutler and which claims that the US Government is constantly conspiring against its citizens. Talk of secret government concentration camps, the FBI working to the orders of the Mafia. Gordon Liddy exhorting listeners to shoot law enforcement officers in the head to avoid bullet-proof waistcoats.

A congresswoman, Barbara Cubin from Wyoming, referring to the Internal Revenue Service as 'the Gestapo'. The film clips moved on to the training camps of the self-styled 'militia' with its leaders' death threats against those who were attempting to exclude sub-machine guns from the closets of private citizens. Men openly advocating warfare and armed rebellion against the government 'thugs'. Intercepted radio traffic and intercepts from Internet showed all too clearly that the threats were not bluffing but part of the defiance of the government. And it was all government that was the target. It mattered not whether it was Democratic or Republican.

When the lights eventually went on there was a long silence and then Joe Healey slowly stood up and, looking at the three men in turn, he said quietly, 'Well, my friends. That's where we're at.' He hesitated for a moment. 'All I can do is leave it to you people . . . and remember . . . no matter how successful you are . . . nobody'll ever thank you for it.' He smiled and Swenson walked with him to the door of the suite.

They moved to Baumann's suite and settled around the long table. Baumann facing Swenson and Crombie, with a pile of papers beside him on the table.

It was Baumann who smoothly took over.

'I thought I'd best tell you of my assessment team's analysis of what's going on.' He looked at the other two. 'Agreed?'

They both nodded and Baumann leaned forward. 'It's our opinion that our only real asset at the moment is Sir Peter's man, Mason. All the indications we have are that the man Rosen is our first target.' He paused. 'All our thinking is outlined in the copies of reports that I'll pass over to you later. We think that Rosen is the source of the denunciations we have all received. My people think it has been a trial run to see if it works. Does it actually destroy the individuals concerned? So far his score has been high. It's working.

'But there's a bigger picture and we think that Rosen is only a trial run for the real thing. The real thing involves violence and terrorism. Probably starting with killing individual politicians and moving on to sabotage and destruction of public facilities.' He paused. 'Fortunately our view is that that's long-term. Could be a year maybe two before they've got their act together for that. When that happens Rosen won't count. It'll be in the hands of people like the neo-Nazis in Germany and Britain and the militia here in the USA.' He paused. 'So our immediate concern is to deal with Rosen. Sir Peter's man,

Mason, is our only lead into Rosen's set-up and I have to warn you that Mason would be in considerable danger if things went wrong. Rosen may not be a violent man but his associates are ruthless.' He paused. 'We need to discuss right now the facilities each of us can make available and the official attitude to our operation.' He nodded to Swenson. 'Olaf. You go first.'

Swenson leaned back in his chair. 'Official attitude none. It's a covert operation authorised by me personally and probably indictable. Facilities? I'll put in our Counter-Terrorism Centre. It's a highly secret group inside the CIA. We have a staff of just under two hundred people and their official remit is disrupting, countering and assisting in the arrest of terrorists. They have high-tech equipment using computers, spy satellites and we get all relevant intercepts from the National Security Agency.' He shrugged and smiled at Baumann.

'Your turn, Franz.'

'All BND facilities are available including SEK, our commando unit that does a similar job to SWAT units, but everything kept to a minimum in early stages for the sake of security. It'll be on a need-to-know basis.' He paused. 'Especially when it could affect Mason.' He shrugged. 'That's it.'

Crombie took a deep breath. 'As I think you both know I have virtually no official backing. One minister virtually knows that I am doing something but although he didn't forbid it he didn't approve it either. I have a small scheme on-going related to the harassment by our media of MPs and the government in general. That has been moderately successful. It was because of the threat from the Stasi documents that we arranged for Mason to try and trace the source in Berlin. It was in the course of this investigation that he came into contact with Rosen and several others. I can use my facilities on a personal basis to provide you both with information but I have no resources I can deploy openly. A specialist here and there, but that's it.'

Swenson said quietly, 'We need someone who can stand on the sideline and give us advice. It's easy for things to get out of hand on games like these. We need a professional, an insider to keep track of where we're going.' He paused. 'We'd like you to take over that responsibility.'

Sir Peter smiled wryly. 'You don't need to find me a sinecure.'

The phone rang and Swenson reached for it and listened. Then he said, 'Yes, he's here. I'll put him on.'

Swenson held out the phone to Crombie. 'It's your wife, Peter.'

Crombie took the phone. 'What's up?'

'Hi. There's another one of those letters. But this time it's more a packet, quite thick. Do you want me to open it or can it wait?'

'Open it. See what it is and ring me back but be careful what you say.'

'OK. You all right?'

'I'm fine. Ring me back as soon as you can.'

It was ten minutes before Lady Diana called back.

'There are about thirty different sheets. All politicians. Both parties and a note that says copies have been sent to two UK press agencies.'

'What sort of accusations?'

'The usual. Sex or fraud but no suggestion that they were informers to those people.'

'When did it arrive?'

'About an hour ago.'

'Anything on the radio or in the papers?'

'No. Nothing. They'll want lawyers to go over it before they use it. Could be very expensive for them if any of it can be proved wrong.'

There were a few moments silence and then Crombie said, 'Seal them up and put them in my desk. Just forget 'em.'

Lady Diana had learned way back that you don't argue with the captain, no matter what.

'OK dearest. Wilco, as your chaps always say.'

As Crombie hung up the phone he had no idea of whether he had done the right thing or not. He wanted to go home and collect his thoughts. He wanted to be back on his own patch again not planning how to control several million dissident Americans. He remembered what the Vice-President had said to Swenson – 'you've got to remember – the United Kingdom's almost as big as the state of Oregon'. So much for the 'special relationship'. The thought made him even more glad that he was a Brit. And even more determined not to let the bastards ruin his country.

He walked back to where Swenson and Baumann were sitting. He told them about the message from his wife.

Swenson looked up at him. 'So much for this crap you were giving us about a sinecure. We shouldn't be here if it wasn't for you. And the message you just had shows all too clearly that you're still in the frame, my friend.' He looked at his watch. 'It's way past midnight but let's spend ten minutes assessing what we're up to.'

Crombie sat down in the free chair and he suddenly realised what needed to be said for his own peace of mind.

'I think it's important to get what we have in mind into perspective. It's a question of facing the facts. We are not going to be able to stop millions of people in the USA from hating their government. Only politicians can do that. And they show no signs of attempting to face the problem. But in Germany and Britain the problem is the same but on a much smaller scale. In the UK we have the same problem as the USA, a media that is irresponsible and we can do something to show the media and the Opposition that enough is enough. In Germany we have the problem of neo-Nazis and terrorist groups and cults. Franz Baumann feels that Rosen is a key figure. We must find out what he's up to and, if necessary, deal with it. All we are doing is a large-scale reconnaissance. We are not going to put the world right. But we can show how to stabilise the situation in two countries and politicians will be forced to take action.' He sighed and looked at Swenson. 'For your people, Olaf, the most we can hope for is to get at the ring-leaders, show that they are revolutionaries. Far more dangerous than the Communists ever were, and hope that the politicians can learn the lessons.'

For long moments the two were silent and then Baumann smiled and said quietly, 'What military men call "objectives and intentions."' He paused. 'But you're right. It would be easy to let things get out of hand. The media and the politicians would claim that *we* were the conspirators, enemies of free speech and against the constitution.' He looked at Swenson. 'How about you, Olaf?'

'It depresses me, but like Peter said, we've got to face the facts. The burden will be on you two and for the US of A we can only help where we can and hope that Congress takes heed of how you've tackled the problems.' He sighed. 'I'm tired. How about we get down to details tomorrow?' As Swenson stood up the phone rang and Crombie walked over and picked it up. He listened for a few moments, said 'Thank you' and hung up, turning to the others.

'It was a call from your wife, Olaf. Said to look at CNN right now.' He walked to the TV set and flicked through the channels to CNN and stood watching, the remote control in his hand. As he brought up the sound, the picture showed a reporter with a microphone and police and medics in the background. There was a small inset picture of a man he didn't recognise. The reporter was obviously repeating what had been said before.

'. . . the police have given no details of the killings, nor any idea of the motives, but the connection between the two victims is all too obvious. Both Senator Ralston and Congressman Fellows were leading advocates of modifications to the gun laws to restrict the size and type of guns that could be owned by individual citizens. I have been told that the Senator was shot at close range by a man in a vehicle using what a witness, an ex-marine, described as an AK.47. The shooting took place as the Senator was leaving the Ford Theatre after watching a rehearsal of a local amateur group. I guess there is no need to remind viewers that it was the Ford Theatre where President Lincoln was assassinated. Congressman Fellows was shot as he was hailing a cab as he came out from a meeting at FBI Headquarters at the J. Edgar Hoover Building on 10th Street and Pennsylvania Avenue. Unconfirmed reports say that he was hit by five shots from a handgun. The attacker was picked up by a black van . . . both victims were already dead when the emergency services and police arrived . . . back to the studio from Mike Calvert on 10th Street, Washington DC.'

The picture cut to a White House spokesman and Swenson said harshly, 'For Christ's sake switch it off'. He stood up slowly. 'I'd better go over to Langley. I'll see you sometime tomorrow.' He looked at the other two. 'Don't be too ready to side-line my problems, my friends.' He pointed at the blank TV screen. 'Maybe the Good Lord was sending us a message.'

When the others left, Crombie looked at his watch. It was 3.30 a.m. He poured himself a whisky and using the remote control switched on the TV and spent a few minutes surfing through the available channels. He settled on The Cosby Show. He liked the programme. He watched it regularly. They were his kind of people. When the show finished he switched off the TV and walked to the window. Even at this hour the city was alive, with lights twinkling as far as the eye could see. It reminded him of the lines of an Arabic poem he had once learned.

'The evening is a black bride wearing silver necklaces.'

It reminded him too of the beautiful girl who had taught him those words. It seemed a long time ago. He sighed as he looked at the world outside. He loved New York, a city alight with energy day and night but Washington seemed characterless, a gloomy place. A place for transients who didn't come for love and didn't come to stay. He drank up the last of his whisky and went to bed.

They had discussed their roles in the operation the following day and by the evening it had been agreed that Crombie would be the central point to disseminate the information and reports from all three countries. There would be obligatory reports on a weekly basis until the scheme was operational and at that point there would be daily reports even if they were nil reports.

Crombie had upgraded himself to the Sunday Concorde flight and lay back comfortably working out what he had to do when he got back.

First of all he had to decide if Harding was really the man to control using Mason in penetrating the Rosen set-up, if there was one. His instinct was that Mason should be controlled by Baumann. A local, the man on the spot and entirely professional. In which case he had to concoct some story for Harding for shifting Mason from his control. He hated to admit it but he preferred Baumann to Harding anyway.

Then he would have to brief Mason himself before transferring him to Baumann. According to the records promotion wasn't due for a year but it would smooth things over. Next on the list must be a meeting with Sam Wheeler and then decide whether his little exercise should be closed down. There was still the Leader of the Opposition's request for a meeting about harassment of Opposition MPs. He'd quite enjoy that.

CHAPTER 23

Major Waring, Royal Artillery, used part of a torn curtain to wipe the thick dust from the old oak table so that he could lay out the Ordnance survey map. Outside the fire engines were pulling out. There had been a small fire in one end of the building. An ambulance was waiting for the two casualties, one of which was serious. the police had taped off the area around the building and the main gates were under police supervision. An area for VIPs' cars had been marked out. An attack on Chequers, the Prime Minister's official country residence, was bound to lead to the place swarming with people once the word got out.

Inside what was left of the building several men had assembled around the table with the Artillery Major.

'Right, gentlemen. Having looked at the bits and pieces we've picked up so far I can tell you that the damage was done by an 81mm. mortar. It will have launched approximately four kilos of high explosives and it will have been fired from somewhere in a radius of just over three and a half miles. The mortar is easily transportable, needs a very small launching area and from the single shot I'd guess the attackers were very sure of hitting their target because they used a Merlin – a terminally-guided anti-armour bomb. I'd estimate that just over half the building has been destroyed.'

The MI5 man said, 'Who was it? IRA?'

'No. It's a mortar limited to special SAS units. The IRA could never have got hold of one.'

'So who do you think?'

'I've no idea. I've already checked with Hereford. All their 81s are accounted for. They don't have all that many.' He sighed and shrugged. 'I'd say you've got to look at either the Ministry of Defence or at the manufacturers. I'll put the stuff we've collected under sealed security and it'll be available to authorised personnel at our equipment

depot at Larkfield.' He pointed to the map on the table. 'I'll leave you
the map. I've drawn a circle to the map scale with a radius of three and
a half miles from Chequers. It covers a lot of land surface.' He nodded
and left the Special Branch man, the MI5 man and the Chief Constable
to continue their deliberations.

The TV news programmes had done their speculating which ranged
from the IRA to Arab Fundamentalists and Japanese cults. It was just
in time for the News at Ten that all media received a faxed message
which they showed on screen.

It said simply – *'Chequers – Government, even in its best state, is but
a necessary evil; in its worst state, an intolerable one.'* It took half an
hour before it was identified to viewers as a quotation from Tom Paine.
Most viewers went to bed wondering who the hell Tom Paine was. But
the morning papers were already pillaging their data-bases and taking
down long quotes from historians and the better-educated political
commentators. The Home Office gave a brief press conference hoping
that it would make the morning papers. The enquiries into the attack
on Chequers would, as it obviously concerned terrorists, be in the
hands of MI5.

Crombie made no attempt to contact his opposite number in the
Security Services but offered assistance if it were required through one
of his liaison team. Crombie was the only man, apart from the people
who had sent the fax messages, who recognised the significance of the
message from the perpetrators. Even revolutionaries, it seemed, could
overestimate the intelligence of their audience.

Crombie's meeting with Harding wasn't easy. There was not only the
removal of Mason from Harding's control but conveying the decision
to reduce the establishment of the SIS in Berlin now that the Wall had
been down for several years. There was some consolation for Harding
in being offered the posting of liaison officer to NATO, a cushy posting
and based in Brussels, which he gladly accepted. He told Harding to
get Mason to come over as soon as possible and he gave his home
number for Mason to contact him. When Mason phoned, Crombie
arranged a meeting four days on, and then phoned Baumann to ask if
he could come over to take over Mason. Baumann said he'd cancel his
appointments to be there.

* * *

Baumann came over the day before Crombie was due to see Mason and it was agreed that Mason would be controlled in the field by Baumann and that BND would provide any back-up that was needed. The same day Swenson phoned Crombie suggesting that he sent over a top man from the CIA's Anti-terrorist unit to give Mason, Baumann and Crombie a picture of the terrorism scene in the USA. They could fill him in on what was going on in Berlin.

When Mason came out of his meeting with Crombie it seemed almost incredible. Sir Peter Crombie was the Director-General of SIS. A man whom Mason had only met two or three times at those routine, internal social gatherings that were put on from time to time so that the lesser lights could look over the men who controlled their lives. D-Gs were seldom chosen from the actual intelligence people. They were always outsiders. Military men. Administrators who could keep the lid on the many pots that were boiling or simmering in the name of intelligence gathering. The gossip he had heard of Crombie was that he didn't interfere very much and was largely ineffective but acceptable to the politicians.

To be working on so close a basis with the D-G himself, with a promotion thrown in as well, indicated that the operation had now moved into a new dimension. To be working with Baumann as his immediate boss meant that he had somehow become a key operator in a much bigger project.

Baumann had a suite at the Park Lane Hilton and had invited Mason over for a working breakfast.

As he stirred his coffee, Baumann said, 'Where are you staying?'

'I've got a small flat in East Croydon, just outside London.'

'I guess Sir Peter made clear when he spoke with you that the BND think that Rosen might be a key figure in a conspiracy of some kind?'

'He didn't give any details. He seemed a bit vague about it.' Mason smiled. 'I assumed he didn't know very much about the BND theory.'

'We're pretty sure that Rosen is a key figure but we don't know what his rôle is.' He paused. 'I'm hoping that you can get close enough to him to give us a lead as to what part he plays.' He looked across the table at Mason's face as he said, 'He mixes with some pretty rough characters. Could be dangerous. How d'you feel about that?'

Mason shrugged. 'I can look after myself.'

'Well, think about it.'

'What is it you want me to do exactly?'

'Get as close as you can to Rosen. Seem as if you go along with his ideas. Not all the way but not against him.'

'Why should he care about what I think or have me hanging around?'

Baumann smiled. 'You're being too modest. You are a catch for a man like Rosen. After all – you're an SIS agent. You know, or you can find out, what your people in London are thinking.' He paused. 'I've had my people check him out. At least I tried to.' He paused again. 'There's nothing. His past is a blank. No birth records, no schooling records, no records of any kind. It was as if he had never existed. The CV he provided to get his chair at the university is a fabrication from start to finish and obviously put together by an expert.'

'That sort of deception can be broken – given time.'

'I'm not sure we've got time. By the way, what may I call you – do you use James or Jim?'

'James, And you're Franz.'

'How did you know that?'

'I looked up your file yesterday.'

Baumann laughed. 'Fair enough.' He stood up and walked over to the tall window that looked over Park Lane to Hyde Park. He looked at his watch and turned to Mason. 'They're due here in ten minutes. Have you met Swenson before?'

'No. He's way above my level.' He smiled. 'I hadn't even properly met Crombie until a couple of days ago. Just seen him around.'

'Swenson's a pro. Knows what he's up to and isn't afraid of the politicians in Washington.' He paused. 'But the guy he's bringing with him, Klein, is the one that matters to us today. He's deputy director of the CIA's Anti-terrorist outfit and they have the widest possible remit. No holds barred. And they can use any monitoring done by NSA at Fort George Meade. That access could be invaluable for us. Klein knows more about terrorism than the terrorists themselves. I've never met him but I've read his commentaries and he's totally committed and totally credible. They're very different people but he and our friend Rosen are fanatics about their totally opposing theories.'

* * *

'The name's Klein, gentlemen. Art Klein. You know about my job and you've asked me to give you a picture of our operation and the people we're trying to eliminate.' He paused and looked around. Klein looked like Al Pacino in *Sea of love*. Untidy and rather doleful but with big brown eyes that took in everything. 'And when I say eliminate I mean just that.' He paused. 'We're here in London so let me ask Mr Mason a question.' He looked at Mason. 'Is it the law in the UK that wearing a seat-belt in a car is compulsory?'

'Yes. It's compulsory. You get a thirty-pound fine if the police stop you and you aren't complying.'

'Right.' He looked at Mason. 'Do you always wear a seat-belt when driving?'

'No'

'Why not?'

Mason shrugged. 'Too much bother.'

Klein nodded. 'So . . . let me tell you that there are people in the USA who refuse to wear seat-belts because they say that it's no business of the state to lay down such laws. Taking away the freedom of the citizen. Making laws that purport to benefit you but take away your freedom to decide for yourself.' He sighed and then said softly, 'And there are hundreds of thousands who deliberately break the law on principle. And there is a smaller number . . . maybe tens of thousands, who are prepared to shoot a law-officer who tries to enforce that law.' He paused. 'I just want to show you that terrorism isn't just the killing of enemies or blowing up buildings. Evil men have persuaded ordinary people that the government, any government, is their mortal enemy.

'There are newspapers in the States, right now, printing stories that it was the government that cold-bloodedly blew up the building in Oklahoma City to get rid of Secret Service agents who knew too much about the President. We are finding that many of the terrorist groups have formed such a complex analysis of so-called governmental repression that even non-extremists can find some appeal in the milder theories where personal liberty is concerned. If you don't like seat-belts or air-bags or motor-cycle helmets it can be turned into a hatred of government.

'We have people today who resent having to have certificates to register births, death and marriages. People who refuse to fill in census forms or forms for Social Security. There are lawyers who support their views. People who are for or against abortion just kill one another and feel righteous about it.' He paused. 'But we've now got to the stage where the militia and others are organised to subvert not only the US government but to subvert the Constitution. And they point out that the twentieth century provides not a single example of a determined populace with access to small arms having been defeated by a modern army. The Russians lost in Afghanistan, the United States lost in Vietnam and the French lost in Indo-China. In each case a poorly armed population beat a modern army. When you bring in religion you bring in the real fanatics – the Islamic fundamentalists – Israeli fanatics – the Ayatollahs . . .' he shrugged '. . . not forgetting Catholics versus Protestants and good old Muslims agin Christians in the Balkans and the Middle East.' He paused. 'You've seen it in Northern Ireland. It's everywhere. Fanatics who torture and kill and claim that *they* are the law.'

When he stopped there was a long silence and then Baumann said, 'A frightening scenario, Art. Tell us what you're doing about it.'

Klein was silent for a few moments and then he said, 'The Anti-terrorism unit is specially privileged. We have our own staff, all of whom are experts in some aspect of counter-terrorism. But we also have access to all the information gathered at the National Security Agency and uniquely we have the same resources at the FBI. We work with both organisations very effectively. I understand from Olaf Swenson that you will share our resources when necessary, the only restriction will be that in certain areas it might need the agreement of Swenson and Sir Peter. The aim will be total co-operation with no element of rivalry. Just as we have with the FBI and NSA.' He sighed. 'We have no such arrangement with any other foreign government or agency. We also hope that your combined work will help us too.'

Sir Peter said, 'What can we do right now?'

'I'd like to discuss that with Herr Baumann and Mr Mason later today and I'm prepared to stay over tomorrow.'

Baumann and Mason waited as Klein went off to make a phone-call and Crombie went off to another meeting.

When Klein came back he said, 'Langley got me a seat on a late-night Concorde test-flight tomorrow.' He paused. 'You hear about the Nelson Overy business? The President's buddy who did a moonlight flit some weeks back.'

Baumann said, 'Yea. I remember it.' He smiled. 'I can guess what your news is.'

'OK. What is it?'

'Killed. Shot or a street accident.'

'Near enough. Beaten up. Been dead several days when they found his body and a couple more days before he was identified. Unknown assailants. Being buried locally at widow's request.' He half-smiled. 'Panic stations in the White House.' He shrugged. 'Back to our little problem.' He paused. 'Provided you agree I'm going to post one of my top men to you. Here or in Berlin. Wherever you think best. He can see what you need that we might be able to provide. Our records are world-wide and extensive. OK?'

Baumann said, 'Thanks. We'll be glad to have him with us. I think here in Berlin.' He paused. 'You must find our problems pretty insignificant compared with yours.'

'One thing we learned way back which you might care to copy. With such a big canvas to go at you can easily dilute the results by trying to cover everything. What we have done is to separate our resources. We have a team that concentrates on one particular group, another that is building up information on a similar group, and the rest of us are evaluating the broad problem. We have the benefits of lots of leads and information from other US intelligence agencies. You've got some restriction by not being supported by the politicians, especially in the UK.' He shrugged. 'You're stuck with that but we'll cover up all we can.'

For two hours the three of them had compared their respective operations and the help they could expect from Klein's man when he arrived. He had also agreed to check their records for any trace of Jakob Rosen and the identities of the Americans Mason had identified as being at Rosen's house for the party. Klein's man was Altieri. He had been chosen for his experience of subversives in America, and would be based at a CIA safe-house in Berlin.

CHAPTER 24

Rosen waited for the traffic lights to change at the Ku-damm crossing. There was the usual collection of punks and skate-boarders around Breitscheidplatz and three lines of cars in each direction. He wondered how many Berliners knew that Ku-damm only existed because Chancellor Bismarck had envied Paris its Champs Elysées. It was meant to enable 'the Berlin population to circulate with ease in the open air' and to facilitate 'the equestrian training of the upper classes'.

When the lights changed Rosen crossed the street and walked slowly to the Kaiser-Wilhelm Gedächtniskirche. The bombed ruins of the old church had been left as a *Mahnmal*, a 'warning for posterity'. Berliners had named the ruins 'the Hollow Tooth' and the new church building with its stained-glass windows was, because of its design, the 'Egg Crate'. Whatever the warning to posterity might be the present inhabitants of Berlin barely noticed either building despite their images being the most sold postcards for tourists.

He noticed the elderly woman sitting on the steps of the ruins with a handwritten cardboard noticeboard that said *'Ficken ist gesund'*, a questionable and rather crude declaration that claimed that making love is good for one's health. Rosen walked on a few yards and entered the new church building. It was Wednesday and the organist was playing Bach. Not some noisy *toccata* or a fugue but a slow, gentle *étude* that induced contemplation and peace. Rosen came most Wednesdays. It was an oasis for his overactive mind. But there was a price to be paid for release from the treadmill of his brain. It was the memories of long ago that he could normally dilute to almost nothing by thinking and working at his plan for a new world. A world where politicians and governments no longer controlled people's lives.

There were no more than a dozen people in the church and the sun shining through the purple-blue stained-glass windows bathed them in its rather melancholy light.

For a moment his mind went to the two Americans. Only one of them understood what it was all about. The other was an advocate of action not words. And action for that man was violence. They nicknamed him The Reaper, but he saw himself as a God-fearing man, punishing those who broke God's laws. The abortionists, the politicians who voted public funds for promiscuous single mothers, the armed men who killed women and children at Waco in the name of the government. Rosen believed that counter-violence would achieve nothing. In the end the politicians would take over again, offering peace and an end to killing. Politicians were the proper targets. They were already universally loathed, but for ordinary people there seemed to be no defence against them. Once every four or five years you could vote for a new lot but that was just shuffling the pack. He and his collaborators had to show that from now on being a politician would be dangerous. A life of exposure, vilification and public disgrace.

He shook his head like a dog coming out of water as if the gesture could get rid of the intrusive thoughts. He brought his mind back to Johann Sebastian. He wondered what Bach had thought of Vivaldi. And thinking of Vivaldi and his 273 concertos. There hadn't been a single recording of any of it until long-play records had been invented. And now there were at least a hundred versions of 'The Four Seasons' in the record catalogues. But he would gladly trade all of it for just the cello concertos.

He closed his eyes and listened to the music, and ten minutes later he left and took a taxi back to the university. He had to call the Englishman. He could be incredibly useful if only he could be converted.

Baumann was flying back to Munich to report to his brass at Pullach and Mason decided to spend an extra day dealing with some routine problems at his flat in Croydon and a quick visit to his parents.

He had taken his mother a scarf from the boutique at Victoria Station and a brooch from the Torq shop. As she slowly and carefully unwrapped the two small packages she said, 'You shouldn't spend your money on me, boy. Just seeing you is enough for me.'

'How've you been? How's the asthma?'

She sighed. 'I'm fine. This dry weather suits me. But your dad's in a bit of trouble.'

'What kind of trouble?'

'The Social Security people. He'd forgotten to mention some money he'd got in a building society. He's got to pay back about four hundred pounds and he's a bit short at the moment.'

He stood up, smiling. 'You know what you always used to do when I said I was in trouble?'

'What was that?'

'You made us a cup of tea. I'll make a cup of tea for us. No. Don't get up. I know where everything is.'

In the kitchen he made out a cheque, while the water was boiling, for five hundred pounds payable in cash. He arranged the tea things on the red plastic tray with a plate of digestive biscuits and the cheque on a saucer. He put the tray on the small table beside her chair and sat down facing her.

'I've made out a cheque for him that he can draw as cash. He'll know how to deal with it. I've had an annuity pay up a few weeks ago so the money's no problem'. He smiled. 'So stop worrying about him. He'll get by. He always does.'

He saw the tears in her eyes as she shook her head, too upset to speak, and her hands were trembling as she poured out the tea. If his father had been around he could have given him the money without her having to know. But his father, no doubt, was paying court to some equally upset woman who was missing her husband. In a way his mother was just another of his old man's victims. But robbed, not of money, but of genuine caring. He neither hated nor despised his father. He was just some figure out of a TV soap, appearing from time to time when the scriptwriters were desperate for something to happen.

Baumann had flown up from Munich to meet Mason's plane at Tegel. They took a taxi to Cafe Möhring on the Ku-damm and talked over sandwiches, cakes and coffee. American efficiency was already working. Klein had got the NSA to give them a high-grade encryption, that was virtually unbreakable without a team of experts, for their messages, and Klein had already sent over details of the two Americans Mason had identified from Rosen's party.

One of them, the scruffy-looking one, was a senior lecturer on computer technology at a mid-west university. Thirty-five years old and much sought-after by other universities and several hi-tech companies. Further investigation would be carried out immediately. The other man was an ex-US Marine with an honourable discharge. He was believed to be a KKK member and made no secret of his membership of a local militia group of 'America-First'. He was a long-distance truck driver employed by a wealthy farmer whose extreme right-wing convictions were popular in all the local small towns. The FBI had information, unconfirmed, that a county-wide militia group had weapons training from the ex-marine on the thousand acre farm.

Baumann smiled as he glanced at the last page of Klein's fax and read out. 'The CIA have over fifty Rosens listed for one reason or another. Seventeen have addresses in Germany. Three of them are Berlin addresses and none of them fit our boy. Two are in their seventies and the other's serving a prison sentence for drug offences. He's in a jail in Dresden.' He shrugged and smiled. 'I guess it's a beginning.'

'What do you want me to do?'

'Just get alongside Rosen. Don't rush or he'll be suspicious. I've got the layout of his place from the Bauamt and I'd like to fill in what the rooms are used for. It's a big place for just one man.'

'What about Freddie Malins?'

Baumann hesitated, then said, 'Yeah. Keep in with him too.'

'Why?'

Baumann laughed. 'I don't know. Just instinct says it might pay off.' He paused. 'I've taken over one of our old safe-houses. It's not far from Rosen's place. I'll give you the address and the telephone number and my contact number.' He reached for his canvas bag. 'I've got you a local cell-phone with a scrambler facility. Might be useful in an emergency.'

'What kind of emergency are you thinking of?'

'None in particular but we're in a different ball-game from now on. And I'd guess that a lot of Rosen's buddies are pretty rough types. It's not politics or philosophies with them. Their pleasure is in beating people up.' He waved to the waiter for the check and when he'd paid he said, 'Let's go to your place and go over what else we want to know.'

As Mason put the key in the lock of the door of his flat he was half-turned, looking at Baumann, as he said, 'When's Klein's man due to arrive?'

Baumann was staring over Mason's shoulder and he said quietly, 'Looks like you've had visitors.'

As Mason's eyes followed Baumann's gaze he slowly pushed open the door. The room had been ransacked. Drawers from the sideboard had been pulled out with the contents strewn around. It was the same scene in his bedroom. Baumann sat in the living-room waiting for Mason to complete his inspection.

When Mason walked back into the living-room Baumann said, 'What's missing?'

Mason frowned. 'Nothing. It's crazy. Nothing's gone.'

Baumann stood up. 'Ah, well, let's have some music while we clear up.'

He walked over and switched on the radio, pressing the buttons until he found some music. Then he turned the volume up high and turned to look at Mason with a warning finger to his lips.

'Speak softly,' he whispered, 'and only talk in this room.'

'OK.'

'Have you got a gun?'

For a moment Mason hesitated and then said, 'Yes.'

'Where do you keep it?'

'Under some potatoes in the vegetable compartment in the refrigerator.'

'Is it still there?'

'I don't know. I didn't look.'

'Go and check.'

When Mason came back he was holding the pistol.

'It was still there under the potatoes.'

Baumann nodded. 'Have you noticed anything odd about all this?'

'No. Except that nothing's missing.'

'If it was a normal break-in the outside door would be damaged. Your clothes would have gone. What's left would have been torn up or cut and the drawers would have been smashed.' He paused. 'And they'd have crapped all over everywhere.'

'So?'

Baumann stood up: 'Have you got a screwdriver?'

'Yes. In a drawer in the kitchen.'

Baumann waved his arm at the scattered belongings. 'This is just a cover.'

'For what?'

'Get me the screwdriver.'

When Mason handed over a small screwdriver, Baumann walked over to the telephone and turned it over to unscrew the base. When it came apart he pointed. 'There's the monitoring bug and I'd guess there's a micro-transmitter somewhere.' He looked around and then moved the TV and took out the wall-plug and unscrewed the back. As he peered inside he pointed and said, 'This gizmo will pick up your general conversation in the living-room and there'll be another in your bedroom. Probably in the bedside lamp. These are quite expensive transmitters. Whoever put them in is a good technician but not much good at faking burglary.'

'Who do you think? And why are they interested in me?'

Baumann smiled. 'For who – I'd guess Rosen's pals – and why you – because you're SIS and they want to keep tabs on what you're up to.' He paused and smiled. 'I suggest you leave them in place and see what happens.'

'No way. I want them out.'

Baumann shrugged. 'OK. I'll get one of my chaps to take them out tomorrow. I've already disengaged both of them.' He grinned. 'Just watch what you say in bed tonight. We'll leave our strategy talk until tomorrow.' He paused. 'By the way we need some sort of photograph of Rosen.'

Baumann left his Berlin address and telephone numbers after he had helped Mason clear up the mess. As he left he said, 'I'll send our guy to remove the electronics tomorrow. He'll be pleased with the two multi-transmitters, they're worth at least five hundred dollars each.' He grinned. 'You'd better turn down the radio volume or you'll have your neighbours complaining.'

Mason answered the bell in his bathrobe. It was Baumann and another man. Mason looked at his watch. 'For Christ's sake it's only six-thirty.'

Baumann laughed. 'We've got a busy day, my friend. Let's get your stuff cleaned up.' Baumann nodded to his man and when Mason walked into the kitchen Baumann followed him and sat at the table as Mason made coffee.

'Klein's guy arrives at Tegel at 09.30 hours. I've said we'll meet him in. OK?'

Mason nodded. He wasn't appeased.

'What's his name?'

'Altieri. Bill Altieri. Senior Agent Altieri to be formal.' He paused. 'He's bringing over a file of stuff that they think might be useful.'

Sam Wheeler had taken Crombie to the house in Clapham to meet the two Americans, and to learn what material was available. After the introductions they sat around the pasting table in the work-room and Sam Wheeler summed up.

'We've got hard evidence to damage about ten constant critics of the government. Only two are politicians and the others are broadcasting people. Well-known names, and editors or political commentators on broadsheets. We've got no problem with the two opposition MPs, it's the media people who are the problem.' He smiled. 'My friends here and I don't agree on the media.'

'Why not?' Crombie looked at the Americans and it was Chuck who responded.

'We've got eight media guys and all the dirt on them is sex stuff . . .' he nodded at Wheeler '. . . Sam says there's not enough variety. Thinks the public will be bored.'

'And you two?'

'Our experience is that the public will lap it up. They always do. And anyway once we've done two or three key ones the others will take the hint and back off.'

'What about libel?'

Sam Wheeler said, 'They'd be "outed" in the Commons or the Lords. Two would be quoted from French newspaper reports.'

'So what's the problem?'

Sam Wheeler smiled and shrugged. 'Just that at least politicians cover all the sins, these press people seem to go in solely for sex, not money.'

Crombie nodded. 'That's why they're always writing about other people's sex lives.' He sniffed. 'They're just dirty little boys who spend their time throwing mud at people who are as tacky as they are themselves.'

'So, Peter. Shall we keep going?'

Crombie nodded. 'I don't see why not. They always say themselves that "the public are entitled to know". Are you using young Hugo for suggesting the MPs to throw the mud?'

'Yes. He's been a great help. Very Machiavellian is young Hugo.'

Crombie shrugged. 'Probably end up as Prime Minister if he's not careful. Knows more about the House than even the party Whips.' He paused. 'What are these people up to – young girls or orgies or what?'

'Three of them are into sado-masochism. Whipping and that sort of stuff.'

Crombie shook his head. 'It's those bloody nannies and public schools get 'em started. Ought to be hung.'

The BND's old safe-house was near the old East German Transport Ministry building off Krausenstrasse and Baumann had taken them there straight from Tegel after meeting in Bill Altieri.

The phone was ringing as they walked into the living-room. Baumann said, 'Make yourselves comfortable,' as he walked across the room to take the call.

'Yeah, speaking . . .' there was a long pause then '. . . are you sure? . . . what's that mean . . . OK. Thanks.' He looked round at Mason as he hung up.

'My people have checked over the electronics they took from your place.' He paused. 'Guess what?' He paused again. 'They say the stuff's all American. Custom-made, patent held by a company that's owned by the FBI. Not available to any other organisation or to the public. No finger-prints. Gloves were used. Very professional.' He shrugged. 'What do you make of that?'

Altieri chipped in. 'The FBI doesn't operate outside the USA. Only the CIA does that. Maybe it's a joint operation.'

'But why?' Mason said. 'What the hell interest have they got in me?'

Baumann looked at Altieri. 'Could you have a word with someone at Langley, Bill?'

Altieri looked unhappy but he said, 'I'll see what I can find out.' He pointed at a box file at the side of his duffle bag. 'That's for you from Langley.' He paused. 'I'll phone my people and get them to pick me up.'

'Stay for a meal,' Baumann said.

'Thanks but I've got things to do. I'll call you tomorrow.'

When Altieri had left, Mason said, 'Where is the CIA safe-house he's using?'

Baumann shrugged. 'God knows. It would be on our side of the old

Wall.' He smiled. 'They seldom ventured over the other side. It's difficult for an American not to look like an American.'

'Altieri looked a bit uncomfortable about the bugs in my place.'

'They almost certainly won't tell him what they're up to and if they did I don't think he'd tell us.' He shrugged. 'Be an interesting test of how much they're committed to us.'

'D'you want to look through the CIA stuff he left for us?'

'Let's wait until Altieri gets back to us.' He paused. 'We need to have you around your usual haunts so that Rosen can contact you.'

'There's probably some messages on my answering machine. I'll keep in touch.'

The House of Commons was crowded. It was the afternoon for questions about the Department of Trade and Industry. The Minister himself was unwell and a Junior Minister would be fielding the questions. Most of them were expected to be about a leaked letter from the Minister to the Treasury published that day in one of the tabloids. It was alleged that the letter indicated that arms on the restricted list were due to be sold to Pakistan.

Howard Gordon, the Opposition spokesman on trade and industry, caught the Speaker's eye and stood up.

'Madam Chairman, I am not surprised that the Minister feels too unwell to face questions about the letter published today. A letter that clearly shows that the government is prepared to flout the law when its friends can make a fortune out of illegal exports of arms on the banned list. What does the Junior Minister have to say on this matter?'

As he sat down the Junior Minister rose but was interrupted by the previous speaker standing up again and saying, 'Madam Speaker, I hope that the government spokesman will not fall back on their standard excuse of refusing to comment on leaked documents.' He sat down with almost a flounce.

The Junior Minister rose to his feet again. 'Madam Speaker, we are not talking here about a so-called leaked document. We are talking about a *stolen* document. Regarding the Minister being unwell, he happens to be in hospital being checked for a possible appendectomy.' He paused and looked across at the Opposition. 'Now back to your stolen document. The journalist used by the newspaper which published the so-called letter is a man named Gordon Lessor who shares a flat in Pimlico with the member from the other side who has just raised the question. This journalist and this newspaper have printed a number of so-called leaked documents from the DTI in the past. Let me advise the House how this document was obtained. Mr Lessor has a lady friend who is a clerk in the DTI. She was offered, and accepted, fifty pounds in cash to provide a copy of any document that might embarrass the government. That was how the document was obtained.' He paused. 'But I have to inform the House that no such letter was ever written to the Treasury. It was a "dummy" letter which along with half a dozen other dummy letters passed across the desk of the young lady concerned who was already under suspicion for previous "leakings". The young lady concerned is at the moment at Chelsea police station . . .' he smiled '. . . as they say – helping the police with their enquiries.' He paused again. 'She has made a signed statement in the presence of her solicitor and her fellow-conspirator is in custody at Savile Row police station.' He looked across at the Opposition benches. 'So much for the phoney indignation about the government flouting the law.'

The Press Gallery emptied, well aware that they could quote the whole story without fear of any action for defamation. Statements made in both Houses were not actionable because of Parliamentary Privilege. And could be quoted by the media once they had been made.

The House was in turmoil, Madam Speaker rebuked both sides and when she was ignored she suspended proceedings for an hour to, as she said with considerable annoyance, 'allow members to calm down'.

By late evening the press agencies were reporting unconfirmed reports that the details of the theft were being passed to the Director of Public Prosecutions. An harassed-looking editor interviewed on TV, coming from the offices of a well-known libel lawyer, said that it was obvious that the government had acted as *'agents provocateurs'*. He didn't sound as if even he believed it. He went on to assert that both he and the paper had acted in good faith. The TV interviewer had grinned as he said that and the grin had not been cut from the usual 22-second clip they showed at the end of the late news to send viewers happy to bed.

*   *   *

There were only two messages on Mason's answering machine. One from Freddie Malins asking where the hell he'd been and one from Rosen asking him to call him at his home number or call in if he was in the vicinity. Rosen was at home until next Monday.

As he pressed the 'Clear' button the phone rang and he picked it up.
'Yeah'

'Baumann. I just heard from Altieri. Seems like the FBI asked for the co-operation of the CIA to check on associates of Freddie Malins. They didn't tell him why. You'd been seen at Malins' club and it was noticed that you always went up to his private quarters.'

'What's Malins been up to?'

'They wouldn't tell Altieri.' He laughed. 'They were more interested in what he himself was doing over here. But it seems that he's being quite open with us.' He paused. 'Any action your end?'

Mason laughed softly. 'A message from Freddie Malins asking where the hell I'd been for the last few days. And a message from Rosen asking me to contact him. I was thinking of going round to his place this evening.'

'OK. I'll give Altieri a meal. See you.'

The gate in the wall at Rosen's place wasn't locked, there was no response when he pressed the bell and he walked in, closing the gate behind him. To the side of the house there was a small orchard with half a dozen fruit trees. Rosen was sitting on a bench with another man and a chess board on a small rustic table in front of them. Rosen looked up, smiled and waved Mason over. He introduced the other man as Heller.

'D'you play chess, James?'

Mason smiled. 'Yes. Badly.'

Rosen laughed. 'Welcome. I need an opponent who doesn't beat me in ten moves and says "what an interesting move" when I make my first losing move.' He patted the bench beside him. 'Sit down. We've nearly finished this game.'

Mason looked at the pieces on the board. Rosen was playing white and it looked like a Guy Lopez opening that had gone wrong somewhere. As Rosen's hand went to one of his knights, Mason said, 'Stop.'

Rosen stopped and looked at him. 'Tell me.'

'Get your Queen out of the corner. She's not only useless there but she's even blocking your King's only move to avoid the mate.'

Rosen looked back at the board. 'You're absolutely right.' He stood up. 'Let's go and have a beer. I've got some Budweiser.'

They sat drinking beer from the can with a CD of Max Bruch's Violin Concerto playing in the background. Heller was a good-looking man much younger than Rosen and he had an air of self-assurance and authority that all too often only came from having been in some military-élite like SAS. He changed easily in and out of German but his accent in English was heavily American. His appearance was *'echt Deutsch'*. Blond, short-cut hair, blue eyes and a solid build.

Inevitably, with Rosen, the talk moved to politics and politicians. Both Heller and Rosen were as one on the subject. Politicians were the power-hungry enemies of ordinary people. When Rosen drew Mason into their talk Mason offered the thought that at least the politicians in their countries were elected. The products of democracy.

Heller looked amused at the naivety but Rosen was clearly angry.

'What democracy? Why should the vote of people who give no thought to politics except for once in four or five years have the same value as that of a man who thinks about what is going on in the world. It's preposterous. They are offered lower taxes and greater benefits – none of which will be forthcoming. It's what some comedian once said – "Like turkeys voting for Christmas".'

'Maybe they get what they deserve.'

Rosen's indignation rose. 'That's a terrible thing to say, James. A cop-out. Just what the Nazis said to justify concentration camps.'

'So what do you do to put it right?'

It was Heller who intervened. 'You eliminate the politicians. You eliminate the structure. Judges, lawyers, the police, the secret service. The structure that keeps them all in power.'

Rosen, now calmer said, 'You go back to square one. You give people the chance to think again. You had a play, a musical in London, that said it. "Stop the world – I want to get off." That's what we've got to do. Stop the world so that we can think again.'

'And what do you put in its place?'

'Individual freedom. We live by our own standards. Each one of us. Not controlled by men in Bonn or London or Washington. Millions of people in America already recognise this. All they need is guidance on how to get what they want. Freedom. Freedom from government. Any government.'

'Could lead to chaos, Jake.'

Mason saw the quick glance at Heller by Rosen and the half-smile on the younger man's face.

Heller said quietly, looking at Mason. 'It's going to happen, my friend. It really is. We all have a part to play.'

Mason smiled. 'Sounds like I'd be on your hit-list.'

Rosen said quickly, 'You wouldn't be here if that was so.'

'So why am I an exception?'

'Because you listen. Because you're a thinker. You set your own standards. You wouldn't do something you believed was evil or even just wrong merely because you were told to.'

'How do you know that?'

Rosen shrugged. 'I just do. I have an instinct about people.'

Mason looked at his watch. 'It's late. I'd better go.' He stood up and Rosen said, 'See you for breakfast at the Europa place. OK?'

'OK.'

He said his farewells and they both walked with him through the garden to the gate in the wall.

Mason walked through to Unter den Linden and down to the taxis at the Brandenburg Gate. He had to wait for a taxi and as he looked across to where the old Reichstag building was lit up it suddenly made him wonder what it must have been like to see that building in Nazi times. He realised that maybe unintentionally to all concerned he had just gone through some sort of examination or assessment. Rosen's attitude towards him didn't match their thinking. Rosen had no grounds, despite what he said, to see him as anything different from the people they wanted to eliminate. The only reason he could be tolerated would be that they wanted to use him in some way. He was some kind of scapegoat chosen to be sacrificed. But which side had decided he should be a scapegoat? Was it Baumann and the others or Rosen and his lot?

As a taxi drove up he asked for the cafe near his flat. There were two more messages on the answer-phone from Freddie Malins. He sounded rather testy on both of them. He looked at his watch. It was 10.30, not late for the Pussy-Cat Club. He had a quick shave and phoned Freddie Malins that he was on his way to the club.

* * *

Back at Rosen's place they were talking about James Mason.

'Why does he keep contact with you, Jake? What's in it for him?'

'Like I told you. His people in London sent him over to look for Charlie Foster's files.'

'So how did he get your name?'

'No idea.'

'Why don't you ask him?'

'I did. But he evaded giving an answer and I didn't want him to know that it mattered.'

'You need some background on him.'

'I've started the ball rolling already.'

'So back to basics. What d'you want him for? Why does he matter?'

'He's a direct line back to an intelligence organisation.'

'That works both ways.'

'What's that mean?'

'He could have been planted on you.'

'They've never heard of me.'

'So how are you going to use him?'

'I'm not sure yet. But I've got plans.'

Heller sighed. 'Well . . . keep your powder dry. And if you get even the faintest idea he's playing games, pass him over to me.'

Rosen smiled. 'I will, my boy, I will.'

The barman took him up to Freddie's place and Freddie was not his usual friendly self.

'Where you been? I've been looking all over for you.'

'I was in London.'

'Why didn't you tell me you were going to be away.'

Mason looked at him. 'Tell me one good reason why I should.'

Malins thought for a moment and then relaxed.

'I had something I needed to discuss with you.' He paused and looked accusingly at Mason. 'In your interest, as much as mine.'

'So . . . let's discuss.'

Malins leaned forward, elbows on the table, his shoulders hunched up.

'I had a visit from a mutual friend.' He paused but Mason didn't respond. 'He was trying to check up on you.'

'Go on, Freddie. Get to it. Who was the mutual friend?'

'The Herr Professor. Rosen. Wanted to know about your background and where you got his name from to connect him with Charlie Foster.'

'What did you tell him?'

'Nothing.'

'So what's the problem?'

Malins looked away for a moment and then looked back at Mason. 'He knows something that if he made it public could ruin me.'

'You mean the black-market stuff you got up to when you were in SIS?'

'No. It was something Charlie Foster knew and he must have told Rosen.'

'What is it?'

'For a couple of years I was a Stasi informer. Charlie found it in their records.'

'And if you don't answer his questions about me, he'll expose you?'

'Yeah. That's the proposition.'

Mason was silent for a few moments and then he said, 'Leave it to me. I'll deal with Rosen.' He paused. 'Anything else?'

'No.'

'Pass me the phone.'

Malins pushed across the phone and Mason checked Rosen's number in his notebook and then dialled it.

'Rosen.'

'Did I wake you up? It's James.'

'No. I was just tidying the place.'

'I'm with Freddie Malins right now.' He paused. 'He tells me you want to know who gave me your name as a connection to Charlie Foster. It was an ex-Stasi chap. He was just a driver. Picked Charlie up sometimes from his home. He just gave me the names of people who spent a lot of time there. You were one of them. He pumps gas at Freddie's garage. I only met him the one time.' He waited for a response but there was none and he went on. 'As for my background. Nothing for you there. Working-class parents, grammar school, army, now SIS and looking for Charlie's treasure trove, and hoping you might help me.'

'I told you. It's not there to find. It doesn't exist.'

'My chaps in London don't believe me when I tell 'em that. They just say – keep looking. You know how these people are.' He paused briefly. 'So no more messing Freddie about – agreed?'

'Agreed. It was just a routine precaution.'

'Bullshit, Jake. If I had something to hide Freddie Malins wouldn't know about it. If you want to know something – ask. Me. OK?'

'OK.'

Mason hung up the phone and looked at Malins.

'OK now?'

Malins nodded. 'Yeah. Thanks. Let's have a beer.'

CHAPTER 25

It was only about twenty-five acres not counting the woods. More a small holding than a farm. About five miles from the racecourse at Goodwood and lying at the foot of the soft curved downs of West Sussex. There were three battery houses each housing 3,000 hybrid layers. Outside there were a couple of dozen sheep and a well-kept kitchen garden.

The seven men sitting around in one of the sheds were dressed in working clothes. The piece of equipment was lying lengthways on an old wooden table and the man standing behind the table kept one hand on the device all the time he was talking. It was like a gesture of affection. Despite his efforts to talk like a civilian it was inevitably much the same as the lectures he used to give back at Hereford.

'It's called the 81mm. mortar for obvious reasons. It's British made and British designed. As you could see when you looked at it just now, it's beautifully engineered. Both the barrel and the streamlined bomb put the 81 at the forefront of mortar design. There's a plastic sealing ring on the bomb which traps the gases instead of letting them go to waste. This cuts out side-to-side yaw and improves accuracy. It has a range of well over five thousand metres. Call it three and a half miles.' The man paused. 'Me and George will take you over the loading, setting and firing procedures on a one-to-one basis.' He smiled a rather forced smile. 'You won't be able to fire one until the actual operation. But believe me you'll get all the training you need.'

He looked at the tall man leaning against the shed wall by the window. 'George, you take over and I'll raise some char.'

The men listening to ex-SAS Sergeant Ames had many things in common but the least noticeable were the letters KAOS tattooed under their left armpits where SS troops used to have their blood groups tattooed.

The meeting was in the FBI's Hoover building. Swenson was in the chair with O'Hara from the NSA and Parsons from the FBI each side of him. On the other side of the table were three senators. Two Republicans and one Democrat. They had been chosen for their reputations of honesty and patriotism. It was the Democrat who waved a hand and interrupted O'Hara's flow.

'What the hell is an algorithm, chief?'

'It's a procedure whereby an infinite sequence of terms can be generated.' He smiled. 'In very basic terms it's the formula, for want of a better word, that an encryption code can be built on.'

'And you say that it's possible to devise an encryption that even your experts can't break?'

'Yeah. There are two at least being used at the moment.'

'Can't you trace the person who's transmitting them?'

'In one case the inventor of the code has given the software to almost anyone who wants it. It's called PGP which is an acronym of Pretty Good Privacy.'

'Why does he do it?'

'He's a very bright guy but he's agin government agencies having the right to listen to transmissions that people don't want to be overhead.'

'So what do you guys want?'

O'Hara pointed at Parsons as he leaned back from the table.

'What we want, Senator,' Parsons said quietly, 'is legislation that allows a person to use an encryption that is private to all others. Except to the NSA, FBI and the CIA.'

'How do you do that?'

'It's a thing called the Clipper Chip. It's installed in all computers then nobody unauthorised can listen-in except the three government agencies.' He paused. 'We've floated the idea several times but it causes a hell of a wave of resentment from so-called "freedom fighters".' He sighed and shrugged. 'We've used the fact that there's pornography on the Internet but it doesn't hold water. There's pornography in magazines, videos, films and even on CDs now. All obtainable and most of them legal. The argument goes – why pick on porn just on the Internet?' He spread his hands. 'Let's face it. They've got a point. And the constitution's on their side. It's censorship.' He put his hands back on the table. 'But it's the other unbroken encryption that we wanted to raise with you.'

'You know who the PGP guy is?'

'Yeah. We're taking action against him but we won't win. The problem for us is the second case. We think we know who the guy is but we haven't a shred of proof.'

'And your people at NSA can't break it?'

'That's right. They're still trying but they know it's impossible.'

'Impossible or difficult?'

'The mathematics, and it's a special branch of mathematics called stochastic maths – the mathematics of randomness. The mathematicians estimate that if we used every computer we have at Fort George Meade non-stop it would take us over a million years, perhaps thousands of millions of years.'

The senior Republican spoke for the first time. 'What do you want from us?'

'I guess it comes down to advice. And your blessing on us taking action that we're pretty sure ain't legal.'

'Like what?'

'Pressuring this suspect until he gives us the code.'

'Why does it matter to you people apart from curiosity?' The Senator smiled. 'And bloody-mindedness.'

It was Swenson who answered. 'We believe that the code is being used for terrorism. And subversion that borders on revolution.' He paused. 'Not just in the USA but at least two other countries.'

'Which others?'

'Germany and the UK.'

'Could you prove this in a court if the guy co-operated?'

'I don't know. We're just going on experience and instinct. There'll be a similar guy in each of the other two countries.'

'Any clues as to who they are?'

'None.' He hesitated. 'Let's say some vibes.'

'And all you're asking is our blessing to putting pressure on this one guy?'

'Yeah.'

'What's his name?'

'Logan.'

'What's he do?'

'He's a very top man at Fort George Meade. And his father's a Senior DA in New York.'

'Is the father suspect too?'

'No. They're not on speaking terms.'

'I think . . .' the Democrat Senator said '. . . I think you should go ahead and do whatever is necessary.'

He looked at the other two Senators and they nodded their agreement.

Swenson said, 'Thanks. We'd have gone ahead anyway but the three of us felt we needed to hear the views of trustworthy people who were not involved in the business. Thanks to all three of you for your time and your thinking.'

They sat around talking about the problems created by the First Amendment but came to the conclusion that way back Madison and the others had no thought that the country could end up with media that was itself subversive.

The long delayed meeting with the leader of Her Majesty's Official Opposition finally took place in one of the ante-rooms at the House of Commons. After a few amiable remarks from both men it was Crombie who got down to business.

'I have to ask you why you didn't choose to have a meeting on this subject with the D-G of MI5. It's really their turf you know. Internal affairs.'

'I realise that, Sir Peter, but I have to say we don't have much confidence in them. After what they got up to with Harold Wilson and then the miners' strike, we're wondering, quite seriously, if it wasn't they who initiated all this scandal stuff.'

Crombie smiled as he said, 'I'm sure you're mistaken, Joseph.' It was a knowing smile between friends talking in code. 'What exactly are you worried about?'

'It seems to me, Sir Peter, and to many of my colleagues, that over the last six months or so there has been a concerted attack by the media on members of my party. We wondered what we could do to establish if this is the case or not.'

'I think that protocol suggests that on such a matter you should be talking to the Prime Minister, not me.'

'That would make it official and I would rather avoid that.'

'Have you any proof to back up these allegations? If you have I would suggest that it's a matter for the police and the law officers.'

'We have no proof. It's just a strong feeling that we are being victimised.'

Crombie half-smiled. 'I've heard that the media feel that *they* are being attacked. And until recently I suggest that the government party members have had more than their fair share of accusations of sleaze and dishonesty. And if I remember rightly, most of those attacks came from your colleagues in the House. Parliamentary Privilege and all that.' He paused. 'It's a wild thought but maybe they're hitting back.'

'How would you suggest that I deal with the problem?'

'Ah now. I'd recommend that you get your party Whips together with the government Whips and suggest a cease-fire.' He smiled. 'Maybe even an armistice. And each party's Whips make it known to their honourable members that it's time to call it a day.' He smiled again. 'It would please the public. Might give your chaps some time to bend their minds to running the country instead of just slandering Ministers of the Crown. Might even get you some votes.'

'You feel that our suspicions about MI5 are unfounded?'

'Absolutely. Out of the question.'

As he stood he said, 'I must say I'm glad we have public servants like your good self heading up these rather mysterious services.'

As he strolled back to the commons' car-park, Crombie was not too happy about his deceit but was satisfied that what he had done was the right thing. It went through his mind that he shared with his enemies his utter disdain for politicians. What had happened to them? Those men like Churchill and Attlee, Ernie Bevin and Joe Grimond. Real men. Men who would have sent a scandal-monger away with a flea in his ear. And no half-decent paper would have spent a penny let alone thousands of pounds for setting up the entrapment of some man's visit to a tart. He still hadn't taken any action on the four Stasi documents that were locked in his desk at home. Maybe they should stay there a bit longer.

It was rumoured among the staff at GCHQ that how you dressed could affect your promotion and security rating. There were those who suggested that casual dressing, especially sweat-shirts and jeans could indicate a matching casualness towards rules and regulations. Others maintained that casual dress indicated lively, independent personalities on the so-called 'cutting-edge' of technology. The analysis of the two other gradations of clothing seemed to have a more logical foundation. Armani suits and Gucci shoes and the like were highly dangerous unless you already had a top security rating. Consensus said that a Viyella shirt and Daks trousers, a Marks and Spencer's pullover or a British Home Stores' striped shirt would see you through better than either of the extremes.

'Pops' Wilson, the man who was to chair the meeting, was reckoned to be a rather snappy dresser. An Austin Reed man. Good clothes but casually worn. He was just over fifty, a bit on the plump side and he sat with his cuff links undone and his shirt-sleeves rolled up. He had always been known as 'Pops', allegedly because of his appearance and amiability but he was, in fact, more avuncular than paternal. Either way he was both popular and well-respected.

He looked at the list of items to be discussed at the meeting in an hour's time. A few of them were old favourites but most of them represented new problems that needed his comments.

1. Intermittent and random mis-function on Rhyolite satellite.

2. Discipline. Two instances have been detected where down-time on Cray computer RSD-135 had been logged as 'servicing'.

3. Liaison with the Public Cryptography Study Group needs to be improved. Increase funding?

4. Operation Shamrock calling for extra mathematician. Minimum Phd.

5. Finalise own input to joint commentary with NSA to proposed US legislation to make Clipper Chip mandatory. How deal with existing computers?

6. Chinese Embassy have changed code four times in last month. No obvious reason. Consider.

7. See separate comments on Internet and use of PGP.

8. Routine consideration of unidentified unbreakable Internet encryption. Random traffic of too short duration to locate and from different areas. Appears to be same code as reported by NSA.

As 'Pops' Wilson closed the file he went to light a cigarette and then remembered the rules and put it back in the packet. He was sure they wouldn't get as far as Item 8. Not that it mattered if they did. And then his committee began to assemble, ID tags and swipe cards dangling from shirt or jacket pockets.

It was just after 8 p.m. as 'Pops' Wilson strolled across the green in Cheltenham towards the Queen's Hotel. He waited at the edge of the kerb for the traffic to clear and then crossed the road and walked up the steps to the hotel entrance. The hotel was not far from the rooms he rented just off the square and several people nodded and smiled as he made his way to the far end of the lounge. He saw that Bailey was already there, their beers already on the glass-topped table.

As he settled down he said quietly, 'Can't stay too long, Frank. I've got to go back to GCHQ for an all-night job.'

'Was it true what we heard?'

'Yeah. I'm afraid so.'

'Tell me.'

'They're making up a special team to try and locate the source of transmissions.'

'OK. We can keep moving locations and transmission times and cut down on length of transmissions.'

'Any problems in Germany or the States?'

'The Germans don't give any indications that they've even noticed the code. Rosen's been very sensible.'

'And the Yanks?'

'Hard to tell. They've identified that they've got a code they can't decipher. That's about all we know. Logan's not a good communicator.'

'Are you ready to take action when you get the word?'

'More or less.'

'What's the problem?'

Bailey shrugged and sighed. 'I'm glad I've got nothing to do with 'em. They're just rabble in my opinion. It'll be them controlling us when the operation gets going. And once they get out of hand . . .' he shook his head '. . . there'll be killings.' He paused. 'What started as groups of disaffected men with genuine grievances, ends up as no more than a front for thugs and psychopaths. They'll be making the politicians' point for them.'

'There's thousands, tens of thousands, who think the way we do. Not given to violence. But if you're fighting politicians and governments it's pictures of rioting on TV that makes them change their ways. Remember the Poll Tax rioting. Bad. But it worked.'

Bailey smiled, ' *"Sed quis custodiet ipsos custodes."* '

'Pops' Wilson laughed. 'You always were a pedant.' He finished up his beer and stood up, turning to Bailey. 'See you at the weekend. Let's go to the races.'

There were more nods from staff and guests as 'Pops' Wilson made his way across the lounge. They knew that he was something very important at GCHQ, and they all knew that Bailey F.W. was the headmaster of one of the better grammar schools in Cheltenham.

CHAPTER 26

Rosen had been waiting for him at the Europa place. He had finished his breakfast and was stirring his coffee slowly when Mason arrived and sat down.

'You're late.'

'Am I. I don't remember saying a time.'

'We didn't but you always get here at a few minutes after eight.' He looked at his rather ugly wrist-watch with its worn leather strap. 'It's eight-thirty.'

'I'm sorry,' Mason said and then the waitress came. He ordered a roll and butter and a fresh peach and then turned back to Rosen.

'And how are you today?'

Rosen looked surprised and said after a moment's silence, 'What made you ask me that?'

'You looked different. I wondered if you were unwell or something.'

Rosen looked away as if he were looking at the people eating at other tables. But the look in his eyes was far away. And when he turned back to look at Mason there were tears at the edges of his eyes.

'But what made you ask me today. At this particular moment? It was routine politeness wasn't it?' Rosen said it as if he needed some sort of reassurance.

Mason spoke slowly, emphasising each word. 'It was not a routine politeness. I asked you because I sensed you were either tired or depressed.' He paused. 'So what's the answer?'

Again, Rosen looked away, his eyes moving from table to table and then back to his own hands clasped around his coffee cup as if for warmth, despite the fact that it was a warm spring day. Without looking up at Mason, Rosen said, 'Have you ever killed anybody?'

Mason sighed. 'It's not something I talk about, Jake. Forget it.'

'That means you have.' He looked up at Mason's face. 'Are you ever afraid that someone might kill you?'

'I said cut it out, Jake. Have another coffee and then I'll have to go.'

Rosen nodded and Mason signalled to the waitress for another pot of coffee. As he was pouring the coffee into Rosen's cup, Rosen said, 'If I gave you some of Charlie Foster's material what would your people do with it?'

'Depends on what was in it I guess.'

'Would you get a promotion?'

'No. I've just been promoted.'

'What kind of people are they – your bosses in London?'

Mason smiled. 'Just men.'

'D'you know Café Belmont?'

'No.'

'It's where you can play chess all night and all day. It's in Kurfürstenstrasse. Number 107. You can eat there too. How about we meet there this afternoon?'

'I can't this afternoon.'

'OK. This evening?'

'What time?'

'To suit you.'

'OK. About eight.'

As Mason walked back to his flat his thoughts were on Rosen. There was no doubt that he was upset about something. The question about killing, the tears in his eyes, were all pointers to some kind of emotional disturbance. He could have pursued it but he reckoned that it was better to let Rosen volunteer anything he wanted to say.

They were sitting in the sunshine in the garden. The two Americans sitting on the grass and Sam Wheeler sitting in an ancient deck-chair they had found in one of the garages.

They had gone through a refined list of projects, all of them aimed at media people rather than politicians to comply with a broad list Sam Wheeler had got from Crombie.

'Anything else?' Sam said, hands ready to ease himself out of the chair.

'Are you interested in Nazis?'

'What Nazis?'

'The real thing. Germans. Neo-Nazis. In London. Doing the rounds of subversives.'

'Tell me more. D'you know who they are?'

Chuck passed him a piece of paper. 'Names and places where they hang out'.

'How did you come to learn about them?'

Chuck laughed. 'We were doing some checking on one of the tabloid's political columnists for our operation. Seems he'd done a rather nasty piece about the British National Party and they were looking for some dirt on him. We kind of came together accidentally in a pub in Brixton.' He grinned. 'We gave 'em a lead or two.'

'Any idea what they're doing over here?'

'They were pretty close but there were hints of helping organise demos and protests in London and other towns. Seems like these particular Germans do that sort of stuff in Germany. HQ in Dresden.'

'I'll pass it on.'

Chuck smiled. 'Wait until your bad guys are being helped by Americans. Then you'll really be in the major league.'

Sam Wheeler had a meeting that evening with Crombie and handed over the details of the German neo-Nazis. Crombie in his turn handed the information to his opposite number at MI5. It was an internal security matter and Crombie saw no reason for SIS to get involved.

CHAPTER 27

They had been to a performance by local German actors of readings from Shakespeare at Theater des Westens and Rosen seemed to be in good spirits as they walked towards Zoo Station for a taxi. The street lights were just coming on but the evening had that special feel that spring gives to the air even in cities like Berlin.

As they turned into the street where the railway bridge overhangs the streets, Rosen stopped at a flower shop that had a display of cut flowers in baskets on the pavement.

'Aren't they beautiful. Look at those daffodils. They're perfect.' He turned to Mason. 'I must buy a couple of bunches to brighten up the house.'

Mason smiled. 'Go ahead.'

As the woman wrapped the flowers she was pleased and amused by Rosen's pleasure at the display outside the shop and she put in a small bunch of forget-me-nots with her compliments.

They were walking away, Rosen looking at his flowers, when a train of freight wagons rumbled and clattered over the bridge and suddenly Rosen's face was distorted. His mouth agape, his breathing rasping as if he was choking. His body was shaking convulsively and he staggered towards the road, his face staring up to the bridge. Mason tried to stop him but he wrenched himself away. There was the blare of a car horn and then the sickening thud as a big white Mercedes threw Rosen's body into the air to come crashing down on the bonnet of the car as it braked.

Mason shouted to the woman at the flower-shop to call for an ambulance and then ran to where Rosen was lying on the bonnet of the car. He was unconscious and one arm was at an odd angle. A man helped Mason carry Rosen to the pavement and a motor-cycle policeman cleared a space around Rosen's body.

The ambulance was there in a couple of minutes and Rosen was put on a stretcher. Mason wanted to go with him in the ambulance but the policeman wanted him to make a statement about what had happened.

As he answered the questions Mason was aware that the radio in the Mercedes was still playing as someone comforted the woman driver. It was playing Dolly Parton singing 'Jolene' and he could see someone picking up Rosen's daffodils from where they had fallen in the gutter.

When he had finished his statement he asked the policeman to use his cell-phone and find out where Rosen had been taken.

As the cop closed down his phone, he said 'He's at Krankenhaus Moabit, do you know where it is?'

'No'

'It's not far. Turmstrasse. Moabit. Grab a taxi, the driver will know it. It's a major Berlin hospital.'

At the hospital the doctor in charge told Mason that Rosen was out of casualty but was still in a coma. He had a broken rib and a broken arm. Both fractures had been treated and Rosen was well-enough known for them to have given him a private room. He was escorted to the room by a nurse who said that he was limited to ten minutes. But they had a problem.

'We have to notify the next-of-kin but we have no idea who they are.'

Mason hesitated. 'He doesn't have any next-of-kin.'

'Everybody has next-of-kin. What about his family? Aunts, uncles and that sort of thing.'

'There are none. None that I know. I believe he was married at one time but that was over long ago.'

'How ridiculous. Even the drunks from park benches always have somebody.'

'I'll see what I can find out.'

'Maybe the university would know.'

'I'll try them anyway.'

Mason stood looking at Rosen as he lay there inert and unconscious with the tangle of tubes and instruments that monitored his condition. He looked deathly pale and his broken arm was stretched out on a support that jutted out from the bed. His torn clothes were neatly folded on a chair in the corner of the room.

On a trolley under the window the things from Rosen's clothes were laid out. There was what looked like a diary, a bunch of keys and the cheap watch with its wide leather strap that he always wore. There was a small wallet with several credit cards and just over a hundred D-Marks in cash.

Looking back at Rosen he wondered what had caused the strange behaviour in the street. It was like an epileptic fit. Mason sat on the edge of the bed and looked at Rosen.

'Jake. Can you hear me Jake?'

There was no response and he stood up. It was only then that he noticed the tattooed number on Rosen's wrist where he usually wore his watch. The rest of his arm was in plaster. For a moment Mason wondered how far he should go. Then he walked back to the display on the trolley and slid the keys into his pocket.

There were public telephones in the hospital reception area and he phoned Baumann telling him what had happened. Baumann said he would meet him at Rosen's place in an hour.

Baumann's car was already there, parked a short walk from the gate in the wall. When Mason paid off the taxi he saw that there were two men with Baumann. Mason looked at his watch. It was 1.15 a.m.

There were no lights on in the house as they let themselves in. Baumann had introduced his two companions as electronics experts but he didn't give their names. They were both BND and both from the anti-terrorist squad.

It was a substantial house with a large sitting room, an equally large dining room and a library. The kitchen gave on to a utilities room and a cold-store with a freezer. There were two good-sized bedrooms, and two smaller bedrooms. There was a quite palatial bathroom and another bathroom off the entrance hall.

The furnishings were sparse and plain. Plain wood and black leather and curtains that looked as if they had been bought ready-made. The pictures on the walls were all black and white photographs, typical of the kind of photographs taken by Magnum photographers. The Spanish soldier, Doisneau's embracing couple, the little Vietnamese girl who had been napalmed, the sailor kissing the nurse on Fifth

Avenue on VE Day and the picture of a pretty, young mother lying on a bed with her baby and a sleeping cat. A picture from the classic book – *The Family of Man*.

They had gathered together in the kitchen an hour later with coffee and sandwiches.

Baumann looked across at Mason sitting opposite him at the kitchen table.

'You notice anything, James?'

'Nothing particular. But it's got an odd atmosphere. There's nobody's personality impressed on the place. It isn't somebody's home. Just a place to sleep and change your shirt in before you go out. There are no clues to whoever lives here.' He paused. 'Except for the pictures. They say quite a lot. I don't know what, but they speak of a person who is kind of sad for humanity.' He looked at Baumann. 'What about you?'

Baumann looked down as he stirred his coffee and then looked up. 'My technical friends haven't found anything that matters.' He paused. 'But we're missing a room. I've asked them to do some measuring, inside and out.'

'How could you tell?'

Baumann smiled. 'I can't. I'm guessing but I'm sure I'm right.'

'How can you be so sure?'

'We've had DF vans, direction-finding vans, at work for the last two weeks. There's both radio and radio-telephone, RTTY stuff, going out of this immediate area. We can't pin-point its exact location but I'm sure it's this place.'

One of Baumann's assistants came in with a builder's tape measure and a scrap of paper.

'You're right, colonel. There's an area about six by six metres at the north corner. All brick and no windows. Got ivy growing all over it. We pulled some off. There were two windows there once that have been bricked in.'

Baumann nodded. 'Grab a sandwich and some coffee.'

As the two of them went upstairs, Baumann led the way. 'It's from one of the smaller bedrooms. And I know where the access is.' He laughed. 'D'you ever read C.S. Lewis's Narnia stories?'

'No.'

'The kids go through a wardrobe into a strange, new world. I reckon that's what we're going to do.'

Mason stood and watched as Baumann opened the double doors of the wardrobe and took out the clothes on their hangers and stacked them on the bed. Most of them looked as if they were from charity shops.

The door at the back of the wardrobe was about a metre wide. A sliding door with an electronic security lock with twenty buttons on it. Beaumann called down the stairs for the two electronic specialists to come up.

The older man shone a torch on the lock and after a few moments turned to his companion.

'Bring the bag up for me, Joe.' As Joe left, the man turned to Baumann. 'It would take a week to decode it but it's badly installed. They always are. But I'll have to cut into the woodwork. Is that OK?'

Baumann shook his head. 'No. Definitely not.'

'I need to make a hole in the door and then cut two wires. We could get it carefully restored.' Then he paused. 'How long have we got? A full day?'

'Maybe. Tell me what you've got in mind.'

'If an alarm goes off does that matter?'

'Here or somewhere else?'

'Just here?'

'That's OK.'

'I can get a laser here in a couple of hours. There'll be no sign that it's been cut. And the owner will still be able to use the lock.'

Baumann sighed. 'OK. Do it.'

When they were alone Baumann said to Mason, 'Can you stay here for the rest of the night? I can be back by nine.'

'OK.'

'How long do you think he'll be in the hospital?'

'At least a week, probably more.'

'Anyway it's got us inside. I'll put a guard inside the wall gate area. Stop any of his mates from getting in.'

Mason wandered around the house after Baumann had left. The phone rang twice but he didn't answer it. He undressed and settled down on the settee for the night with a cushion for a pillow. He realised that all the lights in the house had been left on but was too tired to do anything about it. The house itself had depressed him. It was soulless. A house but not a home. And that revealing crockery on the draining board by the sink. Only one of everything. One side-plate, one dinner plate, one cup, one dessert plate and one knife, fork and spoon. All arranged as if they were ready for inspection. And when he closed his eyes all he could see was that sad tattoo on Rosen's wrist, and the wide watch-strap that was worn to hide it. He had said nothing to Baumann about the tattoo. He wasn't sure why. His instinct said that it would be a betrayal, an outrage. An invasion of a man's privacy when he was help-less and defenceless. He would think about it. Wait, maybe, until at least Rosen was out of hospital.

Baumann shook him awake. He and his two experts had been in the concealed room for over an hour.

'Come and have a look.'

Mason groaned. 'Let me wash first for God's sake.'

'OK. Two minutes.'

Baumann was obviously pleased with whatever he'd found.

The walls and ceiling were painted white and Mason half-closed his eyes against the sudden brightness.

The older technician pointed out the various pieces of equipment. There were two Icom transceivers, two computers each with keyboards and monitors, a small but sophisticated Casio calculator and three tele-phones all with different numbers. Over the work-bench were four clocks. One showed UCT, one local German time, one London local time and one showing local Washington time. And there was a Racal transceiver.

'Both the computers have got modems and are set up for Internet.' The man pointed at half a dozen sheets of computer print-out. 'Those were left over in the buffer. I'm not a code expert but I'd say that they're in one of those codes that nobody's been able to break as yet.'

Mason nodded. 'Does the print-out help to break the code?'

'No. All that that does is provide proof that the guy was involved in using an unbreakable code.' He shrugged. 'Would take some explaining. It's mainly kids, hackers, who play those games. Not university professors.'

'Will he know from the lock that we've been in here?'

'No. We've fixed it so that the lock functions normally. It just won't give a warning alarm even if it's misused.'

By noon Baumann had colour-shots of the room and each piece of equipment with its function and serial number. Copies of the sheets of computer print-out were taken and the screen showing various stages of logging-on to the Internet was photographed, and Rosen's log-in name and his E-mail and TCP addresses were recorded.

Mason phoned the hospital and was told that Rosen was responding to treatment but it would help a patient in a coma if somebody he knew could talk to him. He might not appear to respond but experience showed that patients in Intensive Therapy subsequently recalled things that had been said to them. Even reading from a book might help. Just a familiar voice could help get a comatose mind back into the real world.

Baumann had phoned Cologne, the BND's cryptology centre and they had sent across one of their specialists who was based in Berlin. He was a young man in his early twenties but he was obviously at home with both computers and the Internet. He didn't even sit down but stood tapping away at the keyboard and checking the display on the screen. Finally he switched off the computer. the screen and the modem that linked the computer to the phone.

He turned to Mason and Baumann. 'He's using Compuserve to get on the net and I can't decrypt the text without the key.'

'What kind of key?'

'A mathematical key. An algorithm.'

'How long would it take to do that?'

The young man shrugged. 'Several million years with a couple of hundred main-frames doing nothing else. You've got a guy at Pullach named Waigel, he can explain it to you. But he can't do anything about it.' He paused and shrugged. 'Sorry.'

There was some mail for Rosen and Mason put it on the trolley beside the bed with the keys. All the keys had been copied by a locksmith and Mason kept the two original house-keys. He was looking after the house and it was obvious that he needed to keep those keys.

He pulled up a chair beside Rosen's bed and looked at Rosen's face.

He looked much the same. For an hour Mason read out slowly Thomas Mann's *Buddenbrooks*. Once or twice he thought Rosen stirred but when he looked at him nothing had changed.

A nurse came in to check the instruments and came back later with a cup of coffee to keep him awake. It was getting light when she eventually shook him awake.

CHAPTER 28

Agent Borinski was about to close the office when the girl walked in. She was a real beauty, a mane of black hair, big eyes and a full sensuous mouth. He'd seen girls like that when he was in Texas in San Antonio. But you didn't see many like that around Baltimore. She was tall and shapely and obviously well aware of the effect her body had on men. There was only one thing that spoiled the picture and that was a livid bruise that went from her left eye down to her mouth. At first he thought it was a birth-mark until he saw the outline of a hand on her face.

'Hi. What can I do for you?'

'Are you FBI agent, yes?'

'Yes, ma'am. Agent Borinski. How can I help you?'

She pointed at the bruise on her face. 'I want to tell you of man who do this to me.'

'I see . . .' he said, not wanting to offend '. . . why don't you have a word with the police?'

'Is not for police I want to talk.'

Borinski pulled out a chair. 'Take a seat ma'am.' When she was settled, he said, 'So tell me. How can I help you?'

'This man who do this is dangerous.'

'The police will take care of you.' He paused. 'What's your name?'

'Is Santos. Angelina Santos. He is planning to kill many people.'

'What's his name?'

'Is named. Martin. Roy Martin. He has killed many people already.'

The thought went through Borinski's mind that if she wasn't so beautiful he would believe what she was saying.

'Tell me about him.'

'He say he and his friends will explode White House and all politicians.'

'Maybe he was trying to impress you or frighten you.'

She shook her head vigorously. 'They have meetings. They have guns and explosives. They talk about what they do.'

'What does he do – this Roy Martin guy?'

'He has scrap place. Old cars to break-up. Stoves, refrigerators. Many things of metals.'

'Where?'

'Here in Philadelphia. Down on the docks.'

'How did you get the bruise?'

'He beat me that I not go on bed with his friends.'

'When was this?'

'Two days ago.' She shrugged. 'He tied me up but I got away when he go to work today morning.'

'Do you have your own place or did you live with him?'

'With him.'

Agent Borinski hesitated for a moment and then said, 'You like tea or coffee?'

'I like coffee. No sugar.'

When he gave her a mug of coffee he excused himself and went into the back office and called Special Agent Howe. She said she would be over in fifteen minutes. Don't let the girl go.

They took her up to a pleasant cabin near the reservoir at Hurst. The girl, Special Agent Lily Howe, a motherly Spanish-speaking woman, and Special Agent Hooper. They had bought food on the way. A police medic had checked her over, wincing as he looked at the bruise on her face, endearing himself to his patient when he said, 'Must be a real shit who could do that, honey.'

At the cabin they sat down to fried bacon, sausage and eggs and as they chatted, keeping away from why she was there, the girl had relaxed and became a small girl again, laughing at not very good jokes and no longer scared at what might happen to her.

She had slept soundly for the first time in months and was ready the next morning to answer all their questions.

By the end of the second day the FBI had formed a team of twelve to start the surveillance of Roy Martin and his fellow thugs. By day three they had found the report on the central computer of the surveillance by the FBI man in the white Bronco in his security check on Logan for his NSA employers. There had been nothing in his movements or contacts at that time to make him suspect and he'd been given a routine clearance. Even now, Logan's odd meetings with Roy Martin were not seen as particularly significant. A PhD in mathematics and a thuggish scrap dealer didn't look like bosom buddies or co-conspirators against the State. The only reason why NSA had called for the security check on Logan was because of the work he was doing on breaking the encryption code.

There was a message for him at the hospital reception desk. Dr Salis would like to see him before he went up to see Rosen.

Mason waited in the reception area until a nurse came to take him to the doctor's small office.

'Do sit down,' the doctor smiled as he pointed to a chair. 'I understand that you're English but speak perfect German.'

Mason smiled. 'My mother was German.' He paused. 'You wanted to see me about Professor Rosen?'

Dr Salis sighed. 'Yes. He's improving. Has even had brief periods of consciousness. Tries to speak but can't quite make it. Seems very concerned about something. His injuries are healing well and there was no damage to the skull or the brain – at least not more than superficial bumps and bruises.' He paused. 'He doesn't really need to be hospitalised. It's just a question of time and mental stimulation. But I understand that he has no relatives or friends at his house or nearby.' He shrugged. 'What do we do?'

'Could some nursing help or supervision be provided at his home if he paid for it?'

'Of course. I can see to that. But we need to know that somebody responsible is around as well.'

'You mean me?'

'I was hoping that might be possible.'

'How long would I need to be there?'

'A week. Maybe two. I don't see it being more. Leave him here today and tonight and we'll ambulance him home tomorrow.'

'OK. If it will help. I'll stay at the house tomorrow onwards.'

'I'm sure your friend Rosen will be grateful when he's back in the world with us again.'

The doctor smiled and stood up, holding out his hand, then walking with Mason to the elevators, where he stopped and looked at Mason, then said quietly, 'What's wrong with this man?'

'In what way?'

'He's suffering deep trauma. He's not medically ill. But his mind's in a mess.' He paused. 'Any idea what triggered it off?'

Mason went over again what had happened and when he had finished the doctor sighed. 'Maybe being back in his normal surrounding will help. Is he religious?'

'No. Not at all.'

'He needs either a priest or a psychiatrist. One or the other.'

'He is a psychologist himself.'

'I know. That's what worries me.' He paused. 'Contact me if his condition deteriorates. But there's no medical problem. He'll be able to use his arm in about a week's time. His rib-cage is already knitting together.'

As he stood by the door inside Rosen's room, Mason saw that Rosen's eyes were closed and he was wearing the wrist-watch again.

There was some mail from the house and when he put it on the trolley he turned as Rosen struggled to sit up, his eyes on Mason as he struggled to speak, his throat working to draw in air.

'To . . . go . . . home.'

'OK. Jake. Don't try to speak. Just nod or shake your head. OK?' Rosen nodded.

'I can take you home tomorrow – is that OK?'

'Yes . . . yes.'

Mason sat with Rosen for an hour, just talking to him about going home and having him and a nurse to look after him for a couple of weeks.

In the end Rosen was obviously pleased and grateful, but, exhausted by his efforts, he fell asleep.

In the lobby Mason phoned Baumann and gave him the news.

Rosen was already sitting in a chair in his room at the hospital, dressed, with his jacket around his shoulders. His arm was in a sling and he could move it from the shoulder because only the ulna had been broken. A small canvas bag was on the floor beside him containing his belongings. He was smiling and he could speak quite normally but very slowly as if searching carefully for each word.

Mason and the young nurse travelled with him in a hospital car. Once they were at the house Rosen walked from room to room, obviously delighted to be back home. Even the garden had to be inspected.

At ten o'clock the nurse left and Mason made an omelette as Rosen sat watching in the kitchen. When he had finished eating Rosen pushed his plate aside and looked at Mason.

'Why did you do all this for me?'

Mason shrugged. 'I was around when it happened, that's all.'

'But nobody else helped.'

'There were quite a lot of phone calls the first day. I just told them you were away for a few days. After that I took the phone off the hook.'

'Who called?'

Mason shook his head. 'I didn't ask them. I think one of them was one of your American friends.' He shrugged. 'They can wait a few days longer.'

For a few moments Rosen was silent and then he said quietly, 'I'm sorry about what happened. You must have thought I was crazy.'

'I didn't think anything while it was happening. Just that you needed help. Afterwards I assumed that something had upset you. Some kind of nightmare.'

Rosen looked up from his coffee cup. 'You're very perceptive. I think you know what it was, don't you?'

'A theory maybe. Just a theory.'

'Was it you who took off my watch?'

'No. The doctors did that to deal with your arm.'

'So what's the theory?'

'That it was something to do with the flowers.'

Rosen looked amazed. 'I don't understand. Why the flowers?'

'I don't really know. They were out of character. You aren't a flower-buying sort of man. I wondered if the flowers represented something romantic in your past.'

For a long time Rosen looked at Mason's face in silence and then he said very quickly. 'Are you giving me a way out? Is that what it is?'

'A way out of what?'

'The number tattooed on my wrist.'

Mason hesitated and then said, 'I assumed at first that you must have been in a camp. And then I realised you weren't old enough.' He shrugged. 'And if you didn't mention it I shouldn't either.'

Rosen was still for a moment and then he lowered his head, his free hand covering his face. Mason impulsively reached out his hand and touched Rosen's hand. He said quietly, 'What is it, Jake? Tell me.'

Rosen spoke without lifting his head. 'It was the wagons,' he said. 'My name's not Rosen. It's Brodski. My father was a Jew. We were Polish. We lived in Konin. We were sent to Auschwitz in wagons – cattle wagons like those going across the bridge. It was the same noise. The clattering and banging. We were in the wagons for fifteen days. Mama, Papa and me. I was four years old. Seven when the Nazis were thrown out.'

'What happened to your parents?'

'My father went into the gas chamber a few days after we arrived. They separated us at the unloading place. I stayed with my mother. She was young and very beautiful. They kept her alive so that they could have her and she kept me alive. We had a room in the SS quarters. Just her and me. And they did it to her while I was there. It was crazy. I used to sit on the floor beside her, holding her hand while they did it. I didn't understand what was going on. I just knew she was frightened so I held her hand.' He lifted his head and looked at Mason. 'I try to forget, but I can't. It goes through my mind like a terrible film.'

'What happened to her?'

'I don't know. About a week before the camp was freed she was taken out and I never saw her again.'

'And what happened to you?'

Rosen shook his head. 'I'll tell you one of these days.' He paused and looked at Mason, his eyes brimming with tears. And very softly he said, 'I shouldn't be here.'

It was a long time before Mason could sleep that night. As he had done when he was alone at the house, he had brought down a duvet and slept on the couch. But his mind was on what it must have been like for a small boy in the terrible conditions of Auschwitz. It didn't bear thinking about. No wonder Baumann's people hadn't been able to discover anything about Rosen's past. At some stage he would have to tell Baumann what he had learned but he would wait until it was essential. Maybe Rosen would turn out not to be important. And considering what he had gone through it was no wonder that he was fanatic about putting the world to rights.

CHAPTER 29

The metal plate on the computer said simply – 'Neptune C3800 5 processor 2 GBytes memory' and Logan pressed the button that linked the computer with five other similar machines. For a few seconds there was that wonderful chattering sound of hardware responding to software. The whole operation took a little less than two minutes, after which Logan returned the computers to their normal function, wiped out the implanted instructions and set them about their standard routine of word-string searching. He looked at his watch and then walked back to the elevator to his office floor.

By the time he had switched on his own computer every telephone exchange in Washington DC had been switched off or the lines re-routed to various cities in Texas or New Mexico. The facilities to the FBI, the CIA, the FCC, the US House of Representatives, the United States Senate, the White House, the Treasury, the US Navy, the Pentagon and the lines to all newspapers, TV stations and radio stations were wiped out.

Logan's encrypted program was timed for two days' duration and in that time politicians and bureaucrats cursed their dependence on electronic communications. In case they hadn't grasped the point, when the TV stations switched on there was an image on screen that just said – KAOS.

A dozen self-appointed committees of investigation had been set up, each with its own particular axe to grind. But underlying it all was the realisation that somebody could bring the government of the United States to a grinding halt by remote control. And there was no way to find out who was responsible. The semantics of KAOS were kicked around by both pedants and pseuds.

It took a few days for the media to realise that Washington and the military of the United States had been out of touch for forty-eight hours. Signalmen in both the US Army and the US Navy who could read Morse were in great demand. The old advocates of CW radio and Morse were vindicated at last.

It was rumoured that when the President was told that he was out of touch with all government agencies he had said that 'he wished it happened more often'.

In Dresden a mob of over two hundred set fire to a row of houses that were the homes of thirty Turkish immigrants. Twenty Turks died in the fire and four of those who fled the burning buildings were clubbed to death on the street. The TV cameras had shown it all and an enquiry was mounted as to how the TV cameras just happened to be there at that time, on that night, at that place. The police who had arrived late had arrested three of the alleged perpetrators, all of whom had worn swastika armbands, and under strip-search at the police station it was discovered that they had KAOS tattooed in their armpits.

When the police used TV footage of the event to identify successfully the three men, the studios of the TV company in Cologne and Berlin had been firebombed. There had been injuries but no deaths and the damage had been assessed as at least a million D-Marks.

The British Telecom van had been stolen two days' earlier and the Volvo had been on a trial run prior to purchase. The explosives in the van demolished the home of the Leader of Her Majesty's Opposition, killing two of his family. The bomb in the Volvo had brought down the building where the Deputy Speaker of the House of Commons lived with his family, and killed the Deputy Speaker, his wife and two teenage daughters.

The caller who contacted the media was said to have an upper-class accent but the message was clear enough. The bombings were only the beginning. From now on politicians were an endangered species. Their days were numbered no matter what political party they represented. If they cared for their families they should resign immediately. The speaker had said that it was a communiqué from KAOS, and had gone on to spell out the word but refused to elaborate on who or what KAOS was. There had been no conversation and all questions had been ignored.

* * *

There seemed to be no significance to the date but on June the fourth in the United States there were fourteen murders at noon local time. All were in different states and at exactly noon, local time.

All the victims were minor politicians or bureaucrats and they included a judge and a sheriff. They were all killed at close quarters by gunshots.

CHAPTER 30

Altieri asked for the meeting and it was held in a small room at the BND offices in Berlin. He sat at the head of the table with Mason on one side and Baumann on the other. Altieri had several buff-coloured files in front of him.

'I thought we'd better meet and discuss the information that Langley and Fort Meade have cobbled together. Is that OK with you guys?'

Mason and Baumann nodded without comment and Altieri continued.

'First of all it looks like the opposition operates under this code-word KAOS. We've had the computers search through a mass of information and this code-word has appeared in several places.

'It was used in the recent communications wipe-out in Washington. It was used in messages to the media after the bombings in the UK. KAOS tattoos in the armpit have been found on observed or arrested suspects in all three countries. The tattoo was on the neo-Nazis arrested after the Turkish fire-bombing.' He paused. 'Most significant of all is the fact that the code-word is used in front of all the Internet traffic that uses the encryption that we can't break.' He paused again. 'We're about to pick up a group of thugs in the Baltimore area that we have had under observation and there is one guy who has contact with them who works for the NSA at Fort Meade. His current task at NSA is attempting to break the unbreakable code. I've got the feeling that if we can make him talk we'd make some progress.

'Finally we've got this guy Rosen. He speaks quite openly in the media against all politicians and all governments. And the BND and CIA attempts at fixing the source of Internet traffic using this code seem to indicate that it comes from Rosen's place. The BND technicians' report indicated that Rosen's computer was using the Internet and when they groped around in the software there was some evidence that this unbreakable code was being used. Not only on outgoing traffic but also on traffic from overseas. It looked as if the operators were using what encryption guys call " a private key". It's quite unbreakable.

'I've discussed this Rosen character with our psycho people but we don't really know enough about him. His CV shows nothing but philosophy and psychology and he'd need to have math to be able to do this encryption jazz.' He looked at the other two, half-smiling. 'And I would be very remiss if I didn't pass on to you both the comments of the CIA's legal guy.' He paused. 'He pointed out that all of us involved in this operation could quite justifiably be accused of being the real villains. He quoted the First Amendment – *"Congress shall make no law abridging the freedom of speech, or of the press . . ."* He added for good measure Article Nineteen of the United Nations, Universal Declaration of Human Rights.' He paused and reached for a piece of paper. 'I'll have to read it to you. I quote: *"Everyone has the right to freedom of opinion and expression; this right includes freedom to hold opinions without interference and to seek, receive and impart information and ideas through any media regardless of frontiers".'* Altieri shrugged. 'You can see why governments won't give us open support.' He paused. 'Nevertheless it's our job to control or eliminate these assholes. No matter who they are.' He nodded to Mason. 'Tell us your views on Rosen. What's he like?'

'He was involved in a car accident so I've been in close touch with him for just over a week.' He paused. 'What's he like? He dislikes all governments, politicians and bureaucrats. I've met people at his house who would easily and happily turn to violence to get what they want. Rosen is not a man of violence but I don't think he would try and stop others from violence. He's got great charm and he is a born recruiter. I think he sees himself as a kind of Messiah.' He paused. 'But for me the most damning evidence is that his radio and computer equipment were in a secret room with a high security lock system.'

Baumann said, 'Our people looked over the print-out we copied and they confirmed that it was encrypted but couldn't confirm if it was in the super code.' He looked at Altieri. 'Maybe your people at NSA could look at it.'

'Sure. Let me have it.' He paused looking at Mason. 'Are you gonna stay alongside him?'

'If that's what you guys want.'

Both Baumann and Altieri had wanted him to stay at Rosen's place as long as possible without making Rosen suspicious.

CHAPTER 31

Special Agent Gardner was listening to his hand-held radio as he was speaking to the men sitting at the cramped desks in the school-room they had taken over for the operation.

'There's seven of them and they're in the shack by the metal crusher. I want the big truck across the gates. Springer, you cut the chain with the bolt-cutters and we go in. Weapons at the port and standard rules of engagement. If any one of 'em goes for a weapon or waves one around you kill the bastard but I want at least two left for interrogation about the big guy. All survivors are to be handcuffed and brought back here for dispersal.' He looked at his watch. 'Right. Five minutes to go. On your way.'

In the shack at the scrap-yard at the docks Martin was just beginning his talk. There were open cases of Uzis and AK47s and a table with about twenty handguns.

He was facing the group of men, hands on hips, jaw raised, reminiscent of Benito Mussolini.

'You men will be responsible for distributing the weapons and for training and drilling. You're all trained soldiers and . . .'

The wooden door of the shack was torn off its hinges and flung aside as four of the FBI men burst in, their guns traversing the seated men.

'Mr Martin, you and these men are under arrest. I advise you to co-operate so that none of you are hurt.'

For a moment it looked as if Martin might do something but he shrugged and held out his wrists in mock surrender.

Photographs and video shots were taken of the interior of the shack and the approach from the outside gates. Two men were left to load the weapons onto the second truck after Martin and his men had been loaded into two police coaches with individual cells.

A specialist rummage squad had searched the shack and Martin's living quarters at the rear of the portable building that served as offices for the scrap-yard. A documents team went through the box files and reckoned that there was more than enough to indict them for a number of serious offences against the state.

Special Agent Gardner took only one agent with him to pick up Logan. Logan was the real target but there was nothing they could charge him with. It could only be a fishing expedition. His infrequent contacts with Martin wouldn't be enough to establish a connection. They had shown a photograph of Logan to Martin's ex-girlfriend but she hadn't ever seen him at the scrap-yard.

Logan owned an apartment in a condo on the outskirts of Baltimore. According to NSA records his salary was 170,000 dollars a year with several additions like health insurance, pension funding and travel discounts. Logan had made three trips to Berlin and two to Mexico City in the last six months but he had only stayed for a couple of days each time. They were recorded as pleasure trips but Gardner was interested. Berlin was a long and expensive trip just for a couple of days. A couple of days was what men did for business reasons, where the cost didn't matter. He frequently flew to Carmel in California to see his mother who ran an art gallery there. Gossip said he was very fond of his mother. He had had no contact with his father, the attorney, for at least six years but nobody seemed sure about what caused the difference between them. Logan was due at NSA at 9 a.m. and he normally left about 7.30 a.m. and did some household shopping on the way.

Gardner showed his ID at the reception desk and said that he was on an official call to the occupier of Suite 25. He didn't want to be announced. The night porter shrugged and led him to the elevator. Suite 25 was on the sixth floor.

There were only four suites on each floor and as Gardner and his girl assistant came out of the elevator Suite 25 was facing them. There was country music just audible as they stood at the door. It sounded like WPOC on 93.1 which was Gardner's own preferred local station.

He pressed the bell and waited. When the door was opened Logan was buttoning up his jacket, the door still on the chain.

'Mr Logan?'

'Yeah. Who are you? How'd you get up here?'

Gardner unfolded his leather ID wallet and held it up. Logan peered through the narrow door opening and after a few moments said, 'I can't make it out. What is it?'

'It says my name's Horace Gardner and that I'm a special agent of the FBI.'

'You're kidding. Who are you?'

'I'm exactly what it says, Mr Logan, and I'd like to come in and talk with you.' He paused. 'I've got a search warrant, Mr Logan.'

For what seemed quite a long time Logan just stood there. And then he unchained the door and opened it to let them inside. As Logan closed the door behind them, Gardner said, 'This is my assistant Agent Parfitt.'

Logan looked genuinely confused and Gardner said, 'Perhaps we could sit down and have a chat, Mr Logan.'

Logan waved them towards some cane armchairs around a low table. When they were all settled Logan seemed more composed.

'You'd better tell me what it's all about, and as you're FBI I think you ought to know that I work at Fort Meade and I've got the highest security rating there is. My work is top secret.'

'I know that, Mr Logan.' He paused. 'Tell me about Mr Martin.'

'Who's he?'

Gardner took out his notebook and turned the pages. When he found what he wanted he looked at Logan. 'You spent an hour or so with him on the ninth of this month and on the twentieth. And last month you saw him twice, the second time you stayed overnight in the city. You spent the evening with him and an hour the next morning.'

'Jesus. Is this the guy at the scrap-yard?'

'That's the one.'

Logan shrugged. 'I'm a car buff. I sometimes check to see if he's got bits and pieces that I need.'

'Need for what?'

'I'm planning to reconstruct a Jag. An XK 120.'

'Have you ever bought something from him?'

'Not that I can recall.'

'How much of the car have you got so far?'

'None. It's just in the feasibility study stage.'

For a few moments Gardner sat looking at Logan without saying anything and then he said, 'I think it would save a lot of dancing around if you took your shirt off, Mr Logan.'

Logan looked in disbelief at Agent Parfitt who said nothing. When Logan looked back to Gardner he said, 'I can't believe this. Is it some kind of personality test or what?'

'I'm quite serious, Mr Logan. Just take off your jacket and your shirt.'

'And if I don't?'

'Then I'll take you back to my office and we'll take it off for you.'

'But this is so bizarre, so crazy. It's like the Keystone Kops and the Marx brothers.' He paused, 'Am I under arrest or something? Are you charging me with an offence?'

'Not at the moment. So long as you co-operate we're just talking.'

'And you want me to take my shirt off?' Logan smiled as he said it and Gardner just nodded as he watched Logan take off his jacket and start unbuttoning his shirt. When he slid it from his shoulders he sat there amused.

'Is that it?'

'Lift both arms up over your head.'

And suddenly Logan realised what it was all about. For a moment he hesitated and then he sighed heavily and raised his arms. Gardner looked and then exchanged glances with his assistant.

Looking back at Logan he said, 'OK, Mr Logan. You can put your kit back on again.'

When Logan was dressed again Gardner said quietly, 'Tell me what it means.'

'What what means?'

'It's not a time to play games, Mr Logan. What does the tattoo mean in your armpit?'

Logan shrugged. 'I don't really remember. I think it was done when I was at college. A fraternity thing.'

The thought of Martin from the scrap-yard being a member of a college fraternity would have been amusing if it hadn't heralded a new stage in the game.

'You'd better pack a case, Mr Logan. Enough things to see you through a couple of weeks.'

'You don't understand. I've got a very important job at NSA. I'll have to contact them if I don't turn up this morning.'

'I've warned them about the possibility already. They won't be expecting you. Not today at least.'

'Where are we going? I thought your offices were downtown.'

Gardner said quietly, 'We'll be out of town for a few days.'

'I'd like to contact my lawyer.'

Gardner nodded. 'You can when I've charged you. If I do.'

A rather subdued Logan, accompanied and watched by Gardner wherever he went, slowly packed a suitcase, and half an hour after he had opened the door to his visitors he opened the door for the three of them to leave.

As the car headed north out of the city on Interstate 83, Logan realised how little he knew outside the city. It was nearly an hour before they left the highway and took a road that led through a wooded area and came to what seemed to be a lake or a large reservoir. The car skirted the lake and stopped at a clap-board house that stood back from the road up an unmade drive. It was less than ten miles from the state border with Pennsylvania. A man with the butt of a gun sticking out of a holster was sitting on a rocking chair on the verandah.

When the call came through to Al Simmons he was looking over the crop-duster.

'When did they pick 'em up?'

'Last night.'

'How many?'

'As far as I can tell, about nine, but since then they've been pulling in dozens of members all over the place.'

'Where?'

'Chicago, Kansas, both Dakotas and Texas.'

'What have they been charged with?'

'The normal crap about overturning the government and the constitution.'

'Seems like it's time to teach those assholes a lesson. Keep me informed.'

Al Simmons walked back to the house and into his office. He made ten calls, each consisting of one word – KAOS – and the number, one. Two more calls were made on the Internet in 'private key' encryption. One call to Berlin, the other to a host address in Bath in the UK.

The next day on CBS's evening news he watched the uproar in Congress as one speaker after the other protested against the killings.

A dozen apparently unconnected killings. Congressmen, sheriffs, judges and bureaucrats from State assemblies to White House aides. Speakers railed at the government and the policies that had led to this discontent and cursed the police and the FBI who seemed helpless in giving protection against thugs and psychopaths.

At 1 a.m. the speaker of the House sent a hand-written message to the President warning him that unless he addressed Congress in person it could be a riot. An hour later the President arrived and although he was obviously the worse for drink he was able to bring some order to the proceedings. He promised that there would be a ruthless crackdown on the people who were committing murder in the name of freedom. The senior Senator for Texas took over the Speaker's chair and led the assembly into a tearful rendering of 'God Bless America.' There were thousands of Americans who shed tears at what they saw on their TV screens, and commentators in the media next day drew comparisons with the country's reaction to the assassination of Jack Kennedy. And strangely enough many people felt a fleeting sympathy for their politicians.

They had been at it for two days. The same questions again and again. And the same answers.

'So tell me about KAOS.'

'I told you it's just a Greek word. The Greek for chaos.'

'No way, sunbeam. The Greek for chaos has an "h" in it. Martin says you are the one who controls the passing of instructions and information for his operations and for the rest of them – the militia, the bombers and the killers.' He paused, 'Just for the record – by the way, who's your next of kin?'

'My mother.'

'I spoke to her yesterday. She wants you to phone her. She's got some problems.'

'What kind of problems?'

'Why don't you have a chat with her.'

'OK'.

Gardner sat beside Logan, listening on the extension as Logan spoke to the hysterical woman whose gallery had been smashed to pieces and the pictures slashed with the word KAOS scrawled all over the white walls. He knew from the look on Logan's face that he'd talk. Men like

Logan kept their distance from the thugs. They didn't ask what they did and they didn't want to know. But Logan wasn't dumb, he would know that it wasn't his mates who had smashed up his mother's place. Both sides could play those games. When Logan hung up his face was drawn and he was near to tears.

'Tell me about KAOS,' Gardner said, quietly.

Logan sighed. 'It's just a loose collection of people who are anti-government and anti-authority. They think our lives are controlled by people who like having power over the rest of us. People who make laws and rules to restrict our lives. And people who help them.' For a moment his eyes were angry as he said, 'People like you.'

'Who's the head guy?'

'We don't have such things. There's two instigators. One for making war and one for the Internet control to consolidate information and pass information. They're just men of the people like Martin and me in the USA. And others in England and Germany.' He paused. 'There's just one key-holder in each country.'

'What's a key-holder?'

Logan sighed. 'For a non-breakable code you need a key at both ends. You can't send the key by Internet because others could read it. The key has to be handed over physically in hard-copy.'

'How many key-holders are there?'

'Three. Me, the German guy and the Brit.'

'Who is the German guy?'

'I don't know his name. I've only met him twice. At Tegel. We had recognition signals both times for security. All I know is that he lectures at one of the Berlin universities. And his subject isn't math or computers.'

'And the Brit?'

'The same applies. I handed over the key at Gatwick in the Burger Bar. I got the impression he was a schoolmaster.'

'What made you think that?'

Logan half-smiled. 'We only talked for about twenty minutes but he used two Latin tags in that short time. Could be a writer of course. Historian or biographer.'

'What if one of you gets hit by a bus?'

'At all three bases there's one other person who knows where to find the key.'

'Where's your copy of the key?'

Logan shook his head. 'That's my insurance against you guys. The other two will already know that I'm not active at the moment.'

'It would make life a lot easier for both of us if you levelled with me about the whole business.' He looked at Logan quizzically. 'You don't look like a guy who gets his kicks out of seeing people shot or blown to pieces.'

Logan shook his head. 'You know, I don't understand how you can utter such shit when you yourself have broken the law by kidnapping me. Maybe you never read the Fourth Amendment.' He paused. 'And don't think I'll forget what you did to my mother. You're a prime example of what's made people, ordinary people see the government as the enemy of the people. You, Special Agent Gardner, are a shit in anybody's language.'

Special Agent Gardner stared back at his victim and said, 'You'd better take an aspirin and slip into something loose and lie down for a couple of hours, you're getting hysterical, my friend.'

Washington had patched S.A. Gardner through direct to Altieri in Berlin. When he had finished his report, Altieri said, 'Do you think this guy would identify his contact in Berlin if we sent over a photograph?'

'I don't know. Can but try.'

'Show it to him anyway, even if he won't co-operate. You might get something from his reaction.' He paused, 'Where are you?'

'Baltimore.'

'Have you got a good fax machine there?'

'Yeah. A Canon.'

'Give me your fax number and it'll be with you in about an hour.'

The only photographs of Rosen they had were taken from a TV screen of an old programme of a talk-show when Rosen was a panel member. Altieri sent them on a state-of-the-art fax machine to the FBI office in downtown Baltimore.

When Gardner showed the photographs to Logan he said immediately that he didn't recognise the man. It wasn't the man he had met in Berlin. But the reaction was too quick and Gardner knew that Logan was lying. He called in one of the FBI photographers and he took shots of Logan which were processed and faxed back to Altieri who passed a set on to Mason to see if Rosen recognised the man. He accepted that Mason would have to wait for a suitable opportunity. If Rosen was the Berlin man and was shown Logan's photograph he would know that he himself was under suspicion and it could be the end of Mason's relationship with him.

CHAPTER 32

The Prime Minister had informed the Speaker that he would be making a special statement at 3 p.m. in the House that day.

At 3 p.m. exactly the Speaker called the Prime Minister and Arthur Ramsey stood up and took his place at the Despatch Box. The House was crowded on both sides and he looked around at his supporters and then across to the Opposition benches.

'I am sure that most, if not all, Honourable Members will have witnessed first-hand or seen on TV the almost incredible scenes around this House that have occupied us all in the last two days.

'What purported to be a protest against proposed changes in Social Security payments was deliberately and maliciously turned into what I can only describe as a riot. Various spokesmen and some of the media have claimed that it was a spontaneous protest against the government.' He paused and looked across at the Opposition benches. 'We have ample proof that the whole thing was planned several weeks ago. It has become the practise of certain groups to take over legitimate and peaceful assemblies and turn them into riots. The people who do this are not protesting against taxes or laws – they are protesting against any form of democratic government.

'The latest information that I have is that seven people died including four police officers and over five hundred people have been treated for the effects of the gas that was used. I must emphasise that unlike what various trouble-makers have claimed, the police were not issued with any gas containers of any kind.

'Twelve main roads leading to Parliament Square were blocked off by articulated lorries that had been stolen the day before. Access by ambulances, fire brigades and other services was completely halted for six hours.

'As if all this was not enough to indicate the careful planning of the instigators then the bombing of this building and the millions of pounds of damage done to this much loved place are proof enough of the lengths to which these people will go. God knows what the casualties would have been if the House had been sitting at the time.

'I have had a long meeting with our service chiefs and the police and I must tell you that I have authorised them to use whatever means are required to deal with the instigators of these crimes.' He paused. 'I have spoken to the Leader of the Opposition and he agrees with me that we must put a stop to this subversion.' He paused and sighed and with a catch in his voice he said, 'As I came in today and made my way through the rubble of what had for centuries been St Stephen's Hall, that saying of Jefferson came to mind – "*As I look around me I tremble for my country when they tell me that God is just.*" '

He bowed to Madam Speaker and sat down. For once, the silence in the Chamber was complete and quite awesome.

If Peter Crombie had needed justification for the things that he had set in motion, he got it the night when he and Diana had stood at their first-floor window and watched the swarms of men shouting and screaming as they smashed the windows of the shops in the street below. There was no traffic, the road had been blocked at Putney Bridge by two stolen furniture vans and it was the rioters who were firing gas canisters, not the police. There were buildings on fire on the Fulham side, their flames reflected in the Thames and on the dark clouds above. Strangely enough it was older people who seemed to cope. They said it reminded them of the blitz.

Diana had said that they looked like savages, their faces distorted in anger and their anger indiscriminate. They smashed ambulances and fire-engines as well as police cars. But what really disturbed Crombie was that most of them were so ordinary. They were just people. People who were wearing Marks and Spencer's pullovers. People who mowed lawns and took their kids to the zoo and waited all night in the Mall for the Queen Mum to come out and take the small posies of flowers from the children on her birthday. Where did it all go wrong? What was the last straw? What, for that matter, had started it all? These new groups, KAOS and the rest of them, blamed everything on the politicians and the system. He himself loathed politicians and lawyers too but killing politicians and bureaucrats wasn't a cure for anything. And it assuredly wasn't the system. They said we needed a Constitution but the Americans had one and they had even more social turmoil. And what did the Germans have to complain about?' A strong currency, a stable government and social services and working conditions that were the envy of every country in Europe. What was it they wanted? Less government, they said. You might just as well suggest playing cricket or football but without any rules. It was juvenile thinking. Maybe that was it. They were just spoilt children. Children who didn't just smash up their toys and the nursery but the whole Goddam world. Like the PM had said to him – it was time to call a halt. Put democracy and all its restrictions on the back-burner for a bit. Teach the bastards a lesson. Get the train back on the track. Get back to what Shakespeare had said – '*This happy breed of men, this little world. This precious stone set in the silver sea.*'

'Pops' Wilson stirred his coffee slowly and looked at his watch. Frank Bailey would already be at the school but he had to be warned as soon as possible.

'Frank, Is that you . . . ?'

'Yes.'

'Good. The county's playing Warwickshire at home. How about we meet there for lunch?'

'Must we?'

'Fraid so, old chap. I'll be there at noon.' He hung up and pressed the bell for his secretary.

'Pops' Wilson had been a member of the county cricket club since he had come down from Oxford and he parked his car in the members' parking area. At the entrance to the members' stand he stopped to buy a score-card from one of the boys and as he fished in his trouser pocket for small change he looked around and saw Bailey looking through his binoculars at the players. He eased his way past members' legs and Bailey moved up to give him room to sit down.

He spoke very quietly. 'We got a problem, Frankie. They've picked up our friend on the other side.'

'Who picked him up?'

'The FBI. Not only our academic friend but several hundred foot soldiers.' He paused and said quietly, 'You'll need to put back your fun and games until I've got a clearer picture.'

'Do you think he'll talk?'

'Don't know. Really don't.' He laughed softly. 'You never can tell with math freaks. Soft targets but bloody-minded.' He paused. 'Your chaps seem to have made their point at Westminster. Looked to me more like the hordes of Ghenghis Khan than political argument.'

Frank Bailey was frequently irritated by 'Pops' Wilson's derogatory remarks about what he himself saw as the simple souls of the revolution. But right now he needed to find out what was happening to their friends across the water.

'I'll have to leave you, "Pops". I've got things to do.'

'OK. I'll hang on till the next wicket goes down. Keep in touch.'

'There's no problem with the code?'

'No.' He laughed. 'Not that I know of anyway. Don't worry about my bit. You've got enough problems on your end of it.'

'What d'you mean?'

'Pops' Wilson looked around but there was nobody within earshot. 'That bloody rag-tag-and-bobtail army of yours. None of 'em wanting the same things. Animal rights, abortion rights, ethnic politics, old-fashioned Commies, psychopaths, schizos – you name it.' He looked at Bailey. 'You can't really believe they listen to your advice, or can you?'

'They do listen. You know that.'

'They need the money you raise for them, kiddo. That's your function for them.' He stood up unsteadily. 'But don't bother about my views. We all have to learn our lessons our own small way.' He sighed. 'I'm gonna move to a seat in the sun.'

CHAPTER 33

When Crombie left his meeting with the Foreign Secretary, Benjamin Porter had left no doubt that SIS could take whatever steps were necessary to deal with what he still only referred to as 'the trouble-makers'. Because it was now obvious that foreigners were involved Crombie would be in charge of even those actions that would normally be the province of MI5 and Special Branch. Two hours after the meeting Crombie was on the plane to Berlin. He had phoned Baumann to arrange a meeting of all concerned. Baumann was meeting him at Tegel and the meeting would be at the CIA safe-house by the Opera House.

Nobody suggested that Altieri should chair the meeting, he just seemed to take over from the moment they were all seated.

'Gentlemen,' Altieri said with the underlying disrespect that drill sergeants have when addressing potential officers. 'I think before we start looking at the details, it's time we had a bit of thinking about our aims.' He paused. 'At the moment we're firing buck-shot at moving targets and apart from finding out a few facts we're wasting our time and efforts. Agreed?'

Altieri looked at each one of them and then went on. 'Seems to me like everybody just got swept or dragged into this hassle and you've never made your minds up what you're aiming to do.' He paused. 'Apart from putting the world to rights and converting apes into angels.' He shook his head, 'It just won't do gentlemen.' He looked at each in turn. 'The only bit of reality I've seen up to now is a single-page commentary by Sir Peter after you had your meeting with Swenson in Washington.' He looked at Crombie. 'Your report said you all had to bear in mind that the problem is world-wide and involved millions of people. The group had to concentrate on much smaller but significant targets.' He paused. 'The problem is, that you've all ignored that report and gone where the wind blows you. In my opinion we should now look at an immediate pay-off in each country. In the UK, the USA and here in Germany. Anybody disagree?'

Nobody responded and Altieri shrugged. 'OK. We've had the sermon – let's have a look at the hymn-sheet.' He reached for a file and took out a couple of sheets of typing, glancing at it before he went on speaking. 'This chap Rosen. Jimmy Mason's done a good job there. We just need a couple more items involving him.' He looked at Baumann. 'Are your people prepared to let us pick him up and wear him down?'

Baumann half-smiled as he shook his head. 'No way. But I'm prepared to do it if it looks like he's really involved. The neo-Nazis have scared my political bosses. They wouldn't interfere.' He smiled. 'Not until it was too late.'

Altieri looked at Mason. 'What we really want from Rosen is what the sons of bitches are planning to do apart from burning down houses. They'll have some master-plan. They always do. It's what holds 'em together.' He shrugged. 'Just keep close to him, James. That's all you can do for the moment.'

Turning to the others Altieri said, 'Right. News from the USA. Two items. We've picked up a guy named Logan. A top guy on encryption at Fort George Meade. We think he was the one who worked out this unbreakable code with some other guy. We suspect the other guy was our friend Rosen. Logan's no hero and he's beginning to talk. One of his regular contacts was a guy named Martin who was the leader of groups of wild boys. Militia, America-Firsts, a spattering of KKK and the usual psychos. We've rounded up nearly five hundred on suspicion of attempting to destroy the government, assassination and the rest of it. These guys are all recognisable by a tattoo under their armpits – the letters K-A-O-S, KAOS. Franz Baumann has checked on the German groups and they use the same sign. It's enough to warrant arrest when you find it.' Altieri looked at Crombie. 'Could you get your people to check on the people who were arrested at the riot in Parliament Square?'

'I'll phone my people to check when we finish.'

Altieri nodded then looked at Baumann. 'Franz, give us your stuff.'

'We've arrested over two hundred suspects. Most of them had the tattoo and at least two of them had connections with Rosen – James identified them from photographs. And tomorrow we are arresting and putting on trial four politicians who were informers for the Stasis and we suspect that the information sent us anonymously about them came from Rosen, who has extensive Stasi and KGB files at his disposal.'

Crombie joined in. 'I'm sitting on a couple of dozen Stasi reports on UK politicians sent to me anonymously. We see Rosen as the source too. One of the things we've got to bear in mind is that devising unbreakable codes and sending evidence that public men were traitors isn't an offence in any of the three countries.'

Altieri nodded. 'We've got to deal with these people in our own sweet way, Peter. No need for court cases. When we eliminate these people those who are still playing games will realise that they could share the same fate. We'll never stop this stuff completely. It's a waste of time trying. But we can put the fear of God into them enough to keep them under control.'

Crombie said, quietly, 'How do you frighten your five hundred suspects, Bill?'

Altieri leaned back in his chair, eyes screwed up as he spoke as he thought. 'Terrible unexplained explosion in an old warehouse building. A nasty train accident on a bridge over a river. Plenty of ways, Pete.'

'Won't your public be suspicious?'

'I hope so. We want all the rumours we can get. we'll be feeding the press ourselves.'

Crombie concealed his distaste of what sounded like authorised mass-murder. And he wasn't too pleased at being called 'Pete' either.

They chatted as they ate sandwiches together and then dispersed.

The following day the German media were full of the arrest of the four politicians and the charges against them. There was much criticism of the government and its coalition partners and there were editorial pieces about the need for an early election. Bonn was taking the matter very seriously. It added to the turmoil when newspapers and broadcasters received a message that there would be more revelations soon. The message purported to come from the KAOS Corporation.

In the UK fifteen men were charged with incitement to riot and just over fifty others were charged with affray leading to actual bodily harm. A prostitute had phoned BBC TV after seeing a newspaper photograph of one of the men charged with incitement to riot. She claimed that the man was one of her regulars who had boasted that he had taken part in the mortar attack on Chequers and had shown her a tattoo under his arm with the word KAOS. It happened that just after her call the BBC was taking a feed from Reuters covering the messages from KAOS to the German media.

CHAPTER 34

There were three cars outside Rosen's place and six or seven of Rosen's biker friends were just leaving as Mason arrived. They glared at him, pushing past him to the cars, giving him the finger as they drove off.

Rosen was standing in the kitchen taking off his sling and cautiously moving his arm. The break in his lower arm was still bandaged and strapped.

He looked at Mason. 'They say I can take it off tomorrow.'

'Good.' He paused, clearly irritated. 'Why do you spend your time with those louts who were just leaving? What have you got in common with them?'

Rosen smiled. 'They have a rôle, Jimmy. They have a role.'

'A rôle in what for God's sake? Jurassic Park?'

'They and others like them are going to change the world. Give people back their freedom to make their own rules instead of being forced to do what Bonn tells them to do. Or London or Washington. There's going to be a new world. It has to be.'

'And who's going to run it, Jake?'

'Nobody. Each of us independent.'

'What rubbish, Jake. It's kind of sick. Like little girls and the tooth-fairy.'

Mason wasn't quite sure why he chose that moment but he reached into his inside jacket pocket and pulled out an envelope. He took out four postcard-sized photographs.

'Have you ever met that man, Jake?'

Rosen looked carefully at each photograph and Mason knew he was playing for time, trying to decide how to respond. Then Rosen looked up at him. 'Where did you get these?'

'Does it matter?'

'Yes it does. I don't want you to get hurt.'

'I don't want you to get hurt either.'

'I beg you to stay your side of the line. Don't get involved. You wouldn't survive. Whatever you do it's going to happen. Nothing can stop it.'

'Tell me about Brodski, the small boy in the extermination camp. What happened to him?'

'Why do you ask?'

'To help me understand you. Maybe I can help you.' He paused. 'Now tell me what happened to that small boy.'

They were standing on opposite sides of the kitchen table and for long moments Rosen stood with his eyes closed without speaking and then he said in almost a whisper. 'You don't understand what matters. It isn't just the terrible things they did to me and my mother and millions of other people.' He paused and started to shout as if he was in pain. 'What mattered was that it was legal. Politicians and bureaucrats made laws that allowed them to do that to us. Men designed ovens to gas people, builders built them, people supplied and installed the gas pipes and built the huts where we lived like animals. They killed human beings like they were an infestation of rats. They had no mercy, no compunction, because what they were doing was legal. The government said so.'

Tears were streaming down Rosen's pale face and he stumbled and sat down with his head in his hands and his elbows on the table. A cup and saucer clattered to the floor and broke into pieces. He looked up at Mason. 'They didn't do it for money. they did it because they obeyed the law. *They* were degraded too. There are people around today who say that it never happened. None of it. I want them to die. All people who control other people's lives must die.'

Rosen sighed a deep sigh and his voice quavered as he said softly, 'All over the world these people must be eliminated. So that others can see that they can never get away with this again.'

Mason's mind went back to its roots in Purley and he walked to the sink and filled the kettle. A few minutes later he was pouring the boiling water into the mugs with their tea-bags. He pushed the milk jug and the sugar bowl across the table to Rosen as he sat down.

'What happened when the camp was liberated, Jake?'

Rosen shrugged without looking up from stirring his tea. For several moments he was silent and then he said, 'They put me in an orphanage.'

'Where?'

'The first was in Poznan. After that . . .' Rosen waved his hand dismissively. 'I don't want to talk about it. It sickens me.'

'Is there anything I could do to persuade you to break off from the people of violence?'

Rosen shook his head. 'It's too late, my friend. Nothing will stop them now. Like they always say – you can't get off the back of the tiger.'

'I can get you off the back of the tiger if you want to get off.'

'I couldn't let all those people down.'

Mason hesitated for a moment and then he said quietly, "Tell me about KAOS.' Mason was watching Rosen's face intently as he waited for a response.

Rosen looked towards the open window, the lace curtain lifting in the gentle breeze from the garden. Still not looking at Mason, Rosen said, 'You tell me what *you* know.'

'It's a word or letters tattooed under the arms of thugs who have been picked up for rioting in England, for other thugs who are charged with sedition in the United States and for home-grown Nazis who set fire to Turkish homes and murdered those who tried to escape. And it's the code-word that somebody uses to put threats to the media about killing politicians and bureaucrats.' He paused. 'Your turn, Jake.' He paused briefly and then said, 'Why did you use the name Rosen?'

Rosen shrugged. 'I didn't know my real name until years after I came out of the camp. I chose Rosen because it reminded me of my mother's favourite song – *"Drei rote Rosen."* Three red roses. It reminded me of her.' He shrugged. 'A bit silly I suppose. Such a small thing to cling to in this rotten world.'

'Your psycho friends don't make the world any less rotten.'

Rosen shook his head slowly, in apparent wonderment. 'D'you really believe in democracy?'

'Beats the shit out of anarchy. Beats the shit out of chaos too.'

'You don't think people should be able to live as they want to? You think it's OK for a handful of people to decide how we all should live? Big brother in disguise.'

'Let's get back to reality. The guy in the photograph. You know him don't you?'

'Maybe.'

'His name's Logan and he's been under arrest for several days. He said he had an opposite number in Germany. The man he described was almost certainly you.'

'So what? Logan's supporters will set him free.'

'Logan's local supporters are all in jail, my friend. Over five hundred of 'em.'

Rosen shrugged. 'There are hundreds of thousands he can rely on.' He paused. 'What's he been charged with anyway?'

'Tell me about the private-key encryption business.'

Rosen smiled. 'They'll never break that. Never in a million years. And that's the part that really matters.'

'Tell me.'

Rosen shook his head. 'You'll find out, Jimmy. It won't be long.' He sighed. 'Do I take it you're on the other side now?'

'If you mean am I agin the random murdering by psycho-killers of people who happen to be politicians or bureaucrats, then you're right.' He paused. 'The problem is that I find it difficult to see you in that gang structure.'

'In a few weeks' time you'll find out what it's all about. You'll be surprised. It's far bigger, far more significant than you imagine. And nobody can stop it.'

As Mason opened his mouth to speak the phone rang and Rosen walked into the living-room to answer it. A few seconds later he came back.

'It's for you. He wouldn't give his name but it sounded like Freddie Malins. Whoever it is speaks terrible German.'

Mason walked through and picked up the phone.

'Yeah. Who is it?'

'It's Freddie. Will you come over here right away. There's a problem.'

'What kind of problem?'

'I don' wanna talk on the phone.'

Mason heard the connection break at the other end.

Back in the kitchen Rosen was cutting a sandwich.

'It was Freddie. I've got to go over to his place. He's got some problem.'

'Are you coming back here afterwards?'

'I'll go to my place and call you from there.'

Rosen shrugged but said nothing.

* * *

It was nearly midnight when Crombie got the call at home from Swenson. They switched over to the double-scrambler circuit once he had responded.

'Sorry it's so late, Peter, but this guy Logan we picked up – seems he's the key figure in the States. Stores their data, passes their orders and instructions and reroutes everything in and out from Germany and the UK. Our people have been working him over and he's given us some dope on his UK contact. Seems like he's a top guy at your place at Cheltenham, GCHQ.'

'Jesus. What else did he tell you?'

'Your guy too is an expert on high-grade codes and sits on a committee that is responsible for working on breaking the code we're after.'

'What's his name?'

'That's the snag. Logan only knows him by a nickname. Seems they call him "Pops". That's about all we've got. He's in his fifties and he works with a local guy who looks after the coordination and orders to the wild-boys at your end.'

'Thanks. I'll get onto it right away. I'll keep in touch.'

'I heard from Altieri and Baumann that your chap Mason is doing a good job keeping alongside the Professor fellow. They're pretty sure he's the German end. But it's all instinct and no grounds for pulling him in.' He paused. 'I guess if the crunch is on we could create some grounds.'

'I guess so.'

'Best of luck.'

'Thanks.'

'Pops' Wilson was watching a video of *The Sound of Music* when the door-bell rang, and he went to the door humming the tune of 'I am sixteen going on seventeen.' He didn't recognise the man who stood there.

'Mr Wilson? "Pops" Wilson?'

'Yeah.' He pushed his glasses back up his nose to get a better look at his visitor.

'My name's Andrews, Mr Wilson. Chief Superintendent Andrews, Special Branch.' He paused. 'Could I have a word with you?'

'What about?'

'Could we talk inside?'

'I suppose so.'

As they walked together into the sitting room Wilson pointed to an armchair as he switched off the TV. He asked to see his visitor's ID and studied it carefully to give himself time to collect his thoughts.

C.S.Andrews said, 'I wonder if you remember a chap named Logan?'

'Does he work at GCHQ?'

'No. He's an American. Like you he's an expert on formulating high-grade code systems.'

'Maybe you're thinking of Zimmerman who devised the PGP code.' He smiled. 'There's more of us around than you'd think.'

'No. The chap I've got in mind is definitely Logan. Says he met you a couple of times. Once in the Burger Bar at Gatwick and once at the Gatwick Hilton.'

Andrews saw realisation dawning on Wilson's face. To confirm Wilson's suspicions he said, 'You talked about KAOS and its plans for the future. Remember?'

'May I make a phone-call?'

'Who to?'

'To whom,' he corrected without thinking. 'Forgive me . . .' he waved the problem aside '. . . just a friend.'

'A lawyer friend?'

'No. I've never stooped that low.' He laughed heartily at his own joke but his eyes were uneasy.

'I'll have to ask you to come with me, Mr Wilson.'

'Where to?'

'We'll be going by police-car to London and you'll be interviewed there by several people.'

'Ah yes. They always call it "helping police with their enquiries". And that really means trying to stop the cops from framing you.' He paused. 'Are you charging me?'

'No. Not yet. Just asking for your help.'

'Just on a bloody fishing expedition.' Andrews saw the anger in the older man's eyes. 'You'll get nothing out of me, my friend. You're wasting your time.'

Andrews watched over him as he went through the ritual of packing a bag, and then handed over the house to a rummage team and a signals specialist.

Two days' later the story of the missing official was 'leaked' to a local paper and from there to the nationals. There were hints that behind the amiable appearance of the lonely bachelor could be more sinister sexual problems. The nature of his problems seemed to range from the exotic to the humdrum. After a couple of weeks the story was dead.

Despite weeks of expert interrogations, drugs and psychological pressure, the rather stout elderly gentleman told them nothing. It was nearly a year later when his naked body was found by a shooting party on a grouse-moor in Scotland. The coroner brought in a verdict of death of an unknown person by causes unknown. The story only made the Scottish papers.

Freddie Malins was waiting for Mason in his apartment at the club, and he was taken upstairs by one of the cleaners.

Freddie was not in the best of moods. 'It isn't me who wants you, it's that bloody Kraut, Baumann. Seems he didn't want to phone you himself while you were at Rosen's place. He wants to see you at his place – wouldn't tell me where it is – says you know already. Also says it's urgent.' He shook his head. 'Tell him I don't want to be mixed up in his little games whatever they are. Just leave me out.' He looked at Mason. 'What are the bastards up to, James? It ain't Charlie Foster any more, I'm sure of that.' He lifted his hand then let it fall. 'You can smell it in the air. And I don't want to be part of it.'

'Did anybody ask you to be part of it?'

'Don't smart-arse me, boy. You watch out for yourself. They're twicing you that's for sure.'

'Who is?'

'Those buggers in London for a start-off. And I wouldn't trust them or Baumann as far as I could throw that bloody piano.'

Mason smiled. 'Thanks for the phone-call, Freddie. I'll treat you to a drink if I can get here tonight.'

Freddie Malins relaxed and slumped into his armchair, shaking his head as if to dismiss what he had said.

'There's something wrong with the whole fucking world. I'm making more money than I've ever made before but there's no enjoyment in it anymore. Can't you feel it? The discontent. The confusion. Every man for himself. Nobody cares anymore.' He looked up at Mason. 'Don't you feel it too?'

'You've been working too hard, Freddie. You need a holiday. A rest and a change.'

Malins shook his head. 'I wish to God that was all I need.'

It was Bill Altieri who let him into Baumann's place. Baumann was on the phone. He nodded to Mason and hung up a couple of minutes later, turning to Mason.

'Things are moving, James. I thought we'd better bring ourselves up to date.' He paused. 'Anything from your end?'

Mason knew that it was time to reveal what he knew about Rosen.

'Yes. First of all Rosen's real name is Brodski. That's why you couldn't trace him. He was born in Poland in a small town called Konin. His family were shipped off to a camp. Auschwitz. His father went to the gas chambers in a couple of days. His mother was young and very pretty. They kept her alive just to have sex with her. Rosen who was about four years old witnessed her being used. He's never got over it. He's got the usual tattoo on his wrist. He's undoubtedly got a mania about people in authority. Politicians especially because they make laws to control people's lives. He said he didn't recognise the photograph of Logan. But he did. He talks as if something special is going to happen fairly soon. Something that they've been planning for a long time.' He shrugged. 'That's about it.'

'My God,' Altieri said. 'That's a hell of a lot more than we've got.' He paused. 'How did you respond to all this?'

'I just emphasised the violence here and in the UK and in America. He tries to defend it on "the end justifies the means", but he doesn't like it. I'm sure of that. He's capable of planning violence but wants to turn a blind eye to it and the people around him who live for it.'

'Any clues as to what the "something special" is?'

'None at all. Just a warning that there's more to it than what's happened so far.'

'Your people have picked up Logan and Rosen's opposite number in the UK but he hasn't said a word. An oldish guy. They thought he would be easy but they've got nothing out of him. Fort Meade have picked up a lot of traffic using this special code and it all starts with this KAOS word in clear and then goes into the code.' He paused. 'How do you think Rosen would respond to pressure?'

'What kind of pressure?'

Altieri shrugged. 'Any kind. Physical or mental.' He looked at Baumann. 'Would your remit from your politicians allow us to pick him up on suspicion?'

'Not at this stage. They might if we knew more about the "something special". Depends on what it is?'

Altieri looked across at Mason. 'When you argue against him what's his reaction? Does he get aggressive?'

'No. He kind of absorbs it. He must have heard it all before – argued more effectively than I do.'

Altieri said, 'You rather like him, don't you?'

Mason thought for a moment. 'More sympathise than like. I sympathise with anyone who was in a concentration camp and I don't find it strange that they end up with plans to put the world right, however crazy the plans may be. Watching men screw your mother isn't the best introduction to philosophy you could get.' He nodded. 'So yes. I guess you're right. I do have a soft spot for Rosen-Brodski.'

Baumann said, 'Why don't you pretend to go along with his views. Not all the way but enough to make him talk about their plans.'

Mason smiled. 'He's not that dumb, Franz. And I'm not that good an actor.' He shrugged it all away. 'I'll see what I can do. But I'll spoil what I've done so far if I rush into being a convert.'

Altieri nodded. 'Best of luck. Any problems contact Franz or me.'

Mason walked through to Ku-damm to find a taxi, then changed his mind and walked on to the Zoo. He paid his 10 D-Marks and strolled down to the area where children could play with the animals and found an empty bench. He could hear the laughter and the squeals of excitement and pleasure as the children fed squirrels and stroked small deer and lambs and goat kids. It was all far removed from what had become his world. A world of random, ruthless killing that was beginning to take over from the imperfect world of law and order, kindness and affection. He had been in the game too long not to realise that it wouldn't be long before Altieri and maybe Baumann too would opt for moving in on Rosen and treating him as an instigator of violence. They would be just as ruthless as Rosen's biker friends and his cohorts of neo-Nazis. And with the instability of that Auschwitz background Rosen wouldn't stand a chance. He himself was left with the choice of betraying a pathetically damaged man to the others or letting some unknown catastrophe happen that Rosen called 'something special.' Bearing in mind the killings and bombings that they indulged in already, 'something special' had the sound of Armageddon. Maybe there was some way that he could get the others what they wanted without sacrificing Rosen. For a brief moment he wondered what Crombie would advocate. But he knew instinctively that Crombie would go along with the others no matter what they did.

He stood up, shaking his head, as if to clear his thoughts, and walked slowly to a kiosk and bought himself an ice-cream. The ice-cream reminded him of trips to Southend when he was a kid and he made a mental note to phone his mother.

CHAPTER 35

Altieri and Baumann had gone out for a meal together and as they tackled their *Wiener Schnitzel* they talked about their jobs and the organisations they worked for. But when they got to their *cappuccini* Altieri put the question they had both avoided.

'What do you feel about Mason?'

Baumann shrugged. 'He's done well. Better than we have.'

'Where do you think he'll stand if we have to move in on Rosen?'

'Depends on what you mean by "move in".'

'I mean use force.'

'Apart from Mason I'd need to be convinced that it was appropriate.' He paused. 'This man is obviously the key man. Logan and Wilson were technical experts carrying out a technical function. Passing orders and information over a vast area in an unbreakable code. But the actual means of sending documents to London and subsequently to Washington and Bonn were undoubtedly initiated and carried out by Rosen.' Baumann wagged an emphasising finger at Altieri. 'Rosen is the key. So we pick him up. Maybe they have some routine in the daily traffic, a check-word maybe, and if it's not in the text they go ahead right away and carry out this special thing that Rosen mentioned. We could be giving the signal for disaster in all three countries.

'So what's the alternative? The first is to persuade Rosen that the whole thing is either reprehensible or non-workable and counterproductive. I don't see even Mason being able to do that.'

'There's only one feasible way. For Mason to get close enough to Rosen to get him to show him. Mason, how the system works, and what they are planning to do in this special operation.'

'How do you think Mason has got as close as he has to Rosen?'

'I don't know. When Rosen was hit by that car Mason looked after him. I guess Rosen was grateful.'

'So where do we go from here?'

'Do what I said. Brief Mason to do almost anything to find out how the system works and what they're planning to do.'

'How does he get that close?'

Baumann shrugged. 'God knows. We can only leave it to him. He's done very well so far.'

Altieri still looked unconvinced. 'OK. But I'm not sure that I trust Mason to co-operate if we end up having to put Rosen through the mincer.'

Altieri, back at the CIA safe-house, and still frustrated, put in a personal call to Swenson. Swenson listened but had enough problems of his own not to want to get involved in a decision where there were too few facts. He was amiable and emollient but his ten minutes of schmooze amounted to – 'you're the expert. I'll go with whatever you want.'

Mason told the taxi to stop at the corner as soon as he saw the long line of motor cycles lined up in front of Rosen's place. He got out, paid off the driver and walked back slowly to the gate to Rosen's house. There were at least a dozen bikes. Two Kawasakis and the rest Harley Davidson's. The wrought-iron gate was ajar and as Mason walked into the garden he saw that the place was crowded with bully-boys like those that he'd seen leaving the house a couple of days before. Despite the summer heat there was a lot of leather clothing and denim jackets. He couldn't see Rosen and he made his way between the groups to the house.

Rosen was in the kitchen with the man he had previously introduced to Mason as Heller. Heller had been in the French Foreign Legion in Vietnam and Mason recognised the wary self-confidence that men got who had survived and prospered after the training at Toulouse or Hereford. He was a good-looking man until you got to the cold grey eyes that missed nothing and he looked at Mason, as he joined them at the kitchen table, with open hostility.

'You look amused, Englishman. Are you going to let us into the joke?'

Mason ignored the German and looked across at Rosen. 'Freddie sends his regards. He's got a small problem.'

Rosen smiled. 'Like what to do with all his new money?'

Mason laughed. 'Something like that.'

Heller stood up, his face flushed with anger. As he made for the door he pointed to the garden and said, 'I'll send them away. They're obviously not welcome here.'

'Thanks,' Rosen said. 'Keep in touch.'

For ten minutes there was the sound of bike engines being revved up to demonstrate their riders' *machismo*. When the noise had died down Mason said, 'Your military friend didn't seem very happy.'

'He's not. They're impatient to get going on the real thing.'

'And you?'

'For me, we stick to the plans.'

'And without you they can't go ahead?'

'Yes. That's what irks them. Logan and the man in Cheltenham had the same problem. Indispensable but resented.'   .

'Was the unbreakable code your work?'

Rosen nodded. 'Yeah. I had Logan and the others just to work on testing it. Logan was very good. A really creative mathematician.'

'Could he break the code?'

'No. With the key he can use the code. But breaking it's something else.'

'How did you authenticate your new identity?'

Rosen smiled. 'If you're an alumnus of Auschwitz, there's a kind of unwritten law. What you Brits call an "old-boys network". We help each other. There are Germans too who acknowledge a debt and pay it.' He paused. 'Heller tells me that there are CIA people wandering around Berlin in the last two weeks. Are they your buddies?'

Mason ignored the question. 'How did you come across Heller and his followers?'

'One of my students who knew I was working on codes for the Internet told him about me. And he had heard me talking on TV against politicians and bureaucrats.' He sighed. 'They seemed to be doing something about it while I was just talking.' He paused. 'So we got together.'

'That makes you an accessory to the things that they do. Turkish children burned to death in their homes.'

Rosen stood up, shaking his head, opening his mouth to speak, gasping, but nothing came out. He slumped back into his chair still gasping for breath.

Mason said quietly, 'Let's go out for a meal.'

Rosen nodded and seemed to relax.

They had eaten at Kempinski's and then gone back to Rosen's place and listened to CDs of Pavarotti doing the high-lights from *Bohème* and *Butterfly*.

Despite the music, Rosen seemed on edge and Mason suggested they played chess. They had been playing for about ten minutes when Rosen suddenly swept his hand across the board, sending the pieces flying with the back of his hand. He stood up unsteadily, sending the chess-board and the small table clattering to the ground. He turned to look at Mason, panting as he said, 'You'd better go. You're driving me mad. I've had enough. Leave me alone.'

Mason stood up slowly and looking at Rosen he said quietly, 'Calm down, Jake. I'll call you tomorrow.'

Rosen was shivering as if he had some sort of fit or ague and he stood watching Mason as he headed for the door to the garden.

When the phone rang Mason switched on the bedside lamp and looked at his watch. It was 4 a.m.

'Yes,' he said angrily.

There was nothing but heavy breathing and then Rosen's distorted voice. 'It's me, Jake. I need help. Please come over. Please.' Each word was punctuated by deep breaths.

'OK. Just hang on.'

It took Mason ten minutes to find a taxi and it was almost an hour before he got to Rosen's place. There were lights on all over the house and the front door was open.

As he got to the living-room he saw that the long wall was covered in black and white photographs, stuck to the wall with Sellotape across the corners. The largest print was the infamous photograph of the gates to Auschwitz with the words *'Arbeit macht frei'* across the arch. There were pictures of trenches full of bodies and others with just skulls and bones. A column of cowed people alongside a cattle-wagon, a shot of one of the huts from the outside and another, an internal shot showing tiers of bunks and emaciated prisoners. There must have been over twenty photographs. In the centre were two pictures side by side. One was a grainy picture of a very pretty young woman's face and the other a young woman at the head of a queue of people, a small boy's hand clasped in hers, his big dark eyes looking fearfully at the camera. The stark sad display was all too obviously a cry for help but it could equally be misinterpreted as only an angry protest.

Mason went quickly through the ground floor rooms and then the rooms upstairs. But there was no sign of Rosen. He checked the answering-machine but it was clear. His thoughts went to the secret room accessed through the cupboard but he had no idea what the code was for the electronic lock.

It was when he was closing the front door that he saw him. Rosen was sitting on the rough wooden bench by the small pond. He was rocking slowly backwards and forwards like an old man in a rocking-chair.

Mason walked over slowly to the bench and sat down beside Rosen. 'What is it, Jake? What's the problem?'

Still rocking slowly Rosen turned his face to look at Mason. Mason was shocked to see how drawn and old Rosen looked. He was panting and every few seconds he closed his eyes as if looking around was too painful. Then Rosen said, 'It's all going wrong. I'm letting them down.'

'Letting who down? D'you mean Heller and his rabble?'

'No. The people I was doing it for. The people in the camps and the people today all over the world.'

'Why are you telling me this?'

'There's nobody I can trust.'

'What about Heller?'

'He would kill me if he knew what had happened.'

'What has happened?'

'Have your American friends killed Logan?'

'I don't think so. Why do you ask?'

Rosen sighed deeply. 'I need to lie down.'

'OK. Let's go in the house.'

Mason lifted Rosen to his feet and with an arm around his waist guided him to where the light shone from the open door. Twice they had to stop to let Rosen draw in breath but finally Mason was able to stretch him out on the leather couch in the living room. He washed Rosen's pale face and drew up a chair beside him.

'Tell me the problem, Jake.'

For long moments he lay with his eyes closed without speaking. Then he said, 'There are code locks into our system if it goes longer than two days without being activated.' He paused. 'In case of illness or some such problem. It's been inactive for over twenty days. In real emergency the circuit can be penetrated by phone to check its status. It can also be penetrated by phone to indicate the level of the problem. I checked it tonight. It's dead.' He paused. 'Logan would never let it get to that stage if he was alive.'

'Perhaps he can't contact it.'

'He only needs a phone contact.'

'They wouldn't let him make the contact. That's for sure.'

'He could do it while seeming to make a quite normal call. Say to his family or an attorney.' Rosen shook his head. 'No. He's dead. He's dead.'

Rosen looked up at Mason's face. 'You or your people went in my room while I was in hospital, didn't you?'

'Yeah.'

Rosen half-smiled. 'But they couldn't break my code could they?'

'No. I don't think so.'

'You wouldn't be here if they'd broken it.' He paused. 'The plan is that if something like this happened I should have to take over the other network.'

'Forget it, Jake. You need a rest. Have you got a private doctor?'

'I won't see a doctor. I'm not ill.'

'Have you got any of the sleeping pills left that the nurse left for you?'

'Yes. They're in the upstairs bathroom.'

'Hang on. I'll get one for you.'

Mason found the bottle of sleeping pills and gave them to Rosen with a glass of warm water. He made no protest and was breathing easily a few minutes later.

Mason waited for another fifteen minutes but Rosen was obviously deeply asleep.

Mason stood in Rosen's secret room and saw the pile of computer print-out on the work-bench. Four pages had been torn off and were separate from the rest.

The first two pages were in code but the next two appeared to be a translation into English. He read the pages several times and then looked at the main pile of print-out that was still on continuous computer stationery. At the far end of the bench was a fax/copier and he printed out a copy of the four separate pages. He then had one more look at the pile of print-out in the hope of memorising it. Maybe it had all gone too far to matter whether Rosen discovered that he'd had access to the material but there was no point in making it obvious.

Moving into Rosen's bedroom Mason sat on the bed and dialled Baumann's number. As he waited he looked at his watch. It was 5 a.m. and it was light outside.

'Baumann.'

'I can't stay long. I'm at Rosen's place. I need a portable phone or a hand-held radio. I need a pistol and a clean shirt. Don't come in. I'll meet you at the gate in the wall in an hour. Understood?'

'Are you in trouble?'

'Not really.'

'OK. I'll be in a white BMW with a driver.'

It was 6.15 a.m. and broad daylight when Mason went out. The car was parked about twenty yards away. He slid into the back seat and handed over copies of the four pages.

'Don't read them now. I've got more to tell you. I'll contact you on the hand-phone and we need to meet, all of us.' He looked at Baumann. 'Don't, repeat don't, do anything. We need to discuss it or we could be really in the shit.'

Baumann nodded. 'OK. The pistol's a PPK. There's a carton of ammo. Two shirts and an emergency number in the shirt pocket.' He looked at Mason who could see that Baumann was worried. 'Is it good news, Jimmy, or bad?'

'Could be bad but I think if we play all the cards right we can neutralise it. But I'm gonna need time.'

'OK. I'll stand by all day. Altieri too.'

It was mid-afternoon before Rosen woke but despite the long sleep he still seemed lethargic and confused.

Mason cooked them a cheese omelette and found some tinned strawberries in a kitchen cupboard. When Mason suggested listening to

Pavarotti and the Puccini arias again, Rosen shook his head. 'They make me sad.'

'I'll make us some tea.' Mason said, and half-smiled because it reminded him of his mother.

'Why are you smiling?'

'When something went wrong my mother always used to make us all a cup of tea. She thinks it cheers people up.'

Rosen said quietly, 'Did you see the picture in the other room of a young blonde woman?'

'Yes. I guessed it was your mother.'

'I used to look at the girls in their summer dresses on Alexanderplatz and wonder how it happened that they are so lucky but my mother had to end her days with two years of nightmare in a concentration camp because she married my father, a Jew. So young and so pretty. But not pretty enough for those animals to save her from the gas chambers.' He sighed. 'I can't forget it. It's like a black and white film running over and over again.' He looked at Mason. 'They say time heals all wounds.' He paused. 'I can tell you it doesn't. I have to remember because everybody else forgets – so easily. To them it's just history.'

'When are you due to have contact with Heller again?'

'In about four or five days. He'll phone. But thank God he's very occupied with his side at the moment.'

'Do you want me to stick around so that I'm here if he comes?'

Rosen sighed. 'How can I ask you to do that? You're on the other side for God's sake.'

'Let's say I do it so that that girl in the photo didn't make her sacrifice in vain.'

'Tell me about your parents.'

Mason chatted about his mother and then about his father's misdeeds. Rosen shook his head in disbelief.

'I can't believe it. You're so different.'

'If I am, Jake, I owe it to them.' He paused. 'I've got a couple of things to do at my place. It'll take a couple of hours or so. I won't go until you're asleep again. Is that OK?'

Rosen shrugged. 'Whatever you want. I'll be OK. I'm used to being on my own.'

Mason sat on the toilet speaking as quietly as he could to Baumann. He would be over at his own place round about midnight but he could only stay for a couple of hours.

*   *   *

Nobody commented on how they happened to be sitting around inside his flat, waiting for him. He guessed that like him somebody had been on a lock-picking course.

They were sitting around the kitchen table and one of them had made some coffee. It was Altieri who cut short the greetings and pointed at the four pages of print-out and the translation. 'Tell us about this stuff.'

'It wasn't possible to remove the pages that are referred to in the summary but I got a quick look at the first couple of pages of the target list.' He frowned. 'They were horrific.'

'Like what?'

'The first targets in all three countries were the TV and radio stations. CNN, ABS and CBS in the States. BBC and ITV in the UK, and RTL, Pro 7 and Vox here in Germany. That was the electronics phase. When it got to the bombing stage it included the White House, the House of Commons and the Bundestag building in Bonn. The NSA and GCHQ were high on the priority list for takeover or destruction.' He paused. 'They must have been planning this for at least a year. And it wasn't done by bikers either. It had the signs of professional soldiers all over it.'

Altieri looked from Mason to Baumann. 'This is incredible.' Then he turned to Mason. 'This is a real prize, Jimmy. Alters the whole game. We could pick him up on this alone.' He paused and looked at Baumann. 'Agreed?'

'Give or take a few misdemeanours on our part – yes.'

Mason shook his head. 'That's not the object of the exercise, surely.'

'What is?' Altieri snapped.

'Stopping from happening what they've planned to do.'

'Pull in Rosen and the party's over.'

'It isn't, I'm afraid. We need Rosen's co-operation if we're to stop this so-called "operation".' He paused. 'At the moment we don't even know when they intend it to start.'

Altieri smiled. 'Give me Rosen for a couple of hours and we'll get all the co-operation we need.'

Mason shook his head. 'That's where you're wrong, Bill. Rosen survived two years in Auschwitz. He was only six or seven years old when he was released.'

Baumann intervened. 'What do you think we should do, James?'

'Let me keep alongside him and see what more I can find out.'

Altieri said angrily, 'Why pussy-foot around, for God's sake?'

'Because he controls the whole damn thing and I think I could stop him.'

'But you could be wrong and it blows up in our faces.'

'Of course.'

'So we pick him up and *then* you try to persuade him to call it all off – yes?'

'He's not that kind of guy, Bill. Use the rough stuff and he'll never co-operate. With me or anyone else.' He paused. 'You don't seem to understand. He's been through a concentration camp. He's seen hundreds of bodies piled up in open graves, he's seen living skeletons being beaten with clubs and rifle-butts.' He paused. 'And he's had to watch men raping his mother. Without quite knowing what they were doing because he was a kid.' He looked at Altieri. 'Do it your way and he'll see you as one more SS man, and he'll clam up. Or he'll go mad. Literally mad. Not angry – mad.' He paused. 'Right now he's on a razor edge. Like that poem said – *"Not waving – but drowning"!*'

Baumann said, 'I think we should try Jimmy's way first, Bill. He knows Rosen by now and he's the one who's got us this far.'

Altieri wasn't convinced. He gestured at the sheets of paper. 'And this crap? We let them start up this shit? I think we should see what Swenson says.'

'He's four thousand miles away, or whatever. If anything we should be asking Crombie's opinion. Jimmy's his man, not Swenson's.' He looked at Mason. 'How long do you think we've got, Jimmy? Before he presses the button?'

'I'd say a week, maybe ten days. But I'm only guessing.'

'Say he got killed in some kind of accident. What happens then?'

'Apart from the unbreakable code there's some sort of built-in system that lets you tell the situation at the three command sites. He already knew that Logan was out of the game. Just from a couple of telephone calls to an anonymous number. He thinks Logan is dead. That Bill's people killed him.' He looked at Altieri. 'Is he dead?'

Altieri hesitated and then said, 'It's possible.' And then he said with a shrug. 'Yes. He's dead.'

'That means that his end of the game is being operated by Rosen.'

'You mean that he's now controlling their plan in the U.S.?'

'Yes.'

Altieri said angrily, 'This is crazy. We ought to have him under lock and key right now. What the hell are we waiting for?'

'Because if it's not under Rosen's control it will start automatically. We'd be pressing the button without knowing it.'

Baumann said, 'What makes you think you can persuade him to call it off?'

'I think he's got terrible doubts about it. I think they've been building up recently. He's looking for a sign. A sort of sign from God.'

'And you could be the sign?'

'Not really. I'll just be a factor. I don't think my efforts, even if they don't work, could make it worse.'

Altieri stood up angrily. 'This is getting ridiculous. It's like these fucking talk-shows on TV about do you tell your girl-friend you've got Aids.' He shook his head in apparent despair.

'Well would you?' Baumann was smiling.

'Would I what?'

'Tell your girl-friend?'

Altieri was not amused and it showed.

There was no real decision made, so by default it was left that Mason would carry on as best he could.

He got a spare phone battery from Baumann before he left and it was Baumann who gave him a lift back to Rosen's place.

Altieri had already paid the bill for the meal but they went on drinking coffee until Baumann eventually said, 'You might as well say it.'

'Say what?'

'Whatever's on your mind. You're wriggling around on your butt like a cat on hot bricks.'

Altieri unwrapped a cube of sugar and put it in his coffee before he answered.

'Can this be between you and me?'

'OK.'

'I don't trust Mason. He's been around Rosen too long. He thinks he's guiding Rosen but I think it's the other way round. Rosen's giving him a schmooze job.'

'You spoken to Swenson on these lines?'

'Very briefly.'

'What did he say?'

'Noncommittal. Doesn't know enough about Mason to form a judgment. Got to be a local decision. He'll back us whichever way.'

'OK. Let's go through the scenario. You pick up Rosen. Then what? Where do you take him?'

'We've got another safe-house. I'd take him there.'

'How many bodies to pick him up?'

'Two and a driver.'

Baumann looked at Altieri. 'You've been planning it, haven't you?'

Altieri shrugged and smiled. 'Just running through the script.'

'OK. You've got him at the safe-house. Then what?'

'I tell him what I want. If he goes along with it – OK. If he doesn't, we put him through the mincer.'

'What is it you tell him you want?'

'To call a halt to this operation and give us the code he's using so that we can take over the networks.'

'But he doesn't play. You eliminate him but you can't control the network. You can't even get into it. Then what?'

Altieri shrugged. 'Then back to square one. But I don't see the negative picture you do.' He was silent for a few moments. 'Sounds from what Rosen told him that we haven't got long.' He paused. 'You got any better ideas?'

'And James Mason. What with him?'

Altieri shrugged. 'He'll have to go along with it or get out of the operation.' He shrugged again. 'Whose side is he on? Rosen's or ours?'

'You don't think that Rosen's terrible life as a child in Auschwitz is bad enough or sad enough to warrant a more civilised approach?'

'For God's sake, Franz. Get real. This guy is at the centre of a conspiracy that threatens to overthrow three governments. We don't owe him anything and if Mason wants to play Mother Teresa let him do it back in London.'

Baumann said quietly, 'If you decide you want to play it solo you'd better warn me in advance.' He paused. 'My organisation has to stick to the law of the land. Kidnapping citizens isn't one of our national sports.'

It was meant to be jocular but Baumann saw the quick flash of anger on Altieri's face as he said, 'Better kidnapping than putting 'em in gas chambers.' He stood up and headed for the door.

Back at the BND house Baumann wondered if it might be sensible to report Altieri's attitude to Pullach. He decided it was premature. Maybe Altieri was just applying pressure and maybe he'd decide against it after reflection. Maybe you got like that if you spent your whole life chasing terrorists.

He reached for his brief-case and took out the pages that Mason had brought in. As he read them again it seemed straight out of some film fantasy. A figment out of some overheated brain.

MIME-Version: 1.0

Content-Type: Text/plain; charset=US-ASCII

Content-Transfer-Encoding: 7bit

Content-Length: 4520

Status: R

—BEGIN PGP KAOS KEY BLOCK—
Version: 2.6
mQCNAjBy9yIAAAEEALt3HEeDAaGLtr6WxWYwuVAo2yhnGx
pmhyHyggLZAYFZFpY+b9XJrB7QjCjxKtrzxMfZMQO5yDk10K
wcvGp7n54phvJuyaILXa8XOO//Iv5uOGOvNTwlOBfjJy5d+zsvNR
RtNND3sqROX6UsGy4ZZxGYssegB5SvuUKbee74ksoRAAURtC
NLYXJsIExvbmRvbiA8a2FybEBib3JnLmRlbW9uLmNvLnVrPg=
==yBk8
Decode copy.
KAOS Corporation.

This undated summary of decisions taken by the three participating groups in KAOS Corporation is the basic plan for K-Day.

Operation Alpha will cover the electronic attacks to paralyse the functioning of government, the police and the security services in all three areas. The teams concerned will be notified of their targets and objectives. When this phase is completed the teams will stand down and disperse.

Operation Beta will cover the elimination of listed targets, both individuals and physical housing of nominated organisations. Participants will report using already established networks and will receive further instructions via KAOS network. KAOS key-holders will be appointed on Beta – 4 days. Operation Beta will cover ten days only.

Operation Gamma will solely concern the three command countries.

Resources to date

Radio and electronics operators are sufficient in all three territories but recruitment and training should continue. The militias for Operation Beta would benefit from further recruitment in UK and Germany. Weapons and explosives availability will be ample. Competent quartermasters have been appointed.

Targets

An appendix K (47 pages) is attached. Part 1 consists of immediate and specific targets for Operation Alpha. Part 2 consists of categories of targets.

Note

No warnings should be given in both operations and there will be no, repeat no, contact with the media other than through the main KAOS administration.

ENDS. DESTROY. DESTROY. KEY OFF.

The information on the four sheets of print-out was bad enough but what made it worse was Altieri's attitude. If they made a wrong move it could start the whole thing off and Baumann wasn't convinced that Altieri's scenario would work. And he, Baumann, was left in the middle to make up his own mind on which way to go. Baumann didn't like being pressured by outsiders, especially on his home ground. He was tempted to see what Pullach had to say but he knew all too well what would happen. If you wanted to do something that was against the law and you asked for the comments of politicians there was no doubt if it suited them they'd urge you to go ahead. Law-makers always feel that they are outside the law themselves, and they were quick to give their approval to breaking the law in a good cause. Their good cause, of course. But if it went wrong, don't look for any support in Bonn. They wouldn't quite remember giving their Good Housekeeping Seal of Approval to kidnapping German citizens. Even Shin Bet had to think twice about kidnapping. He decided to leave any decision for a couple of days and wait and see what developed.

*   *   *

Altieri had been around terrorists long enough to share their disregard for the niceties of civilisation. They, and he, happily shot sitting ducks. They recognised no closed season for their opponents no matter whether they were fish, fowl, game or human beings. On their games board there were no snakes, only ladders. And anyway the dice were loaded. And with a bit of help and a bit of luck you didn't have to throw a six to get out of jail. Altieri decided that his next move had to be a by-pass operation contacting Crombie direct. Crombie wasn't as clued up as Baumann and he was a bit old-fashioned, but Altieri had long experience of dealing with men like Crombie. Touch the right button and all that old-world charm could melt away in seconds. They weren't exactly bigots, more patriots who could be quite easily tempted to step over the line. Back home you waved the Stars and Stripes and for the Brits you waved the Union Jack. Only in a good cause, of course.

Altieri phoned the airport. There was a late plane to London in an hour's time. There was no problem in booking a seat. When he replaced the phone he looked at his watch. For a moment he hesitated, wondering if he should let Baumann know what he was doing. He decided against it. With Mason against his proposals and Baumann no better than vaguely neutral, he'd do it his own way if he could persuade Crombie to go along with his thinking.

At Tegel he used his card and dialled Crombie's number. His wife answered and said he would be home any minute. With only a duffel bag there was still ten minutes before the flight would be called. He waited until the last minute before phoning again. This time it was Crombie who answered. He would come out to Gatwick himself and would be pleased to put him up for the night.

It was just after midnight when Altieri was clear of Immigration but despite the hour Crombie insisted on taking him for a drink at the bar. Crombie had a malt whisky and Altieri had a Bloody Mary.

Altieri wasted no time. 'I've got a problem, Sir Peter. I need your advice.' He paused. 'But it has to be between you and me. Is that OK with you?'

Crombie smiled. 'I'm sure it is.'

For ten minutes Altieri explained the current position and the differences of opinion about how to deal with it. Crombie listened attentively and then said, 'Let me just get this straight.' He paused. '*You* think Mason is under the influence of Rosen and half on his side.' He paused again. 'And you think Baumann won't do anything that is against the law – or nothing substantial. You think this so-called Operation Alpha is very near the starting-gate and you want to go in and remove Rosen in the hope that you can scare him into co-operating. Am I more or less right?'

Altieri nodded. 'More or less.'

'So what is it you want from me?'

'Your off-the-record approval and one of your swat guys who knows Berlin well.'

Crombie was silent for long moments, his eyes on the other people in the bar. Then he turned back to look at Altieri.

'I can see some sense in your analysis of what's going on and what should be done. But this is a three-country operation, why should your views prevail over the other two who don't go along with you?'

'Just one simple fact, Sir Peter. In the UK you've probably got a couple of thousand real hard-core subversives aiming at overturning the government. The Germans have got five or six thousand thugs who use politics as a front for their thuggery.' He paused. 'In the US of A we have at least two or three million people who resent any kind of government control, who are being manipulated into bringing down any form of government and law and order.' He shrugged. 'Our stake in the game's the biggest. We've got more to lose by far.'

Crombie looked down at his hands, fleetingly aware of the tea-leaf stains that showed his age and mortality. He sighed as he raised his head to look at Altieri.

'You say Mason doesn't believe that Rosen will respond to the rough stuff.' He paused. 'What's your answer to that?'

'It worked with the guy from NSA – Logan – he wasn't the hero for long.' Altieri smiled. 'And you broke your guy from GCHQ. They all start out as heroes but when they realise you really *will* go all the way. . .' he shrugged '. . . they fold. They all do.'

Crombie nodded. 'I guess you're the expert. But tell me. Why do you think Mason is sympathetic to Rosen?'

'Seems like Rosen's mother and father were killed in Auschwitz and he was there himself as a kid for just over two years. Mason thinks it's a key factor in persuading him to a rational solution.'

Crombie nodded. 'He could be right, of course.'

'We haven't got the time to play games. Even Mason thinks we've got a week at the outside.'

'As tight as that, eh?'

'Yeah.'

'When are you going back?'

'I'll hang around here the rest of the night and get the first flight back to Berlin. But I need an answer. I need your nod and I need that guy.'

Crombie looked at Altieri. The big American looked back, unflinching. Indifferent to much harsher inspection.

Crombie said softly, 'With some reluctance I give you my blessing – unofficially, of course. And the man can be with you in Berlin, late today.' Crombie hesitated, then said, 'He'll do whatever you require, but . . .' Crombie waved his hands as if brushing away what he was about to say. 'Let's go to Immigration. I can use their phones.' He half-smiled as they walked together to Immigration. 'You must be tired, Bill.'

'No way. I need to be on the ball.' He smiled back at Crombie. 'If I make a cock-up of this lot it's "Goodnight Vienna" for all of us.'

CHAPTER 36

Mason had watched Rosen as he took the phone call. The call had
lasted six or seven minutes but Rosen barely spoke beyond a shrugged
'no' at long intervals. There were no salutations when he finally put
down the phone and looked across at Mason.

'That was Heller. He says if I back out they'll come for me.' He
sighed. 'Says they'll "persuade" me and if I don't respond they'll kill
me as a traitor.' He looked at Mason. 'Do you believe they'd go that
far?'

'I'm sure they would. You need to get out of here, and soon.'

'Give me an hour to think about it, yes?'

Before Mason could reply the doorbell rang and Mason walked over
to open it.

Freddie Malins was standing there obviously agitated.

'Who's in there, Jimmy?'

'Just me and Rosen.'

'I had to come myself. They'll be monitoring all the phones. Can we
go in the garden?'

'OK.'

Outside in the sunshine they stood by the pond.

'I gotta tell you, Jimmy. Your bastards in London are twicing you.
You're gonna end up in some bloody canal if you ain't very, very
careful.'

'Tell me more.'

'Two guys came into my club last night. Early this morning really.
One was a Yank. Built like a grizzly bear, stank of CIA or Special
Services. They were there, talking, for two hours and then the Yank
left on his own. The other guy stayed.' Malins paused. 'He was one of
your lot. I'd met him before. The last time I saw him was at the Pussy-
Cat the night before he killed Charlie Foster. His name's Maguire.

A cold, efficient psycho who used to be something in SIS until they couldn't stomach him any longer. He works freelance for them now. And for anyone else who'll pay the right money.'

'Who do you think he's after?'

'Don't be fucking stupid, man. He's after you.'

'Rosen could be the target.'

'Get real, man. There's fifty people, locals, here in Berlin, who'd knock off Rosen for the cost of a night with one of my girls.'

'Where's he staying?'

'He wouldn't tell me, but I had him tailed. He's holed-up at one of the CIA safe-houses. One just off Alexanderplatz. I'll give you the address.'

'Why are you telling me this, Freddie?'

'First. You're a mate of mine. Second, for years I've walked around wondering when London were going to close their account with me. Anything that I can do to give London the finger is fine by me.'

As Mason stood silent he was aware of a thrush singing somewhere in the orchard. He had no doubt that Freddie Malins was right. The American with Maguire was obviously Altieri who already didn't trust him so far as Rosen was concerned. And Baumann played things by the book. He wouldn't suspect that Altieri would go in for a bit of private enterprise that ignored half the statutes of the Federal Republic.

Finally, sighing, Mason said, 'I need to get Rosen out of this place. Will you help me?'

Malins hesitated, but only for a second. 'Tell me what you want.'

'Just for a start I need a car. Something old. A Ford. And I need a couple of places where I can hole up with Rosen.' He thought for a moment. 'Could I borrow your chap from the garage? The Stasi guy, Laufer. He'll know the back-streets better than I do.'

'That lot's OK. Anything else?'

'Could you find me a private eye? Somebody used to surveillance.'

'I know two ex-detectives from the Kripo. One of them'll be free.'

'How much will it cost?'

'How long for?'

'At least three days. Not more than a week.'

'OK. Leave it to me. We can square things later.' He looked at Mason. 'Why's Rosen so important all of a sudden?'

'I can't tell you, Freddie. It's best you don't know.'

'What are you going to do with him?'

'God knows. I've just got to keep him away from the rough guys.'

'What do you want the private dick for?'

'That American is a CIA guy. Supposed to be on my side but it sounds like he's reneging. If he's with Maguire you could be right and it's me they're after. I want the American under surveillance with a radio. Reporting back on the hour. Tell your chap it's a divorce job. If he knows he's doing surveillance on a CIA guy he'll back off. Have you got enough hand-held radios to go round?'

'Yeah. What frequency shall we use?'

'452.750. That's what I'm using now. When can I get going?'

Malins looked at his watch. 'Two hours OK?'

'Yeah. But tell Laufer to park away from this place and be prepared to hang around until it's dark. And what about my covers?'

'The Pussy-Cat Club. My home in Grunewald. Then there's another club I own back of the Zoo station. Laufer knows where it is.' He shrugged. 'It's a real dump. Nobody'll look for you there. If you need more things just contact me on the portable radio. If you can, use a public phone to the public phone at the Pussy-Cat. Those are checked for bugs every day.'

Malins turned to look at Mason. He put his hand on Mason's arm. 'I hope whatever you're involved in is worth all this, Jimmy.'

Mason nodded and shrugged. 'I hope so too, Freddie. Either way I won't forget the help you're giving me.'

'I'll be in touch in a couple of hours.'

Mason stood watching Freddie Malins walk slowly to the gate in the wall, and suddenly he felt very much alone. He wondered if he should contact Baumann or even Crombie, but he was sure that they must know what was going on. They wouldn't stomach the CIA man playing dirty tricks. But Crombie must have agreed to let Altieri use Maguire for some move against Rosen. He felt that he had too little time to convince Rosen that he should abandon at least his own role in the KAOS business. But he had to try. Rosen was a sick man. Confused and haunted, and seemingly impervious to rational persuasion. He wasn't really protesting against politicians, he was protesting against the ghastly flaws in mankind.

If it had just been a question of Altieri playing games there would have been no problem. He could have cut him off from Rosen easily enough. He was at home in Berlin. Altieri was like a fish out of water. Most of the Berlin CIA agents were too. And if all else failed he could have used Crombie to stop the American. But the advent of Maguire put it in a different league. Maybe Maguire was on some mission for SIS that was nothing to do with Rosen. But it didn't seem likely. There was nothing in Berlin or anywhere else as important as the KAOS operation at the moment, and as Freddie Malins had reminded him, it was Maguire who SIS had used to finish off Charlie Foster. Nobody he had met seemed to have any doubts about that. And if Rosen had been the target, then, as Freddie had said, there were dozens of thugs in Berlin who could do it for no more than 500 D-Marks and with no diplomatic problems if they were caught.

It was 'make your mind up time' for Rosen and if he wasn't going to co-operate there was no point in trying to protect him. Either Heller and his thugs would kill him or somebody from the ranks of the defenders of law and order would finish him off. He'd better get started. For a moment Mason stood still, looking up at the sky and then at the daisies on the small patch of lawn. It was a typical late Spring day. Spring waiting for the call to be summer. Blue sky, no clouds, green grass, blossom on some of the trees. Not Apocalypse now. Apocalypse wasn't until next week.

He said *'Scheisse'* as he kicked a stone and walked into the house, closing the door behind him.

Rosen was standing in front of the stone fireplace, looking at the photographs on the wall. Mason saw that Rosen had taken down one of the photographs from the centre. The faded, grainy photograph of his mother.

As Mason walked up to him, Rosen glanced at him and then back at the photograph.

'What was her name, Jake?'

'Anna Maria,' Rosen said, without taking his eyes off the photograph. 'She was twenty-one when we went into the camp. My father was crazy about her and he persuaded her to marry him when she was barely seventeen.'

'How do you know that?'

'I went back to Konin when I left university. I talked to the few people who could remember those days. They had to elope. Her father was against the marriage because my father was a Jew and they weren't. And he thought she was too young and inexperienced in the ways of the world.' He paused and said bitterly, 'Of course, the Nazis put that right.'

'We need to talk, Jake. We haven't much time. Only hours.'

Rosen half-smiled. 'OK. You always like to talk around the kitchen table. Let's go in there.'

Mason made tea and they settled down at the small table.

'We haven't got much time left, Jake. Hours rather than days. The authorities know about your KAOS set-up and Operations Alpha and Beta. They don't know when it's planned to start but they are assuming that it's a matter of days.' He looked intently at Rosen's face. 'You understand what this means, don't you?'

'Tell me.'

'There are two lots of people about to hunt you down. Not next week but today. Heller on one side, to make you press the button on Operation Alpha, and government authorities on the other side, ready to pressure you into telling them how to stop it.'

'What government authorities?'

'The BND here in Germany. The CIA in America and the people I represent for the UK.'

'Heller might kill me. But not government people.'

'Do you remember telling me that a man named Maguire who worked for SIS was the man who killed Charlie Foster?'

'Yes.'

'He arrived in Berlin last night.'

'To do what?'

'I've no idea.' He paused. 'But I can guess.' He sighed. 'But what matters now is that unless you move out of this place you'll probably be dealt with by Heller or the others. Why waste your life. I'll get you somewhere safe – but only if you agree to stop this crazy KAOS thing.'

'If they killed me it would still happen. It would just go back to being uncoordinated.' He shrugged. 'All that KAOS does is bring it all together.'

'What happens if you don't shut it off?'

'Like I said. It'll just revert to individual groups doing it in their own good time.'

'Do you really want to press that button? And be a new-age Hitler who gives the order to wipe out tens of thousands of innocent people. It won't do what you want it to do anyway. You know that, don't you?'

Rosen nodded. 'Yes.' He shrugged. 'I loved the planning and creating the code system. It made me feel I was striking back at them.' He shook his head. 'You're right. I can't do it.'

'What happens if you don't give the signal?'

'Nothing. It will just lose its momentum. People will go on as individual groups but it will be local and uncoordinated.' He paused. 'That's why those like Heller will never forgive me.'

'Will you destroy the code and the system?'

'Yes.'

'Right now?'

'Yes.'

'Let's go up to your room and do it.'

'It's no big deal, Jimmy. A few minutes and it's done.'

'Let's go then.'

Mason stood beside Rosen and saw the computer monitor screen fill with line after line of random numbers and characters. Rosen moved the cursor from one line to the next and the background to each line turned from white to blue. For a few moments Rosen stood looking at the screen and then he pointed at a key on the keyboard. 'You do it. Just press that key.'

Mason touched the key and the screen was instantly clear. No blue colour, no numbers and letters. Nothing. A blank. He turned to Rosen. 'Is that all you have to do?'

'That's all.'

'Could you re-install it.'

'No. It's wiped out of the memory.'

'Nobody, not even a computer expert, could get it back?'

'There's nothing there to reconstruct. It's an empty box.'

'Could you reconstruct it?'

'Give me four or five years and I could come up with some sort of unbreakable code. But that one has gone into limbo and it can't come back for anybody.'

'And the people on the ground. In the States and the UK and here in Germany. Could any of those reconstruct it?'

Rosen shrugged. 'Except for a handful of people nobody even knew that the programme or the organisation existed. They'll just carry on as they always did.' He smiled. 'It's like that old existentialism conundrum. Look at a table in an empty room – close your eyes – does the table really exist if you can't see it? If you think yes – then prove it.'

Mason was in no mood for philosophy and he said, 'Pack a bag and include your passport and any money, cheque-books and credit cards you've got.' He looked at his watch. 'You've got thirty minutes.'

Mason went to the phone and dialled Baumann's number. It was Baumann himself who answered.

'Baumann speaking. Who is that?'

'It's me, Franz, Mason. Rosen's closed down the operation. It won't go ahead.'

'Altieri's with me, let me put him on the other line.'

'Altieri.' Mason recognised the American's voice.

Baumann said, 'Tell him what you just told me.'

Mason repeated what he had said but Altieri interrupted. 'You mean all these lunatics in USA, UK and here are going to stop being naughty boys. Come off it, Mason. He's shitting you.'

'I didn't say that. What I'm saying is that these people no longer have a network. They may go on operating as individual groups but there's no central organisation. The thing was closed down while I watched and he's wiped out the unbreakable code. Even *he* can't use it any more.'

'Look, fella, that bastard has been at the centre of a conspiracy to overthrow my government – and yours too for that matter. He's got to be punished for it.'

'How're you going to do it – punish him?'

'The least he gets away with is standing trial on serious charges.'

'What evidence have you got?'

'The code. The network itself. His contacts. I'll make that bastard talk don't you worry.'

'And if he won't talk? What then?'

'You just bring him in Mason or I'll come and get him. I want him here inside twenty-four hours.'

'What shall I charge him with?'

'Just bring him in.'

'Does Baumann agree with that?'

'It's not Baumann's call. It's mine.' The anger and frustration was obvious in Altieri's voice. 'And for your information your boss goes with my thinking too. I've spoken to him personally. He'll back me. Your feet won't touch if you cock this up, believe me.'

'Let Franz tell me that he agrees with you.'

The phone crashed down at the other end and Mason knew that Baumann didn't agree with Altieri's thinking or he would have chipped in. It looked as if friend Altieri might have made contact with Crombie without telling Baumann.

Mason called up the stairs to Rosen.

'It's time. Let's get going.'

Chapter 37

The street lights were on and the weather had changed bringing lowering clouds and a drizzle of rain as Mason made his way to the street gate. There were several cars parked in the street and Mason had walked about fifty yards before the sidelights of a car just ahead of him flicked on and off. Mason opened the rear door and slid into the back seat. Laufer turned in the driver's seat to look at him.

'There's a gun in the side-pocket where you're sitting and two cartons of ammo, and there's cash in two plastic bags under the two back seats. Two thousand D-Marks in each packet. Freddie says you can have more if you need it. He says to take you to a place he's got, three rooms over a junk-shop. He owns both places. He's given me two other addresses you can use and he wants me to stay with you as long as I can be useful. OK?'

'Fine. I'll go and get my friend. A couple of minutes.'

Rosen was standing in the middle of the living-room. He had a canvas bag and a brief-case and looked lost and apprehensive.

'Are you sure this is the right thing to do, Jimmy?'

'Yes. Just follow me. Leave all the house lights on and when we're in the street just walk alongside me as if we're talking. OK.'

'Yes.'

Mason picked up his own leather bag and took Rosen's arm, closing the house door behind him before they headed for the gate. A quick glance to check the street and a brisk walk to the car. Rosen was an awkward passenger and it reminded Mason of family trips to Southend when his father had a Ford Anglia and his mother would be fussing about who would sit where and where the bags should be stored. Then they were off, Laufer making a U-turn, checking the mirror to see if they were being followed. Mason had caught sight of Alexanderplatz from at least four different points of view before Laufer went across the pedestrian underpass at Karl-Liebknecht Strasse until they were obviously heading for the slum district called the Barn with a long-established Jewish population. They passed the old Jewish Cemetery and the Neue Synagoge and finally turned into a cobblestoned alley of undiluted squalor. The junk shop was unmistakable, the window hung with pots and pans, a battered violin, several piles of books, and cobwebs leading to goods inside the shop. The open door of the garage beside the shop provided just enough space for the car alongside battered electric cookers and vacuum cleaners. Mason and Rosen had to get out of the car before Laufer could manoeuvre it into the narrow space. Laufer just managed to ease himself out of the car and handed them their bags. There were two modern locks on the shop door and Laufer let them in, pushing aside a tattered lace curtain that trailed from a brass rod over the door. They stood in the darkness until Laufer found the light switch and the sight that greeted them was of a clutter of damaged furniture, pieces of rolled-up carpets and dozens of things whose use could only be guessed at.

A steep wooden staircase led to the living quarters upstairs. There seemed to be more rooms than Laufer had said. The living room and kitchen were combined and there were two other rooms with a bed in each. The place was clean but depressing and reminded Mason of the deserted villages that SAS used for mock attacks. Planned as places, not sites of human activity.

Laufer made several trips down to the car and brought back the gun, wrapped in an oily cloth, the two cartons of ammunition, and two plastic-wrapped packets of money. He also handed over a note from Freddie Malins. The note was brief and gave two telephone numbers that Mason could use to contact Malins and two more addresses that could be used as safe places.

Mason looked around the kitchen. It was quite clean and tidy with most of the things they would need for simple cooking. When he remarked on it to Laufer the German shrugged and smiled and told him that the place was sometimes used by the girls from Freddie's other night-club.

When he unwrapped the gun he was surprised. It was an almost new Smith and Wesson 1006 double-action auto chambers for 10 mm. with a 9 shot magazine. He re-wrapped it and put it in a saucepan on a shelf over the electric cooker. Laufer busied himself putting food from a brown paper bag into the refrigerator.

As they ate an omelette together Mason talked mainly to Laufer.

'Is there a post-office open all night?'

'Only the central one at Zoo Station. That's open twenty-four hours a day.'

'I'll want you to take me there about twelve-thirty and wait for me. I'll be about an hour.'

'Whatever you want.'

Mason took Rosen into one of the bedrooms. There was just a single bed and a wash-basin and a fold-up canvas chair. Mason took the chair and Rosen sat on the bed. He looked tired, pale and drawn.

'Jake. We've got to talk. We've got to get you back in the real world.' He paused. 'Can we do that?'

'Can I ask you a question?'

'Sure. Ask away.'

'Why have you helped me? You're on the other side.'

Mason smiled, rather wryly. 'I got stuck with you, Jake. Listened to a man with great charm who argued with a strange sort of logic, something that in real life was obviously crazy. I wondered why this guy didn't see it.' He paused. 'And then there were those bloody wagons at Zoo Station and as you told me later about what had happened in the camp I realised what your stuff was all about. And it wasn't just crazy, it was dangerous. People with mild grievances against government or the police were being turned into fanatics. As individuals or groups they could be dealt with. But put them all together and have them coordinated, then the psychos, the killers, would take over. It was my job to stop it happening. You were being used, conned, by sick thugs. I gave you a safety-net because I knew you were beginning to back off from KAOS and all that.

'There are other people who feel that they have to eliminate you before KAOS can be wiped out.' He sighed. 'I don't agree. I want to do a deal for you that will allow you to live in peace. Is that OK with you?'

To Mason's surprise Rosen smiled, if rather wanly. 'You drive me back to my philosophy and Isaac Babel, another Jew. He said ". . . *the army of words, an army in which all kinds of weapons are on the move. No iron can enter the human heart as chillingly as a full stop placed at the right time*".'

Mason smiled briefly and then said, 'I need to know some hard facts, Jake. You won't be able to live in Germany for some time or Heller and his thugs will get you. So where do you go and how will you live – money I mean?'

'I'm due a year's sabbatical from the university on full salary. I guess I can get work of some kind.'

'What about Amsterdam? They're pretty civilised in Holland.'

'What about your people?'

'I'll work out a deal that gives you a complete amnesty.'

'Can you really do that?'

'Yeah. I think so. How much capital do you have?'

'Enough to give me a small income.'

'And you'll go with anything I can arrange?'

Rosen smiled. 'I don't fancy the alternative.'

'OK. Get some sleep. I'll be out most of the night.'

Mason bought a 20 D-Mark telephone card and went to one of the line of blue telephone kiosks. The place was almost empty and Mason assumed that that was because it was after midnight. He checked for Baumann's number in his notebook and dialled the number. It rang many times before it was answered. No name, just the number.

'Franz. Mason speaking. Are you alone?'

'Yes.'

'You heard what Altieri was saying to me on the telephone?'

'Yes.'

'Did you know that Maguire is here in Berlin?'

'Who's Maguire?'

'It was Maguire who killed Charlie Foster.'

'I remember now. What's he doing here?'

'He's with Altieri. Been seen together by several people.'

'Is Maguire SIS?'

'He was, but they use him now only as a free-lance when it involves something they daren't do themselves.' He paused. 'I don't trust Altieri. I think he's quite ready to do it his own way. And his way will destroy any chance of stopping this KAOS network.'

'He was talking about paying a visit to you and Rosen. Has he made any contact?'

'No way. I wouldn't see him without your being there.' He paused. 'I think I can do a deal with Rosen.'

'What kind of deal?'

'Can we meet? Just you and me.'

'When?'

'Right now.'

'Where?'

'At the Gedächtnis Kirche.'

'It'll be closed at this hour.'

'No. There's a small door. It's open all the time.'

There was a short silence and then Baumann said, 'OK. An hour from now.'

'Just you,' Mason said. 'Nobody else.'

'OK'.

There were still lights on inside the church but Mason sat in the shadows and went over what he would say to Baumann. The German would be angry that Altieri had taken things into his own hands and was probably already planning actions that were serious crimes against the law in the Federal Republic. But stopping Altieri didn't mean that Baumann and his bosses would agree to a kind of amnesty for Rosen.

When Baumann had not arrived half an hour after the time arranged, Mason began to wonder if it had been a mistake contacting Baumann. Not that he had much choice. Maguire could only have come to Berlin with Crombie's blessing. Altieri wouldn't even know of him or how to contact him. Did it show some doubts on Altieri's part about the action he was intending that he didn't use a CIA hit man? It also confirmed that Altieri was intending to put physical pressure on Rosen. He could have seen Rosen alone if all he was planning was persuasion or an appeal to Rosen's good sense.

It was nearly an hour after the agreed time that Baumann came into the church, looking around cautiously until he heard the sound of Mason's steps as he walked from the shadows towards him.

Baumann said, 'I'm sorry I'm late but I had another problem to deal with. Do you really want to talk here, we could go to a hotel?'

'Let's see how it goes here first.' They sat down on a bench against the wall.

'I've got bad news for you. I had Rosen's house checked out. Rosen isn't there. Altieri has been there with Maguire and he swears that Rosen wasn't at the house when they arrived. And they'd barely arrived when a gang of thugs came storming in and grabbed Altieri and his guy and when they too couldn't find Rosen they literally wrecked the place. They roughed up Altieri and Maguire and left them tied up. They're both having medical treatment at the CIA place and Altieri is out to get Rosen no matter what I say.'

Mason smiled. 'Rosen left the house some hours ago. He's in a safe-place. You can threaten Altieri with making a diplomatic row with Washington if he doesn't toe the line.' Mason shrugged. 'He doesn't matter any more.'

'D'you think Swenson knows what Altieri was planning?'

'No. Not for a moment. Even if he agreed with it, he wouldn't give him the OK without you agreeing too. If Altieri wants to play the Lone Ranger he'll be doing it on his own.'

'I hope you're right. Tell me about this deal you want.'

'At our first joint meeting it was recognised that all we could do was to eliminate the network that brought all the subversive groups together. There was no chance that we could do anything about the groups themselves apart from carrying on against them individually. Agreed?'

Baumann nodded. 'That was Swenson's view. Crombie's view and mine.'

'So if I can get Rosen to break up the network we've done what we set out to do?'

'Agreed. But what we aren't agreed on is how to do it. How to make Rosen do what we want.'

'Let's forget Altieri for the moment. If you, representing the Federal Government, pick him up, arrest him. What would you charge him with?'

'Something between treason and attempting to bring down the government.'

'What evidence would you have?'

'Not much. But we know what he's doing.'

'It isn't not much, Franz. You don't know a thing. Using an unbreakable code isn't an offence. You can't prove anything against him that a court would accept. Technically he's doing nothing criminal or even illegal.'

'You're making Altieri's case for going in and pressuring him.'

'You mean beating him up?'

'I guess that's what Altieri wants to do.'

'And you?'

Baumann sighed. 'No. Those days have long gone. We value the protection the law gives us all. The whole world watches us to see if we might revert to type. As a nation we never were that type.'

'And I can assure you that Rosen wouldn't succumb to physical violence or even the threat of it. After Auschwitz anything Wild Bill Altieri can do is nothing.'

'So what's your solution?'

'Say I could get Rosen to wipe out the network including the unbreakable code so that the whole KAOS operation no longer exists. Would you leave Rosen in peace? Guarantee him an amnesty and no further harassment and no exposure of what he's been doing?'

Baumann was silent for several moments and then he said, 'Is it technically possible to wipe out that unbreakable code? And if he did couldn't he just come up with a new one?'

'He tells me it would take thousands of years of computer time to devise another. And he can wipe out the network just pressing one key on the keyboard. It will wipe out the US and the UK end at the same time.'

'What about the thugs who do the killing and the beating up behind all this? They'd kill him as a traitor to their cause.'

'He'd move to another country and live under another name. We'd have to give him the necessary paperwork.'

'Which country?'

'Holland or Ireland.'

Baumann said, 'You've got this all worked out, haven't you?'

'More or less.'

'How will you persuade him to do this?'

For a few moments Mason said nothing, his eyes closed as he thought about how to respond and then opened his eyes as he decided to level with Baumann.

'I've done it already. The network doesn't exist. I watched him wipe it out and the unbreakable code went too. The code didn't exist except in the software of the computer.'

'Where is Rosen now?'

Mason shook his head. 'I'll tell you when you've agreed the deal.'

'I'll need to consult others. Computer experts, encryption people. Swenson and Crombie. It'll take me at least two days.'

'Can you control Altieri meantime?'

'I'll do my best. I'll put all the CIA detachment under twenty-four hour surveillance.' He paused. 'How can I get in touch with you?'

'I'll give you my cell-phone number. And I'll need one for you.'

Baumann looked around. It was beginning to get light and there were a few people now in the church. He turned to look at Mason.

'Isn't it crazy,' he said. 'Sitting in a church where people come to pray and we are talking about stopping people all over the world from killing other people.' He shook his head. 'You know, when I first met you I thought you would be the one who would advocate the rough stuff.' He paused. 'I was quite wrong.' He paused again. 'How did you do it?'

Mason thought for a moment. 'I came to realise that this charismatic man, the philosophy man, the professor – was a ghost. None of it was real. He was a victim. He didn't really survive the camp. He had a guilt-complex a mile wide because he had survived. The camp guards kept his mother alive because she was young and pretty and they could have her for sex anytime they wanted. And that small boy, Jakob, sat by her while they had her, holding her hand because he knew she was frightened. It was that kid I helped, not the professor. He needed help and I gave him a little support. He trusted me. He still does.'

'Are you married, Jimmy?'

Mason laughed. 'No. No way. Why do you ask?'

Baumann shrugged. 'Just interested.'

Mason took out a pen and scribbled a number on a page from his note-book, handing it to Baumann.

'That's my frequency. I've got yours if it's not been changed.'

'No, it's still the same.' He looked at Mason. 'If it's necessary would you let me meet Rosen with one of our coding people?'

'So long as I decide the meeting place. Yes?'

'Could that be late today? If that goes OK I'll start clearing with Bonn and Pullach about the deal with our friend.'

'That's OK. I'll tell you where to meet us when you contact me.'

Mason lay awake on the bed, looking up at the flaking paper on the ceiling. Wondering if the stain in the centre was more like a Rorschach blot or the shape of South America. Laufer and Rosen were in the other room. He could hear them talking and wondered what the hell they had to talk about. He had slept for three hours with the radio phone on the floor beside the bed. It was 4 p.m. when it rang. He let it ring a few times and then pressed the 'Speak' bar.

'Yes.'

'Where do you want us to meet?'

'D'you know the café at the Europa-Center?'

'Yes.' There was a pause. 'What time?'

Mason looked at his watch. 'How about five o'clock.' He paused. 'No questions beyond the wipe-out of the code. Agreed?'

'Agreed. See you.' And Baumann had hung up.

Rosen stayed in the car with Laufer while Mason strolled around Breidscheidtplatz and then checked out the café. Baumann was already at one of the tables with an academic-looking type with a beard and glasses. Mason threaded his way between the tables and eased himself into a chair at Baumann's table. Baumann introduced him to his companion. Not by name but as an encryption expert.

Mason looked at Baumann. 'Only questions to satisfy your colleague about my friend's technical capability. Yes?'

'No problem. But you can tell your friend that my expert here is from London, from the Royal Holloway College. I'm told that that is authentication enough among code experts.'

Mason nodded. 'I'll go and get him.'

Laufer was parked a block away from the Europa building and Mason slid into the back-seat with Rosen.

'Remember the only reason for this meeting is to satisfy Baumann's encryption expert that you have wiped out the KAOS code. He's from the Royal Holloway College in London, is that significant?'

Rosen nodded. 'Very significant, they do a lot of work for intelligence organisations and several governments on encryption and code-breakers.'

'OK. Let's go. He doesn't know your name or anything except about the KAOS code.'

When Mason and Rosen joined Baumann and his expert it was obvious that the two computer experts recognised one another. They didn't say so but it was evident that they had great respect for each other. They chatted for a few moments about other people who were involved in encryption and the steps that the USA and UK governments had tried in their unsuccessful attempts to make unbreakable codes illegal.

Finally the man from London said, 'I've only two questions to put to you. I've looked at print-out using your code. Would I be right in thinking that it used the same kind of algorithm as Zimmerman's PGP?'

'Yes. You're right but the software was more complex.' He paused. 'What was the other question?'

'I'm told that the problem is – did you or did you not wipe out the total software package of your KAOS code? If you did, it must have been incredibly disturbing to do.'

Rosen shook his head. 'Yes. I wiped it completely. But no, it didn't disturb me. What had started way back as an intellectual challenge had got out of control. I was abusing something that was originally creative and – if I might say so – elegant.'

The man from London looked at Baumann and shrugged. 'I'm satisfied. It's done.'

Baumann and his colleagues left and Rosen and Mason ordered cakes from a trolley and coffee.

Rosen said, 'It's like old times when we had breakfast together.'

Mason said, 'Let this be the last of those days. This is a new start. You can be yourself again.'

As they got out into the street Mason saw a crowd of people at the windows of a shop. He waved on Laufer and Rosen and walked the few yards to see what the people were looking at. It was an electrical shop and there was a large-screen colour TV in the centre of the window display. The screen showed ambulances and what looked like a golf-course, then came back to a reporter. It wasn't possible to hear what he was saying but there was a news-flash band at the bottom of the screen. It said – 'President assassinated in Florida' and the pictures moved to the entrance to a hospital and then to a reporter outside the White House.

Mason hurried to the car and as he closed the door he told them what he had just seen. Laufer switched on the car radio and it was tuned to Deutsche-Welle whose Washington man was reporting that the President and two friends had been shot and killed on a golf-course where they were playing during a break in Miami. The President's body had been put on Air Force One and was on its way back to Washington. The Vice-President had been sworn in and his first appearance as President Healey would be in an hour's time in the Senate.

Mason reached over and switched off the radio and turned to Rosen. 'Do you think that was KAOS?'

'I've no idea. As you know I haven't operated the network for several days. It's the kind of thing they talked about but I always put it down to trying to impress one another. But that was over here. I know very little of what the American end was doing.'

Mason closed his eyes to concentrate his thoughts. What had happened in the States could affect Bonn's thinking on an amnesty for Rosen and also Altieri could see it as justification for an attack on Rosen. He would have to wait to hear from Baumann. Meantime he would have to keep Rosen under constant supervision.

Back at the rooms Mason went straight for the kitchen and took the gun from inside the saucepan on the shelf alongside the cooker. The plastic-wrapped cartons of bullets were inside the toilet tank and Mason took one of them and put it with the gun on the kitchen table. Weighing the gun in his hand he realised that he had to have a holster. The gun was so heavy and so bulky that it would be all too obvious in a jacket pocket. He called in Laufer from the next room.

'I want you to go to the club and tell Freddie I need a holster. A shoulder holster. OK?'

Laufer nodded and said, 'Anything else you want?'

'No. That's all.'

It was two hours before Laufer got back with a well-worn, soft, leather holster. The gun slid in easily and came out smoothly. Laufer had also brought back a scribbled note from Freddie Malins. It seemed that both Altieri and Maguire had visited the club in the last two days. Both of them looking the worse for wear and Altieri still with a plaster across his forehead. Malins had also thoughtfully sent him a packet of freshly-made sandwiches wrapped in a damp cloth.

Rosen had produced a small chess-set from his bag and they had, all three of them, taken turns playing chess as Mason waited for the call from Baumann. Laufer beat both of them consistently.

Mason was worried when there was no call by midnight. He lay on the bed in his clothes and had eventually slept through the night. Laufer had woken him at 8 a.m. the next morning with a mug of tea.

The phone rang at 11.15 a.m. but when Mason pressed the release bar there was nothing at the other end. He tapped out Baumann's number but there was no reply. He tried again at 2 p.m. but there was still no response.

It was 6 p.m. when Baumann's call came through. His voice was lowered and barely audible. He wanted to see Mason alone as soon as possible. They agreed to meet in two hours' time in the bar at Kempinski's.

Baumann heard out Altieri's diatribe about the reluctance to use force against Rosen.

'First of all we have no grounds for even arresting Rosen.'

'For Christ's sake man, those bastards have just assassinated the President of the USA. What more do you want?'

'There's no need to shout Bill. You've got hundreds of different groups in the USA who could have done it. On CNN this morning there seemed to be a consensus that it was most likely Cubans who did it.'

'I don't give a shit what CNN says, nor anyone else. We know these KAOS bastards are part of a network that uses an unbreakable code that's operated by Rosen. That's enough for me.'

'Calm down, fella. If you made a move against Rosen right now you could be indicted for God knows what offences under our laws.' He looked at Altieri. 'You don't need me to tell you that it would be in the headlines as a diplomatic row between your government and mine.'

'It doesn't have to be me. I've got Crombie's guy, Maguire. He'll do it if I tell him to.'

Baumann shrugged. 'OK. So Maguire is arrested. He won't carry the can for you if it all goes wrong. And it will.' Baumann paused. 'I think my boss has spoken to Swenson overnight. I gather that Swenson will go along with what my HQ decide to do.' He smiled. 'It happens that we're talking about one of our citizens who, so far as we know, *know*, not speculate, has committed no offence. We need his co-operation, not his antagonism.'

Altieri leaned forward, his big fists clenched as they pounded the table, to mark each word. 'Let me tell you, my friend. If Rosen isn't pulled in in the next forty-eight hours by your people I'll pull him in myself and his feet won't touch.'

Altieri's face was blotchy with suffused anger, his anger made worse by Baumann's calm disagreement. He turned away abruptly and as he stormed out of the room Baumann heard him shouting for Maguire.

Baumann had already ordered a bottle of wine and was waiting for Mason. He seldom had an excuse to indulge in a visit to Kempinski's, but he loved the place. It was old-fashioned, pre-war, even pre-Hitler. It was as much Vienna as Berlin. It just lacked violins and *sachertorte*. When this business was through he'd have a long weekend here with Magda and the twins.

He saw Mason come in to the bar and waved to him. He liked Mason. Tough and reliable. And calm. He poured wine for Mason as he sat in an armchair alongside.

'*Prost.*'

Mason smiled and said it back.

'I apologise for taking so long. But this thing in Miami had its repercussions over here. Do you think Rosen knew it was going to happen?'

'I'm sure he didn't. To him the KAOS thing was a rather fancy way of punishing politicians and the like. The actual violence was nothing to do with him. He was just the lightning, the others were the thunder.'

'It could have been his KAOS people in the States.'

'When you look at the terrible mess they've got over there it could be any group from anti-abortionists to the Klu Klux Klan. I heard on the radio coming here that three entirely different groups have claimed that they did it. The *L.A. Times* gives it to the Mafia and the *Washington Post* put it to Arab fundamentalists and that lets all the home-grown thugs off the hook.' He paused. 'Will it affect our deal with Rosen?'

Baumann shook his head. 'No. My people go along with me. We've struck a mortal blow at an attempt to internationalise terrorism and that's as much as we could have expected to do. The thugs themselves, wherever they are and whatever their motivation, we shall have to combat piece-meal. Crombie realised that right from the start. He said so at one of our early meetings in Washington. We can learn from one another how best to deal with that and at least we've taken away the sophistication that could have made them invincible.' He paused. 'What's Rosen's real name?'

'Brodski. Jakob Brodski. Born in Konan about 1941. I guess he's really a Pole.'

'The documentation I'm having prepared makes him German. We shall hand over a valid passport, social security documents, and all the usual crappy papers one has to have these days, and we are prepared to fund him through the university at his current rate for the rest of his life. We'll also buy him a house or apartment or pay the rent. Whichever suits him. And finally we'll notify the Dutch authorities that he's a special status citizen so far as Bonn is concerned.'

'That's very generous.'

Baumann shrugged. 'Worth every pfennig as far as we are concerned.' He looked at Mason. 'And what's your next move after you've tucked friend Brodski up in bed?'

'I'll probably get a rocket from Crombie and get posted to our embassy in Helsinki as Third Secretary in charge of passports.'

'What I'm going to say is quite improper.' He smiled. 'Nevertheless I'll say it. If you ever feel like a change of job we can offer you a career at a much higher level than you're at at the moment.'

Mason grinned. 'Sounds like you think he's going to boot me out.'

'No. I don't think that. But he's a strange man is Crombie. Shrewd, nice in some ways but strangely mean-minded and naive in others. I don't really understand that kind of Englishman.'

'He's not an Englishman, Franz. He's a Scot and there are a lot like him in Edinburgh.' He sighed. 'But thanks for the thought and the offer.' He smiled. 'Let's see how we go. When can I get Rosen out of the country so that Altieri can't get his hands on him? Or on me for that matter.'

Baumann smiled. 'I'd put my money on you, my friend.' He paused to think. 'Let's say in two days. Sunday OK?'

'Fine. We're in a terrible dump in Schwendelgasse and we're all beginning to need a bath.' He paused. 'One other thing. Freddie Malins and one of his employees named Laufer have been very helpful. Could you keep a kindly eye on them. They don't know anything about what's been going on.'

'That's OK. Leave it to me.'

The Prime Minister had decided that protocol demanded that the Foreign Secretary and the Leader of Her Majesty's Official Opposition should also be at the briefing meeting with Crombie. It had been arranged at 10 Downing Street and in the PM's private sitting room.

A small mahogany table and four chairs had been brought up from one of the downstairs rooms. Before they came in the room was checked for bugs and was cleared, and although they were not aware of it only Crombie was not checked for a wire as they came into the room.

The PM looked calm but serious, the Foreign Secretary looked as if he were well aware that a government agency for which he was responsible had done a good job, and the Leader of the Opposition, Ryan Appleby, looked faintly aggressive or perhaps just defensive, it was hard to tell which.

'Right, gentlemen,' the PM said. 'No notes if you please and I should be very concerned if there was even a hint in the media that this meeting had taken place. My Press Office has issued a neutral statement that today's meeting is a routine meeting to discuss the subject of how nominees are selected for the Honours List. They will be told after we finish that we are considering setting up a select committee on the subject.' He smiled rather frostily at Ryan Appleby. 'They know the Opposition have a positive instinct for select committees.' He paused. 'Let's see. At the last count the Opposition benches had demanded just over a hundred select committees in the last couple of months.' He shrugged. 'But to business, gentlemen.' He looked at Ben Porter, the Foreign Secretary. 'You stop me if I'm not on the right lines, Minister.'

The PM looked at each of the others before he started to speak. He was an expert at making people feel uneasy with just a glance from his pale blue eyes.

'Sir Peter's people in SIS became concerned about the rising resentment in the general public of all forms of government and in particular the politicians who make the law, and the bureaucrats and organisations enforcing those laws. Civilised societies had assumed that political assassination was a thing of the very dist int past. With the assassination of two Presidents and scores of groups inciting violence against Washington, the United States bore most of the burden of this violent discontent. In the Federal Republic Bonn suffers from its very generosity towards immigrants, and murder by subversives has been increasing.

'In this country it has been obvious for some time that the derogation of government ministers and government policy by the media and the Opposition have played their part in making politicians – all politicians, including the Opposition – into objects of derision and contempt.

'However, Sir Peter's specialists discovered recently that the thugs and subversives in the USA, the Federal Republic and the UK were linked in a conspiracy – an attempt – to join forces into a multi-national campaign of what amounted to revolution. Not revolution by the ballot-box but by the usual weapon of the ignorant – murder, arson and bombing.

'The good news is that Sir Peter assures me that this international link has been destroyed. I have not asked for the details of how this has been achieved but I can tell you that it was a combined effort with the Americans, the Germans and ourselves.' He looked at Crombie. 'Anything you want to add, Sir Peter?'

'No, sir.'

'I hope that all of us around this table might reflect on what I've told you. There are going to be no prizes for anyone who wants to go back to old games. I shall be watching the scene very carefully and I can assure you, gentlemen, that anyone who crosses the line will be dealt with. One way or another.' He paused. 'Thank you, gentlemen. There's tea in the ante-room.'

Freddie Malins had told the bouncer to insist on seeing their membership card if either Altieri or Maguire tried to get into the club. No matter what they said or threatened he should turn them away.

The bouncer recognised Altieri as he pushed aside the curtain. When Altieri demanded to be let in the bouncer had refused, politely but firmly. When Altieri grabbed at the bouncer's T-shirt he lashed out at the American. He hadn't noticed Maguire on the other side of him. They were both wearing black track-suits and as the bouncer gripped Altieri's top, Maguire struck him behind the ear with the butt of a Magnum and the bouncer went down with a groan. It was Maguire who found the swipe-card in the man's back pocket and

they went through the open door into the club. It was a Saturday
night and the club was busy and crowded. They eased their way
through to the bar, throwing back the flap in the counter, pushing
through the curtains behind, then up the stairs and along to Freddie
Malin's place, flinging the door open and heading for Malins who
was sitting at his desk talking on the phone. Malins' right hand
reached for the bell button on his desk but his hand had barely
moved before the pistol butt had smashed down on his fingers. The
telephone clattered onto the desk as Malins tried in vain to put it
back on its cradle. Altieri put it back in its place, his eyes on Malins'
face.

'What's going on? What's all this about?'

'Where's Mason and Rosen?'

'How the hell should I know. They haven't been in the club for
weeks, either of them.'

Altieri grabbed the front of Malins' shirt, his big fist under Malins'
chin. 'Don't shit me, little man. You know where they are.'

'They'll be at Rosen's house maybe.'

'No way. We've been there days ago.'

Malins shrugged. 'Sorry. I can't help you.'

He never saw the blow coming as Altieri's fist smashed into his face.
Half-blinded, with his hands to his face, Malins tried to stand up but
Maguire shoved him back into his chair thrusting his face close to
Malins' face he said, 'Tell us where he is or we'll wreck this fucking
place.'

Malins, despite his pain, shook his head and Maguire's hands
grabbed at his throat. 'You like us to go out to Grunewald and talk to
your old lady? Maybe she's got more sense than you have.'

Altieri said, 'Let go of him.'

As Maguire released his grip on Malins, Altieri stood looking at him,
blood pouring from his nose and mouth, splashing onto the papers on
the desk.

'Malins, you've been around these games long enough to know you
can't win. What are Rosen and Mason to you?'

Freddie Malins looked up at his tormenter and said, 'I've been long
enough in this business to know that your turn will come. Both of you.
You're fucking Nazis the both of you.'

Altieri nodded to Maguire who seized Malins' left hand by the wrist
and spread the fingers over the edge of the desk. Altieri held Malins'

other arm and one by one Maguire broke the fingers of Malins' left hand. Malins screamed as he struggled. 'OK. OK. It's enough.'

Altieri said, 'Right. Where are they?'

Malins sighed and took a deep breath. 'They're in a junk shop in Schwendelgasse.'

'Where the hell's Schwendelgasse?' But Malins had passed out.

Altieri turned to Maguire. 'D'you know where it is?'

'No idea. This ain't my patch. Your guys should know.'

Altieri shook his head. 'I can't ask them.'

'So we take a taxi.'

'No. That would pinpoint us if there are any repercussions.' He shrugged. 'Let's ask somebody in the street.'

Mason answered the phone himself and at first he couldn't identify the speaker or what was being said.

'Who's speaking please. I can't hear very well.'

'It's Freddie, those bastards, Altieri and Maguire, have beaten me up. I've got to go to a doctor. I had to give them your address. They'll be coming for you and Rosen. Get away. Quickly. Got to go I'm . . .'

There was a clatter of the phone falling at the other end and Mason turned to Laufer.

'Get Rosen out immediately. Now. Now. Take him to the airport, to Tegel. Wait for me or Baumann at the British Airways desk. Don't wait for anything. Just go.'

A few seconds later as he dialled Baumann he heard the two clattering down the wooden stairs.

'Baumann.'

'I've just had a call from Freddie Malins. He says Altieri and Maguire have beaten him up. They made him give my address away and he thinks they're already on the way here. I've sent Laufer to Tegel with Rosen. They'll be waiting for you at the British Airways counter. Will you get Rosen away on a plane, with his documents and if possible an escort? Anywhere in Europe. Just the first place out. I'll meet you at Tegel when I've dealt with Altieri and Maguire, OK.'

'OK. Will do. I'll get the police around to you. Give me your address.'

'No. I'll cope. I got to go.'

Mason hung up and went down to slide the bolt across on the street door before he snapped the magazine into the Smith and Wesson. He slid off the safety-catch before he lay it on the table. Finally he switched off all the lights and moved a chair to the window that looked out on the alleyway. There was a faint shine on the cobbles from a light at the far end that led to the main road but there was no movement in the alley until a drunk stumbled his way along, guiding himself with his arm stretched out and his hand on the wall. The drunk was followed by the vague outlines of a couple of cats.

Mason looked at the illuminated dial of his watch. It was 1.15 a.m. He turned the watch on his wrist so that the illuminated face was hidden. Then there was a light at the far end of the alley and the faint thumping of a diesel engine. There were raised voices and as the vehicle moved off the 'Taxi' sign came on.

Mason had no doubt that the two figures making their way up the narrow street were Altieri and Maguire. The two were obviously uncertain of their target, checking both sides of the alleyway. Finally they were right below the window. Then there was knocking on the door, heavier banging, muttered words and then the noise of splitting wood as the door crashed open. Some stumbling around in the darkness of the shop and the flashing of a torch as they made their way through to the stairs. It was a good sign that they hadn't switched on the light downstairs. It meant that they didn't want to be seen so they were free-lancing, not acting officially.

Mason moved silently to the space between a cupboard and where the door from the landing opened inwards. The floorboards of the landing squeaked and groaned as the two made their way along the landing. He wanted both of them to be already in the room when he acted. No loose cannons. They'd open the door, wide. Fumble for the light switch. Switch on and then come inside to look around. After that it was up to him. More Wagner than Irving Berlin.

A few seconds later they did it. The door was flung back. A pause. A hand feeling around on the wall for the switch. Some heavy breathing and a voice with a Glasgow accent says 'The bastards have skipped. That asshole Malins twiced us.' It was like enticing a fish to the bait willing them to come right into the room. Then Altieri's voice just the other side of the door. 'What's that box on the table. Looks like ammo to me.' They went forward together, Mason kicked the door to behind them, holding out the Smith and Wesson and waving it slowly from one to the other, he said, 'The box is empty, my friends.' As Maguire moved, Mason said, 'Don't move. Don't do anything. The slugs are ten millimetre and they'll make a mess of you.'

With the gun still trained on Maguire but with half an eye an Altieri, Mason said, 'I'll give you the choice. I'll ring for the police and put a holding charge on you both for breaking and entering. Possession of a weapon. Etc. Etc. Or you can try playing silly buggers and I'll shoot your fucking heads off.'

'You'll hang for this, Mason.' Altieri said.

'Don't kid yourself. Your little mission down here is already on the record. Freddie Malins is tougher than you thought.' Even as he spoke he saw Maguire's hand move to his hip and he fired off two rounds. One at Maguire's face and the other into his chest. That's what they taught you in the business. Don't fire unless you have to. Defend yourself at all times. And if you have to fire, no fancy stuff. When you shoot you shoot to kill. It seemed a long time with Maguire standing there before the blood flowed out of his forehead as if someone had turned on the tap on a cask of red wine. Altieri stood transfixed, his mouth wide open. Maguire's head hit the table as he crashed to the floor. He knew Altieri wouldn't do anything. He had a violent temper but it was only *macho* bluff. Men like Altieri relied on their rank and their status. Middle-aged drill sergeants. Swearing and cursing, bullying and barking on the parade ground but when the rookies were trained soldiers they could recognise an Altieri a mile away.

It was a couple of seconds after Maguire had fallen before Mason waved the Smith and Wesson at Altieri and pointed to the kitchen chair. 'Sit down, sunshine. And put both hands flat on the table.'

Altieri did as he was told and Mason sat down facing him across the table.

'You're a sitting duck, Altieri. But you know that, don't you?'

Altieri just shrugged.

'You got a gun on you?'

Altieri nodded.

'OK. Take it out very very slowly and put it on the table in front of you.' He smiled. 'Don't be tempted, my friend.'

The pistol was a traditional Luger and Altieri could barely disentangle it from the armpit holster. For all his size and bluster Mason realised that Altieri was really a desk man. Probably did quite well on the firing-range. But not much use when it was for real. When the Luger was on the table, Mason took it and slid out the magazine, emptying the slugs and chucking them into the kitchen sink.

With his left hand he took out his radio phone and dialled Baumann's number. He counted thirteen rings before a breathless voice said, 'Baumann.'

'It's me, Franz. Where are you?'

'At Tegel.'

'Is Laufer with you?'

'Yep.'

'Can you send him back to pick me up?'

'Yes. No problem. Anything else?'

'Yes. I'll be bringing back our colleague, Altieri. He's here with me now. So is Maguire. But Maguire got shot while attempting to do something foolish. Altieri has committed a number of criminal offences. I'll tell you about them off the record. It'll be up to you what you do with him.' He paused. 'Where's my friend?'

'He's on a plane.'

'Where to?'

'Bangkok.' Mason could hear the edge of a smile in Baumann's voice. 'But the plane picks up passengers at Frankfurt and my people will look after him until you take him over. I'll explain when I see you.'

'Shall I go to your place?'

'OK. *Tschüs.*'

Mason laughed. '*Tschüs.*'

Altieri had sat with clenched fists as Laufer drove them to Baumann's place. When Baumann appeared Altieri started complaining but Baumann said, 'Forget it. I've been in touch with your people here, they're expecting you.' He paused. 'I've also put Swenson in the picture.' Altieri banged the door to behind him as he flounced out. Baumann smiled. 'My daughter used to do that when she was four years old.' He paused. 'There's no other plane to Frankfurt tonight, or this morning to be precise, and you'll need to collect your things and get some sleep.' He paused. 'Tell me what happened.' He listened without comment as Mason went over the days' events.

Baumann said, 'Have you heard what happened to Freddie Malins?'

'No. I assume they must have got the address from him. He phoned me and warned me that they were on their way. It allowed me to get Rosen away.'

'They beat him up. He's in hospital. He passed out when he was speaking to me on the phone after he'd phoned you.'

'Is he badly hurt?'

'Broken nose, missing teeth, a face like a balloon and four broken fingers.'

'Oh my God. What bastards. What hospital is he in?'

'The same one Rosen was in.'

'I'd better go and see him. Can you people give me a lift?'

'Wait until the morning and we can go over together. By the way, the passport and the rest of his documents are in his real name Brodski, so don't use Rosen from now on.'

'How was he?'

'Shit-scared but no trouble.' He looked at Mason. 'I've brought Crombie up to date and I've made clear that it was your judgement and your efforts that finished off the network business. Swenson also sends you his thanks. I'll fill him in about Altieri's little capers.' He paused again. 'I gather that Maguire is no longer with us.'

'Can your people clean up the mess at the junk shop?'

'Yeah. He'll just disappear.'

'The same way that poor Charlie Foster disappeared.'

'You got it.' He put his arm round Mason's shoulders. 'Come on, I'll take you back to your place.'

Back at the apartment at Marburger Strasse Mason took a bath and arranged a phone-alarm call for 7 a.m. that morning.

He had breakfast at the café a few doors down the street, at 9 a.m. he phoned Crombie's number. They had talked for fifteen minutes and it was obvious that Baumann had already been in touch with Crombie. Crombie's praise was genuine but by no means fulsome. He made no mention of Maguire and when Mason set out what he wanted for Malins' help and courage, Crombie had agreed immediately.

He would be left to deal with Rosen in conjunction with the Germans and when he got back to London he would be given two weeks' leave after a brief meeting with Crombie.

An hour after his phone call to Crombie, Mason took a taxi to the hospital. It seemed strange to be there again. He had bought a small Sony combined radio and cassette player and four tapes for Freddie Malins. Good classic nostalgia from Ella Fitzgerald to Fats Waller.

Freddie Malins looked a mess. Heavily bandaged around the head, one hand in a plaster cast and an assortment of tubes. It took him some effort to speak, and to avoid looking at him Mason rigged up the small radio, put in a tape and placed it alongside Malins' good hand.

'All you do is press the button. It changes to the other side automatically.'

Slightly tearfully Freddie said indistinctly, 'I had to tell 'em, Jimmy, they said they'd do the family.'

'It's all right, Freddie. I'd have done the same.' He smiled. 'Anyway I settled your account with friend Maguire. I settled Charlie Foster's account at the same time. And they're shipping Altieri back to the States today.' He paused and put his hand on Malins' arm. 'A couple of bits of good news. All, repeat all, your documentation at SIS is being shredded and wiped out at SIS with the compliments of Sir Peter Crombie. And the same with your records here in Germany. Old stuff and current stuff. A clean sheet all ready for you to mess up.' He smiled. 'Thanks for all your help, Freddie. If it hadn't been for your call I'd have been wiped out.' He paused. 'By the way – you never knew a guy named Rosen. He never existed. OK?'

Malins nodded. 'When you going back?'

'This afternoon.'

Malins touched the small radio. 'Thanks for the contraption. I'll enjoy that.'

'When are they letting you out on an unsuspecting world?'

'They said two or three days.'

Mason stood up. 'Baumann's got my number. Any time, any place. I'll be right over.'

It had taken a couple of days to clear up and pay a few bills and Baumann had gone to the airport with him to see him off. He was due to stay one night in London when he would have the meeting with Crombie and then take over Brodski in Frankfurt.

As they waited for his flight to be called Baumann said, 'We've agreed with the Americans that we'll buy a house for Brodski and pay him enough to live decently. The Americans are contributing half and your lot and mine a quarter each. We'll go with whatever deal you do.' The Tannoy was calling his flight and Baumann took his hand. 'Don't forget what I said. Any problem in London and you can double your salary with us.'

Mason smiled. 'Thanks. I won't forget.'

It was still light as they came in to Gatwick. Mason's favourite airports were Schiphol and Gatwick. They had a kind of cheerfulness as if they knew something good was going to happen to you.

As he hauled his one and only bag from the carousel, a young man approached him. 'Are you Mr Mason?'

'Yes'.

'I'm Special Branch. There's a message for you at our office. Shall I show you the way?' He reached for Mason's bag and walked with him to the corridor, vouched for him with the security man and took him inside the partitioned section.

'A drink sir? A whisky, a gin?'

'I wouldn't mind a cup of tea.'

'By the way, my boss has arranged for one of our drivers to take you into town.' He pointed to a card on the table and said, 'The phone's alongside the chair on the trolley.'

The card just said for him to phone Baumann and gave his Berlin security number.

He dialled the number and after a couple of rings it was answered.

'Baumann. Who is it?' He sounded rather testy.

'It's Mason. I'm at Gatwick. I've got a message to phone you.'

There was a long pause and then Baumann said. 'I won't elaborate but Rosen slipped away from my people in Frankfurt. It seems he got back to Berlin, I don't know how.' He paused and sighed. 'Anyway he went back to his old house where you were with him. His thuggish friends had burned it to the ground some days ago.' There was a long pause. 'He was found hanging from one of the apple trees in the garden. He had an envelope pinned to his jacket addressed to you. I opened it. The note just says – I quote – "I'm sorry but I know you'll understand" –unquote. There was a faded photograph in the envelope too. Very old. It was a photograph of a very pretty young woman.' He paused. '*Do* you understand?'

It wasn't easy to speak but Mason said quietly, 'It was a picture of his mother. She died in the camp.' He paused. 'I'll call you in a few days. Let me know when the funeral is. I'll come over.'

'I'll do that. Take care.'

The meeting with Crombie was obviously just a formality. A marker to the end of his assignment in Berlin. The congratulations were tepid and it was clear that Crombie's mind was on other things. But in the last few minutes Crombie had raised the subject of Maguire.

'Does it worry you about killing Maguire?'

His anger was cold and contained as he said, 'I guess it worries me about as much as it worried Maguire when he killed Charlie Foster.'

Crombie nodded and stood up and shook his hand as they stood at the door. 'Have a good leave, Mason,' Crombie said, with all the sincerity of a New York shop assistant saying 'Have a nice day.'

He was too tired to deal with tickets and train times and a taxi at the other end, so he took a taxi all the way. He had phoned his mother to say that he'd stay with them for the night. She was delighted.

She came out into the road as he paid off the cab-driver and gave him a tip.

As the taxi drove away, she said in disgust, 'You could have had a taxi all the way from London for that money. The thieves.'

'I did have it all the way from London.'

She looked shocked. 'You never did. You're joking.'

He laughed and picked up his bag and looked at her. 'Just a little treat.'

She laughed and kissed him. 'I hope you deserved it.'

TED ALLBEURY

THE LINE-CROSSER

SIS agents are expendable

Charlie Foster runs an SIS network into East Berlin. When three of his couriers are arrested and London is ready to let them rot, Charlie, in anger, does his own deal. He trades his own services to the East Germans and the Russians for their release.

From his collaboration he builds up a complete picture of all those in Europe who were Stasi and KGB informers. When the Berlin Wall comes down Charlie Foster has something everybody wants. SIS itself, the West Germans, the Americans and all the collaborators. They are all determined to get Charlie Foster's list. Or Charlie Foster himself.

'A very good book, which explains and makes sense of a series of tangled events, both real and fictional.'
Books Magazine

'Deft plotting, sad but gutsy characters, atmosphere of constant menace ... Ted Allbeury carries it off masterfully.'
Daily Telegraph

HODDER AND STOUGHTON PAPERBACKS

TED ALLBEURY

AS TIME GOES BY

It was a time of courage, of danger, of excitement and heartbreak ...

In 1942 three young women are parachuted into the Dordogne to work for a Special Operations Executive network. Their leader is Harry Bailey, a young man who loves one of them and fears for them all.

Paulette, the passionately committed Frenchwoman, who never forgets her need for revenge against the Germans ... down-to-earth Vi, motivated by an unselfish sense of obligation ... Jenny, the least committed of the three, and the one who must find the most courage.

As the months of dangerous waiting turn at last into active combat behind enemy lines as D-Day approaches, the three heroines' story moves to its unforgettable climax.

HODDER AND STOUGHTON PAPERBACKS

TED ALLBEURY

BEYOND THE SILENCE

George Carling was the spymaster's spymaster, the man who knew all the secrets of the Cold War. Now a newspaper says he was a traitor – that his espionage was too good to be honest.

But Carling's real secrets are deeper, and more astonishing. He is the man who knows about Kim Philby's last great coup: the ultimate deception of the Cold War.

Beyond the Silence is the startling story of a spy who wanted to be a good man – and therefore changed the course of history.

'Ted Allbeury delivers the best plots ... a good story.'
Mail on Sunday

'A superb story ... Allbeury's best for years.'
Bertie Denham, Glasgow Herald

HODDER AND STOUGHTON PAPERBACKS